P9-CRJ-921

ENDINGS

ALSO BY LINDA L. RICHARDS

The Madeline Carter Series

Mad Money

The Next Ex

Calculated Loss

The Kitty Pangborn Series

Death Was the Other Woman

Death Was in the Picture

Death Was in the Blood

The Nicole Charles Series

If It Bleeds

When Blood Lies

Anthologies

Vancouver Noir

Thrillers: 100 Must-Reads

Fast Women and Neon Lights

ENDINGS

A NOVEL

LINDA L. RICHARDS

SARASOTA, FLORIDA

ISBN 978-1-60809-420-2

Published in the United States of America by Oceanview Publishing

Sarasota, Florida

www.oceanviewpub.com

10 9 8 7 6 5 4 3 2 1

PRINTED IN THE UNITED STATES OF AMERICA

It is always important to know when something has reached its end. Closing circles, shutting doors, finishing chapters, it doesn't matter what we call it; what matters is to leave in the past those moments in life that are over.

—**PAULO COELHO,** *The Zahir*

ENDINGS

CHAPTER ONE

I AM ON a plane. There are always planes. That's an important part. They say it's inefficient and ineffective to break cover in your own community. Me, I say it a different way that means the same thing: shitting in your own backyard makes no sense at all.

So, I am on a plane. It's a hop this time. The where does not matter, but if I say "Atlanta" you'll get the idea. In the terminal, when I pick up the rental car that's been reserved for me, I look it over approvingly. It is dark and somber. Unremarkable. Mid-sized. A sedan. If I turn my head quickly, I'll forget what it looks like. I tell the oily-haired kid behind the counter that I'll take it and he nods without concern because there was never any question.

I leave the airport and I drive like someone who knows where she's going. I don't, but I fake it. I've got SatNav in the rental, Google Maps on my cell phone, and I've got the general idea.

I end up in a beautiful neighborhood with wide, tree-lined streets. You can tell it's an affluent neighborhood because even the supermarket has trees and plants right next to it and the bagboys look pale and well scrubbed, like they're home during midterms, working to make beer money. It's a nice place.

I find the house without difficulty. It looks as I'd imagined it would. The house is antebellum, with columns in a big yard with a well-manicured lawn. The house is a white so bright, it's like a clean tooth in the center of a big green mouth. A long driveway curves through the lawn and ends at the entrance to the garage where a porch swing is idle next to the closed front door.

I circle the block a couple of times. Not much is going on. If anyone is home, they're keeping quiet inside and their car is tucked into the garage.

I pull my dark and perfectly nondescript sedan up across the street from the house. It's warm here in "Atlanta." Somewhere, someone has a window open and strains of a Strauss waltz float across the air. Behind the house, I see a pool. It gives me an idea.

I sit in the car and dial the number I was given. It seems to ring for a long time. Finally, someone answers. I force on a clean and happy smile and I make it touch my voice.

A man answers and sounds exactly as I'd anticipated.

"Hi there," I say, the chirp in my voice at a careful place. It echoes the smile. "This is Brandee calling from Super Bright Pools. I wanted to make sure you were happy with the servicing you got earlier today."

There is a pause, but it's not very long. I feel I may have tipped my hand too far. I tell myself it doesn't matter. I tell myself it won't matter for long.

"Listen, *Brandee*, we don't have any pool service. I clean the pool myself."

"I'm sorry," I say in the same odd chirp. "But are you certain. Maybe if you checked with your wife . . ."

"My wife's not here," he says. I hear the call disconnect sharply. And though he'd meant to be rude, I feel myself smile into the phone. He's given me more information than he knew, including the fact the he is alone in the house. Now I know what to do.

I leave the car, approach the house. I am silent. Like a cat.

The first two windows I try are locked, as is the garage door. The third window is not latched, and it doesn't take much for me to open it all the way, slide through. Had I not found the window open, it would have slowed me down, but it would not have stopped me. And, in any case—in almost all cases—there's a window open somewhere. Not in my house. Not anymore. But, what the hell: I like to think you can learn from other people's mistakes.

Once through the window, I'm in the prettiest laundry room I've ever seen. The walls are white and pink, striped, and the room smells good. Clean. There's a little desk in one corner, the surface of it in tidy disarray. There are clothes, neatly folded, on top of the dryer. His and hers, nothing for children. It wouldn't have made any difference if there were, but still. I'm relieved. There's a part of me that can't help it.

When I leave the laundry room, I think I'm mouse-quiet, but he must have very good ears.

"Desiree," he calls out. His voice is honey and old scotch. Oakwood: gnarled and rich. "I didn't expect you for a while."

He turns a corner and he doesn't see Desiree. Instead, he sees a woman in her thirties, someone he possibly wouldn't look at twice were he to pass her at the mall. She is neither tall nor short. If someone were to ask him to describe her, he wouldn't be able to recall much of anything in detail. Though, of course, he does not get that chance.

"How the hell did you get in here?" There is no panic in his voice. No fear. Only surprise.

"Vince Landry?"

He gives a small, almost imperceptible nod but doesn't say anything.

"I'm Brandee," I say, going with my original story, despite the fact that I probably don't look much like anyone's idea of either a pool service person or a customer service rep. Also, despite the fact that none of the story I've woven for him will matter in a few minutes.

"But I told you . . ." The confusion is clearing from his face now. A thundercloud is on the way.

"I'm sorry, but I have some papers . . ." I reach into my purse. It is Coach—authentic Coach, not something you'd buy on Canal Street—and my fingers touch the cold skin of my Bersa Thunder .380. I can feel the cold of the steel even through the nitrile gloves.

I see Vince Landry's eyes widen when he gets a whiff of the Bersa. It's a pretty gun, but I know he's not admiring her beauty.

I don't give him any warning and I don't give me any, either. Not much, anyway. Just before I plug three silenced shots into his chest, I think about my son, now gone. I think about my flat iron and the hair that didn't actually benefit much from straightening on that day. I think about what I then had and what I do not now have. It's like a life flashing in front of my eyes. And for about twenty seconds, I feel good. I feel whole again.

And then Vince Landry is dead at my feet, the light fading from his eyes as the blood begins to drain from his body, and I get a move on because I know that if I want that feeling again—the feeling of good wholeness—I have to shorten the distance between where I am now and where I want to be.

CHAPTER TWO

Five years ago, I was someone's wife and someone else's mother. Their names don't matter now, though they mattered a great deal then.

I had a job. Let's say I worked in an office, because that's close enough to what it was. I got up early in the morning, anyway. Put coffee on while I was still wearing my bathrobe, then hurried through the shower while the coffee brewed. Every day.

Before I left for work, I'd stop by his room. We had a big house, far out of the city and that commute, it gave me hell. I had to leave for work an hour before he even got up for school. So my routine: I'd drop by his room and lay a kiss on his forehead.

"Rise and shine, sleepyhead," I'd say, or some other dopey thing like that.

And mostly he'd fuss, because what nine-year-old kid wants to be woken up long before he has to get ready for school? But I'd wake him up anyway, usually with a glass of juice or milk. And I'd demand a hug and a kiss, and while I roared down the highway on my way to the city, sometimes I'd think about the sweet smell of him. And I'd smile at the memory and at the hopes and dreams I had in my heart, because that was the thing that pushed me out the door in the morning, that kept me running when maybe I could have walked. There was going to be a future, and I was going to make it happen, and I didn't think about the fact that I was buying that future with my own youth. I only thought about the need and desire and must-haves that were right in front of me.

It all seems so stupid now.

That last day, though, that was different.

I was running late. I didn't stop by for a hug and an infusion of that sweet smell. I didn't even stop to grab a coffee or do any of the things I usually did.

I flattened my hair. It seems an odd detail to remember. I used the flat iron on my hair. I can still feel the hot weight of it in my hand. I remember because I've wondered about it since. Wondered about it every single day. Did I leave that iron on? Is *that* how it happened? The insurance people—and the cops—they didn't say so: they couldn't pinpoint it quite that way, and me . . . well, I didn't dare ask. By then it didn't matter anyway, because it was all too late. Don't ask a question, that's what my mother always said. Don't ask a question unless you really want to know.

Cause and effect, right? That's what it boiled down to. And, whatever the cause, here was the effect: the fire killed my child very quickly. At least, that's what they told me. And I've never been sure if they told it to me because it was true, or because they wanted to try and wipe the haunted look out of my eyes. I don't think that it did.

The fire killed my son, but it didn't kill my man. Not right away, anyhow. It half-killed him just enough that he never recognized me—not ever again. But before he died, I owed everything we'd had and shared and more for the medical bills that would make it all right again. That would *try* to make it all right again. And it was then—of *course* it was then—that the world lined up and showed me the way it would be from then on. Life is good that way. It takes care. It shows you symmetry when you never thought you'd see it again. That's the thing I tell myself.

And now? Well, now my life makes no more sense than it did then. But there is occasional purpose. And there is money—at least I never want for that. And there are times—really, just moments so brief you can almost hold them in your hand—when you don't feel the pain or regret or loss for the future you worked so hard for, you practically shoved it out the door.

CHAPTER THREE

After the accident—directly after—there was only pain. When I think back on that time, I see a cold, dark hole. I think, for a while, I still had a job. I know there was someplace I went in the morning, without kisses. Without coffee. I don't remember exactly where I was, but it rained a lot. At least, I think I remember a lot of rain. All my world was very gray.

I would sit at the hospital, with the man who had been my husband. Who was then still my husband.

I would sit with him and I would lift his half-dead hand and I would talk to it and to him. I knew it was useless, but I did it anyway. If I hadn't had him to talk to, I would have been alone. I wasn't ready for that.

It was not a private hospital room. The money was all gone by then, and the bills were piling up more quickly than I could even count. So, in the hospital, my husband had a roommate. The roommate was tall and effete, with long-fingered hands and remarkably long hair. The man's wife was the most beautiful woman I had ever seen, have still ever seen, with dark, kohl-rimmed eyes. I'll always remember the slash of deep red lipstick in her waxen face on those days. Those early days. She wore worry and fear like a cloak.

In the days I sat with my comatose husband behind the curtains drawn around his bed, I gathered that the tall, effete man's name was Julian and that he was in desperate need of some expensive surgery that the couple couldn't afford. Their desperation was palpable and stemmed from the fact that they had been bilked out of a great deal of money by an art dealer. Julian was an artist, and proceeds from his work had been withheld. Had this not occurred, the surgery could have been afforded and their future altered. Assured. It was all, quite literally, a matter of life and death.

They could not have known I listened. They would have been too self-involved to even think about there being anyone beyond the curtains that surrounded my comatose husband most of every day. They would not have known I was there, praying at my husband's bedside at a time when I still had a God to pray to. But in between praying and talking softly to my husband who could not, in any case, understand, I would listen to their hushed discussions. It passed the time.

Over a period of days, while Julian became ever more delicate and haggard, the two of them hatched a plot. They would hire someone to kill the person who had done them such an injustice. In doing so, their funds would be released back to them and the surgery could go on. That was their thinking. But the wife, Clara, couldn't find anyone to do the deed. Over the course of the days I listened, she reported that she had made discreet inquiries but, in truth, she didn't even know where to begin. Who does, when you think about it? What "nice" people know where to look to hire someone when they need someone killed? It's just not generally a middle-class activity. That's not a bad thing.

"You couldn't find anyone?" The rain on the window was a live thing that day. You could hear it beating rhythmically on the glass, some dark jazz tattoo. It didn't drown out the desperation in Julian's voice, though. I could hear that desperation from across the room, louder even than the sounds the words themselves made.

"I'm sure there's someone out there, but I don't know where to look." I heard something dire in her voice and I peeked out from a join in the curtain. Her eyes looked smokier than ever. Twin pools of despair. "Think about it," she said to him. "Even asking the wrong person could land me in jail."

"But, surely, for ten thousand dollars we can find *someone* willing to put a bullet into him."

"It's not the money, Julian." Their voices were hushed, their tones low, but the polished linoleum carried the words to me on ghost hands. "Like I said, I don't know where to look."

"I'll do it." My own voice surprised me, and they looked surprised, too, seeing me step out from behind the curtain in that way. My voice had a disused sound, like I hadn't spoken in a while. Maybe I had not.

Their heads swiveled towards me in a single motion. It was as though neither of them had ever seen me before, though by then Julian and my husband had been roommates for weeks.

"Where did you come from?" she said.

I pointed back at the curtained area. "My husband is in a coma. I sit with him sometimes. I . . . I've been listening. For a while. For days. I know your story."

"And you said you'll . . ." Clara was searching but she didn't find the words she was looking for. I helped her out.

"The man. Who took the money from you. He needs to be dead. You can't find anyone to do it. I have nothing more to lose." I indicated my nearly dead husband and thought about the child they could not see. The house. The dreams. The life. I said it again: "I have nothing more to lose. And I need money. Ten thousand dollars?"

They both nodded, without speech.

"All right, well, I need that, too. Tell me what you want done." I thought about it for a few minutes more, but that was enough. And then, "Tell me what you need me to do."

And so it begins.

And so it began.

CHAPTER FOUR

SEVENTY-TWO PERCENT OF hits are contracted due to matters of the heart. I saw this fact on CNN, so it must be true.

Oh, sure, sometimes those matters of the heart extend to money or the protection of children or some other connected matter. But in seventy-two percent of cases, there is some element of love and loss. CNN says it, but I've seen this, also, with my own heart.

I think about that sometimes. About what would be different if I'd done the sensible, contractual thing in my own marriage. It hadn't been about love for a long time. There had been the child to raise—and I may not have loved his father anymore, but our son sure did. So the child to raise and the shared life to protect.

What if I, in good seventy-two percent style, had not straightened my hair and made coffee on that day? What if, instead, I had taken out a contract on my husband's life? This story would have had a happy ending then, do you see? No massive loss, no soulless searching, no wandering the landscape, a gun in my Coach. One could argue: Well, what of the husband? But he's dead now, you see? And the going was not without discomfort.

And a great deal of pain. Oh, I killed him in the end anyway, of course. But that was a different matter. By then it was a mercy killing, and I don't think that's the sort of contract CNN means.

The news piece had other facts, different statistics. For instance, they said, the most common method of fulfilling a contract was with a firearm.

No surprise there. There is nothing that kills as efficiently as a gun. There have been times when I've used other means, but only under duress or instruction. If for no other reasons than practical ones, firearms make the most sense in my case. I am, after all, generally much smaller than my targets. Physically, I mean. And a gun? Well, it evens things up.

That first hit, for Julian and Clara, was not as difficult as one would imagine. Not as difficult as I feared it would be. I felt soulless in that moment. I felt as though nothing would ever matter again. Truly, in some ways, it has not.

Julian and Clara had told me something about the man's habits, about where to find him; where it might be best to do the deed.

I didn't even have a gun then. Not at first. And I knew enough to understand I didn't want it in my own name. But I needed one.

I went to a bad part of my town, large bills in my purse. I found a guy—a fairly random guy—and I told him what I wanted. I took a risk doing that, I knew, but by then almost everything I did was a risk. It was the only thing keeping me alive.

After Random Guy tried to sell me some meth—I declined—he said I should talk to someone named Rick, a regular at Bud's bar.

Bud's was close—just a couple of blocks from the place Random and I were standing. My first instinct was to walk, but the area was dodgy, plus I had the feeling to put Random in my rear-view, so I drove the paltry two blocks and got rock star parking right outside because it was early; not quite six o'clock.

Inside, the bar was so dim I was both distressed and relieved. A dozen or so guys sat along the battle-scarred bar, propping it up with cheap drinks and baleful-looking conversation.

A couple of heads turned when I sat at the bar, but it didn't take long for them to turn back to their televisions and desultory conversation.

The only other female in the place approached me, a pale brunette in her thirties who asked if she could get me anything. I thought about being pert and asking for a gun, but ordered a beer instead. Once the beer was delivered, she slid a menu in my direction and asked if I wanted any food. I spent some time pretending to look at the menu but realized once I saw the pictures of surreal-looking hamburgers and French fries that the last thing I wanted to do was eat. When she came back for my order, I didn't tell her that. Instead, I told her that a girlfriend of mine had met a guy named Rick and that he'd told her he knew someone with a cheap car for sale.

"I need a cheap car," I said. "So I thought I'd look him up."

She smiled at that, so I knew I'd chosen the right words.

"Sure," she said. "Everyone knows Rick."

She pointed out a guy at the other side of the bar. He was all alone in a booth meant for six, a Sox baseball cap pushed far back on his head.

I thanked her, grabbed my barely sipped beer, and headed in his direction.

"I hear you can get me a cheap car," I said as I sat down.

He looked up from the papers he'd been leaning over, the surprise on his face only mild. I noted clean, neatly trimmed nails with fat, healthy cuticles. Whatever else Rick did, he liked his manicures.

"I need it to be in good condition," I said, meeting his eyes. "And something I can handle on my own."

I could see his confusion clear. It was almost too easy.

"How much experience do you have with . . . fast cars?" he asked.

"None. And speed is not my main concern. I would like . . . I would like it to be accurate."

"That's kinda the point with this kind of . . . car," he said without expression. "Accuracy. But, yeah. Whatever. I have the perfect one for you. Come back on Wednesday. Same time. With $1,200. Cash."

"Obviously."

"Here's my number. Text me when you're outside and I'll meet you."

I did as he asked. On Wednesday, he came out at my text. We walked the few blocks in companionable silence.

His car was a late model Subaru Outback in a pretty shade of green. It looked so solid and reliable and practical, I nearly commented, then opted to keep my yap shut. It didn't matter anyway.

I nervously passed him a sealed envelope. Inside it, I'd carefully placed a dozen one-hundred-dollar bills.

He ripped open the envelope and nodded when he'd finished counting.

"Excellent," he said, then politely, "Thanks," while he pulled a bundle out of the back of the Outback.

I peeked inside and saw a gun, a suppressor, and a couple of boxes of ammunition.

"It's a Bersa Thunder," he said, clearly reading my hesitation for confusion. "It's a good gun for a woman."

I thanked him for his thoughtfulness, then bid him goodbye.

Later, when I felt the heft of it, felt its compact weight in my hand, I could tell he was right. It *was* a good gun for a woman. I knew I'd be able to kill a man with that.

Once I got it, I didn't even really know what to do. It made me think maybe I should have somehow gotten my hands on a new gun. Presumably new-out-of-the-box, it would have come with instructions. But this wasn't that—it had scratches, and I was pretty sure the serial number had been filed off.

I brought the Bersa home and sat and looked at it for a while. It was one thing to think about using a gun. That's what I discovered. Quite another to actually own one.

After a while, when looking at the gun and poking at it produced no sudden rush of knowledge, I had the idea to see if anyone had made a video about how to operate my purchase. It turned out, there were lots of them online. The videos all made loading and operating the Bersa look pretty simple, plus I learned from watching that it was "high quality and reliable," which was something of a relief since I didn't really know what I was doing.

One video showed someone shooting the gun again and again. An intense-looking bearded guy in a watch cap kept shooting and shooting, though the video never showed what he was aiming at or if he was hitting it. After watching the video a couple of times, I had a strong sense that the tidy-looking little gun was very powerful. The guy in the video looked strong and was quite a bit larger than me, but every time he fired the Bersa, I could see the gun jump and buck in his hands. Enough of a jump that I figured you'd have to hold on very tightly with both hands and maybe even expect some bruising after the gun was fired.

It took me a while to figure out where to test the gun. Where would be private enough? Quiet enough? Where could I feasibly practice shooting this gun without anyone seeing me? Somehow this last part—not being seen—seemed very important.

I spent a few days pondering this, meanwhile getting used to some of the mechanics of the beast. I taught myself how to load the magazine. I learned how to screw on the silencer, which the video had taught me was actually called a suppressor. I learned, from watching, that I'd need to hold the gun very tightly when I shot, so it didn't jump right out of my hands. What I hadn't learned was where I would get the courage to actually do the deed, but, as I had so many times of late, I put my head down. I moved forward and on.

Finally, right down to the wire and with no more time to waste, I forced myself out the door. I'd done some research. About forty minutes out of town, there was an old garbage dump that had been shut down twenty years earlier when the city added a fancy waste transfer station at one edge of the multi-acre property. Now garbage got shipped to who-knows-where instead of getting piled up as it had in the old days.

At the other end of the large property from the waste transfer station, trees had begun to grow up where open pit garbage had once stood. The mountains of landfill had been covered over with dirt and were now home to trees and grasses. The driveway was blocked off by a severe-looking gate, but there was no fence. I figured the gate was to keep teenagers out: no parking or racing. And everyone knows teenagers don't like to walk.

I'm not a teenager, so I made a hike of it, parking a mile or so away. Once I got to the property, I quickly left behind any signs of civilization beyond the occasional fast-food wrapper and—encouragingly—shotgun shell casings. Clearly, I'd chosen the right place.

Out of sight of the traffic-less road, I sat down on a rock and screwed the suppressor into position. Now that I'd done it a few times, it was pretty easy. I loaded the gun. For the first shot I decided not to worry too much about hitting anything. The shot itself, that was the thing. Getting a round to leave the gun. Seeing how that would feel; figuring at the same time that my management of it would determine if I could go through with this at all.

It took both more and less than expected to pull the trigger. At first I touched it gently, gingerly and nothing happened. Thinking I'd squeeze it harder, the gun jumped and bucked on my way to shooting it, exploding in my hand milliseconds before I thought it would. I managed to hang onto the gun, but I had a vision of it hitting a rock, spinning around, then sitting in the dirt, watching me. Judging me. I packed that vision away and carried on.

Subsequent attempts went more smoothly. Ready for the jump and buck, I held the gun in a firm grip, then squeezed smoothly. By the sixth shot, I was ready to try a target. I sited a tree perhaps twenty feet away. I was sure that the first shot missed by a substantial amount, as did the next and then the one after that. But the fourth shot hit home. Even from a distance, I was certain of it.

Up close, I could see I was right: a thin trail of sap ran thickly down from the place where the bullet had hit its target. Satisfaction mixed with a regret so sharp I could taste it on my tongue. It tasted metallic. It tasted like loss. As I scurried around, collecting my spent cartridges, I felt some panic: If I experienced regret causing a tree to bleed, how would I ever be able to end a human's life?"

I got over it. That's what we do, right? We suck it up and move on. I had committed to something. And I was raised that way: commit to something, you see it through.

* * *

Julian's dealer lived in a loft near the edge of town. There was a gallery downstairs, an apartment above the gallery. Julian and Clara had told me that before I went there. They told me everything they could. Everything I'd need—that was the hope.

I watched the gallery for a couple of days before making a move. During the day, employees were there—a couple of willowy young women who helped sell art, a young man who handled framing and the loading and unloading of trucks—so I figured that during the day was less than ideal. At night, though, it seemed as though Julian barricaded himself into the building. Later, I'd tell myself it was because he knew he wasn't safe. How could anyone be safe who'd treated people as he had?

On my third night watching, there was an exhibition in the gallery. People came—lots of people—caterers, people I took to be artists, still others who I thought were probably moneyed patrons of the arts.

Late in the evening, I let myself in, fusing myself to a group of young women entering the gallery in a gaggle. I knew I didn't quite fit with their group; angular flesh poured into designer evening wear, their giggles and squeals as much of a covering as the wraps thrown over their shoulders. But it was a gallery and I was all in black. I didn't think anyone would take special note of my arrival. I was right.

Before long a glass of champagne was placed in my hand. There were crackers and cheese. Canapés and petits fours and tiny chocolate tarts etched with lavender *fleur-de-lise*. I wasn't hungry, but I ate some of what was on offer, crackers under cheese turning to sawdust in my mouth. Meanwhile, I moved carefully around the concrete floors of the gallery, looking at the art while keeping an eye out for my target. Max.

"Do you see anything you like?" He'd come upon me so quietly, and from a side entrance. I hadn't even felt his approach.

"Oh, so much," I said, only slightly surprised that it was true. I found myself looking at him. He was tall and slender with a cleft to his chin and a glint in his eye. This close, I could see he was an attractive man.

I could have taken him there. Perhaps I should have. But I hadn't done it before and, in that moment, the thought of taking someone's life clawed at my heart. He must have seen something in my eyes—some sort of glitter, maybe. A feral light, like a fever—and mistaken it for something else. It was by then the end of the evening, and almost everyone had gone. I could—so easily—have taken him right there.

"Will you join me upstairs?" he said. "For a drink?"

I understood his intention. I saw what he saw, as well. I think I was stalling. Waiting for the "perfect moment." All this time later, I understand that they almost never come.

I walked with him to his apartment over the gallery. We sat in a small but elegant living area and chatted for a while. His conversation seemed to fill a spot in my intellect that had been neglected for a long time. He was brilliant. Funny. And he desired me. That was plain on his face. Plain, I think, in the scent he gave out. I hadn't encountered that scent for a long time.

He brought wine and a small plate of canapés I recognized as being leftover from the event and placed them on the coffee table in front of the sofa we sat on. He poured two glasses; handed me one. Conversation was not difficult. We nibbled and drank for a while. It was pleasant—or would have been—had not my mission been demanding so much of my attention.

We talked late into the night. It's a phrase one hears. At one point, he moved towards me as though he had an intention to deepen what we were sharing. I put him off. Conversation, that was all. Maybe the promise of something more.

Eventually though, I let him lead me to his bedroom. We lay fully clothed in each other's arms on a bed as vast as a garden. A dark green duvet enhanced the feeling of being outdoors. That and the modernist landscapes on his bedroom walls. One of them was signed by Julian. That brought me back.

After about an hour, we drifted off to sleep, still in each other's arms. When I woke, I listened to the night sounds for a while. The squeak of wet tires on asphalt. The occasional bleat of a horn or a siren's scream.

I extricated myself and moved to the bathroom, picking up my purse on the way, wincing slightly at the weight of the gun nestled in the soft leather.

In the bathroom, I splashed water on my face, examining it in the mirror as I did. Was there something different there? Something I couldn't erase? But, no, there was not. Not yet, at any rate. I thought that later I might see something, but I didn't then.

I screwed on the suppressor. I didn't think there was anyone in the building, but I knew that a "silenced" gun was anything but silent. I eased the slide back to ensure there was a round in the chamber, then checked the magazine even though I knew I'd filled it before I left the house. I took off the safety and put my hand on the door before I could change my mind.

He stirred when I reentered the room, the gun in my hand. I stopped and stood perfectly still, another piece of art in the room. In the silence, he settled back into slumber. I was glad. I didn't want him to be awake. Before I could change my mind or he could fully wake, I cocked the Bersa and plugged three rounds into him—two into his chest, one into his temple—to be sure the job was done.

In the bathroom, afterwards, I washed my hands in the sink. I could see a drop of his blood on my upper lip. I licked it away.

CHAPTER FIVE

THERE ARE TIMES, in all of our lives, when everything is very difficult. The paths we take, the jobs we do, the choices we make, all result in difficulties. It is as though we are constantly swimming upstream.

At other times, we take a corner, make a choice, and everything falls into place—bing, bing, bing—like dominoes, falling into each other in an orderly fashion. After my time of swimming upstream, after I killed Max, my life was like that. Everything fell into place. Dominoes. Black and white. All fitting together as they should.

My husband died. Let's leave it at that. There was the fire. Then there was a lot of suffering. And then there was none.

My husband died quietly. In his sleep. I was there.

Afterwards, I bent my head to his chest and wept. The tears came from deep inside me. I didn't see it coming, that grief. The sobs ripped from my chest with a violent intensity. It was a primal thing. Primitive. There was nothing of control about it. I cried for the life we had built together, in ashes now. I cried for the splendid young man I had met and later married. I cried, of course, for the child we made together and whom I had buried alone. And then I cried for nothing at all beyond the vast whiteness of feeling that overcame me, enveloped me. I sobbed beyond the point when my body had anything at all to give.

Nurses came. Pulled me from him gently. Said words of comfort and made me drink something. Patted my back. Held me.

None of it healed me, of course. It wasn't meant to. But after a while, the crying stopped and, after a while longer, my hands stopped shaking and the shuddering breaths settled into something more like normal breathing. Later still, I walked into sunshine, amazed to feel my skin react to warmth from the sun and the scent of flowers on the air. Astonished to still feel good to be alive. Astonished and questioning. It didn't seem right, somehow.

How could it be right?

But for a while, after my husband died, it was the last difficult thing. Then the falling into place began. I didn't even see it coming until it was all there, ordered neatly around me.

Dominoes.

I arranged for an agency to represent me.

Those words simplify a lengthy process. Lengthy but not difficult. I just had to think it through. In the job I had in my previous life, I had provided a service, but someone else had done the marketing. It is important in life, I think, to know your strengths, understand your limitations.

So now, again, I had a need: a livelihood. The ability to keep a roof over my head, even though I was now alone in the world and so didn't need much of a roof. And I now had a previously undiscovered skill. I just had to work out how to put those things together: the need and the skill.

I knew that the likelihood of overhearing another conversation as I had in the hospital room Julian the artist and my late husband had shared was unlikely, if not impossible. But what could duplicate that circumstance? Where could I be or go to find someone who might be looking for my particular talent?

The Internet, at first, didn't provide an answer. It produced spoofs and jokes and even video games along with loads of links to film and fictional hit men. It became clear to me that no hard and fast advice that was found there could be taken with anything but a lot of salt. I was coming up dry when an oblique reference to something in an article related to assassination triggered an idea. "The subject said he had found a hit man advertising in a mercenary magazine." I knew I didn't want to start advertising in magazines, but it made me think; maybe others did.

I drove to the one store in my city that still sold a deep selection of magazines and looked for the mercenary section. It wasn't difficult: hunting, fishing, killing. There proved to be not one but six different magazines that I thought might contain what I was looking for. I took a deep breath and waded in, buying all six, then heading home with the idea of continuing my research.

It was clear from that first reading that I was not the intended demographic of the magazines I brought home and then spread out on my bed. Large-breasted women posed in ads for shotguns and off-road vehicles. "In-depth" pieces brayed lustily about traveling across the world to work for Saudi princes and Russian mobsters, but I wasn't here for the articles. I kept skimming, hoping I'd know what I was looking for if I saw it. After a while, I was pretty sure I'd come up empty again and started preparing to make a new plan. Then I turned a page, and something clicked.

At first, I wasn't entirely sure what I was looking at. The language in the small ad wasn't clear, but that seemed intentional:

I knew that the very nature of the thing would force misdirection. It wasn't clear from the words, but I understood right away that they represented the end of my search.

Have what it takes?

Not many do. A steadfast heart. A steady hand. A talent for invisibility. E-mail for more information.

I stared at the ad for a while, willing the words to make sense. Or to not make sense. Sometimes you reach out and find what you are looking for. And I just couldn't think what else these words in this order might mean.

So I responded.

I have the things you've asked for. More. Can't imagine what you request next, but I'm ready.

Then I sent it.

Then I waited.

By the time the response came, I'd imagined I'd gotten it all wrong. Getting the terse note in return didn't entirely reassure me. I assumed this was the nature of the beast. I accepted that they'd have to start somewhere.

Resume? SSN? We're going to look you over.

Requesting the same stuff they might if I were applying to be a clerk at Home Depot surprised me. But then fair enough, I thought. If it *was* what I was hoping, they'd need to look me over pretty carefully, too.

I sent the package off by return e-mail. Then waited some more. It was a shorter wait this time. Just a couple days. And then:

We'd like to look at you in person.

They listed an address near me. A park. I told them I'd show and then I did. But they—or he or she or whatever it or they was or were—did not. I sat in the park, on the designated bench between a water fountain and a kid's play area and waited for . . . something.

While I sat, I kept a sharp eye out, but I didn't see anyone who seemed like someone I might expect to meet. A few moms with little kids heavily engaged in park play. There was one old bum parked on a bench across from me. About the time I figured he might be my contact, he sat up and barfed a violent stream of distressingly green puke directly onto his shoes. That seemed too intense a detail to fake, so I ignored him after that and willed away the memory of what I'd seen.

I sat there for exactly an hour. I didn't look at my phone. I didn't really fidget or even move a whole lot. I went to a kind of meditative place, accessing an oasis of calm I hadn't known I possessed. My eyes were busy, but my body was mostly still. Just as I registered with some surprise how long I'd been sitting there, I felt the vibration of my phone. A text. I didn't recognize the number.

Thank you for your time. We have everything we need.

I sat and looked at the words for a minute, maybe two. Trying to decide what they meant. When I couldn't make sense of them, I texted back.

I don't know what that means.

I wasn't surprised when there was no reply.

CHAPTER SIX

Then all of the money was gone. Not that there had ever been a lot, but now there really was none, plus the cards were maxed and people were starting to bang at the door. I stopped answering the phone.

Not long before my life as I'd known it had ended, we had refinanced the house for a remodel and the remodel had been completed. Polished stone countertops. Walk-in refrigerator. Two dishwashers—two! There had been a reason for the brace of them when we designed that kitchen, but I can't think of it now.

The remodel had demanded new furniture. Truckloads of it. And an outdoor kitchen next to the Pebble Tec pool. All the trappings of a beautiful life. My heart contracted now even at the words "Pebble Tec." In my new reality, I don't remember what they mean.

My husband's income had died with him. He'd made good money when he was on the job but hadn't had the kind of career that offered any type of security. Before long, the money that came to me during my stress leave stopped coming, too. We hadn't carried insurance, not on our lives. Later, I realized we'd been counting on all three of us living forever. Anything else hadn't seemed like a possibility. And now here we were.

Here I was.

I could have gone back to work then. They would have taken me. But I could not go back to work. The very thought of doing it made me weep again; made me wring my hands in despair. The deep, silent, sincere sympathy. The pity. And then, beyond that, the hours of meaningless *function* that would lead to a biweekly *paycheck* in order to purchase more empty *things.* And *why*? And for what? It seemed troublesome now for me to catch my breath, let alone get up and get myself ready to work, or actually go there. No sleepy kisses. No hurried coffee or straightened hair. Going back to work was out of the question. But staying where I was no longer seemed an option, either.

I was a ghost. I wandered around the empty house, sat in the media room with the big TV off, or went outside and trailed my hands through the pool as I watched it turn a little more green every day. In the house that had been my home, there was no longer anything for me. In that house, in that yard, on that street in my hometown. Everything had stopped adding up to sense.

There was no more money coming in, so I stopped making the mortgage payments and paying the insurance and water bills. I could have scraped some of that money together, but why? And for what? There was nothing left I wanted to keep, even if I'd had the funds to do it.

I could have gone along like this for quite some time. Pulling my hand through an ever-more-murky pool until the bank came to take the house back. But I didn't leave it that long. I don't recall there being a decision. Just one day I packed my laptop and a few suitcases, stowed them in my minivan next to some blankets, pillows, and a cooler stuffed with the contents of my refrigerator.

The single item I hesitated over the longest was a photo album. Pictures of parents. Then young love followed by wedding pictures. Next me, swollen with the life growing inside of me, my face foreign to me now. Unfamiliar. A beatific smile. A healthy glow. I didn't recognize that woman at all.

Then baby pictures. First day of school. Visit to Santa. First steps. First bike ride. All those firsts. All of the light on that sweet face.

All of the light.

I left the photo album on the antique table in the foyer. And then I drove away.

CHAPTER SEVEN

THERE WERE HIGHWAYS. And there were roadside rest areas. There were sights to see that I mostly didn't see.

Sometimes I would sleep. More often at rest times, I would lie awake, willing my body to relax. The shift into slumber mostly never came.

I didn't feel as though I was searching. But I didn't feel I was hiding, either.

I could have taken my own life, then. I could have done it easily. But even that seemed like too much bother and maybe, too, the rest I thought that end would give me was better than I deserved. But this limbo, this ghostly drifting, this was what suited me now. This was what I was for.

I might have floated, anchorless, like this, endlessly, but it seemed that, just at a pivotal moment, when all hope had drained away, they contacted me again.

Enough time and activity had passed that I had forgotten about my hour in the park. Whatever had happened was inexplicable, but it was in the past. I had the feeling of a near miss. Like I'd been close to something that had slipped away.

I don't remember where I was when the text came, but that part doesn't matter. I recognized the number, though. Still, I was unprepared.

Download a Tor browser. Then visit aligatormail.onion. Login as newfish, password 12345678. More instructions at that time.

I had no idea what any of this meant. It seemed like a foreign language. I didn't even know what a Tor browser might be. But I've never been slow, and moss doesn't grow on me.

And so, even though I really had no idea what I was getting into, or entirely what I was agreeing to, I texted back:

OK.

Upon Googling, I found that the Tor browser was my "gateway to the Deep Web," which proved to be an unregulated Internet space that was available to me via means of which I was not at that time quite clear. Downloading the browser was easy and free. And aligatormail.onion was also easily accessed. By the time I typed in the password they'd fed me, I was nervous, though I wasn't sure why. I didn't know what was waiting, really. And, yet, part of me knew very well.

To: newfish@aligatormail.onion
From: Nevermind
Subject: First Assignment

You passed the first tests. We'll see if you pass this one. Odds are against you (nothing personal) but we like the cut of your jib.

Location: 41.9028168 -87.624505

Subject name: Alistair Pattison

Method: Your choosing

Expediency: At your discretion, under 30 days please

Payment: Via Bitcoin. Please establish Bitcoin account and leave details via this e-mail address.

Please alert via text when the job is complete. Payment will be made in full at that time.

And that was it. It wasn't nearly enough information; though, in some ways, it was way too much.

We like the cut of your jib.

I googled that, as well. The language was redolent of someone of a certain class. *The cut of your jib.* I pondered that until I couldn't anymore. East Coast, prep schools and Ivy League. Then I focused on the rest of what was said. Maybe the jib pondering had helped me avoid the more pressing issues right in front of me.

It didn't take much googling for me to realize that Alistair Pattison was the scion of a successful contracting firm in a city a two-hour flight from where I'd lived with my Pebble Tec pool. Pattison was a father. A grandfather. He'd been a husband, but was now a widower—small mercies. And someone wanted him dead. A spouse, a lover, a child, a competitor. It was not my job to think about that part. I knew that before I even really began.

I searched a bit further, wanting to know more about him, thinking it would help with my mission. There was a fair amount of information floating around. News stories and items from the society pages, a few of court documents, an op-ed page in the newspaper with a lot of unpleasant comments. From all of that I got the idea that, whatever else was true, Alistair Pattison was a nasty piece of work who had, in his fairly long life, pissed off a lot of people.

He was old now and feeble, but old injuries can die hard and, from what I could see, any number of people might want him dead.

The difficult thing for me was going to be how I did it. Though the address that had been sent to me was a luxury condominium on the lake, I discovered Pattison was now in a nursing home. I was imagining that even the fairly tame "woof!" the Bersa made when silenced might attract attention in the hospital setting. I needed something else.

With a bit more research, I determined I would use ricin to kill him. It sounded super easy to make, so I ordered castor beans on eBay and had them delivered to a UPS store near the hotel I reserved at the same time.

I booked my flight. And, after only a small struggle, set up a Bitcoin account, only half sure I got it right. And there was an irony that almost made me smile for the first time in weeks: figuring out how to get the Bitcoin thing right seemed more daunting than making the deadly toxic poison was going to be.

Tomorrow was coming; was nearly here. And I was standing there with one foot through the doorway. I could have drifted, sure. But this? It just seemed like the next correct thing. I set out and it was like everything changed in that moment. Like nothing was ever quite the same.

CHAPTER EIGHT

THE NURSING HOME has that smell. Not quite urine. Not exactly dust and disuse. A waiting smell. The smell of roads not traveled and forks not taken. The smell of termination.

I arrive in the evening, just as visiting hours are ending. I slip into the unguarded hallways unobserved, thinking that walking as though I belong will get me anywhere I need to go.

It is not difficult to find what I am looking for. The hallway is conveniently marked with the name of the residents who live in each room. And fourth door on the right, I find it: Pattison, A.

I slip through the door quickly and quietly from an empty hallway. No one has seen me arrive. Except Pattison, of course. He is sitting up in a hospital bed on the far side of a large private room, blue eyes bright in a wasted face. He looks pleased to see me. Like a lot of people in his position, I am betting he doesn't get many visitors.

"Ella," he says when I am standing at the foot of his bed. His voice makes me falter. There is such joy in it. Such relief. It almost makes me feel ashamed, though I don't quite understand why. "It is so good of you to come."

"Of . . . of course," I say. Not correcting him about my identity for so many reasons.

"Do you need money? Is that why you are here?" The words are delivered without rancor: as though that would be the natural course of events.

"No." I wonder what to say to keep him from suspecting I am not who he thinks I am, then realize it probably doesn't matter.

"Oh. How funny. I don't think I've ever seen you when you weren't looking for money."

"Well, I'm not now." I say it evenly, with no extra weight on any syllable.

The sound he makes indicates he is digesting this. I settle into the visitor's chair across from the bed. I tell myself I am doing this to make sure he doesn't suspect anything, and no alarms will be sounded, but a part of me knows I am just stalling. I am here to do something, but now that I am here, I am no longer sure I have the gumption.

"How is Thomas?"

The simplest question is difficult when you have nothing to go on. I opt for the oblique.

"How is he? He is Thomas," I say. "You know."

He laughs at that. A scratchy, hollow sound, like he hasn't laughed in a long time, and I figure that's probably true. From what I can see and from what I know, he hasn't had much to laugh about. "All true. You've said it very well."

The ricin is in an envelope in my purse. The creation and drying of it had gone like clockwork, exactly like the instructions I'd followed so carefully had advised. I'd had some vague plan of blowing it into his face, preferably while he was sleeping. I hadn't expected wakefulness or welcome. Hadn't anticipated joviality. Hadn't expected kind of *liking* him and his intelligent blue eyes.

I'd read about the effects of ricin poisoning. It would be an ugly, painful death. Inelegant. In my mind's eye, it had all seemed very easy. Seamless. Sitting here across from the frail old man, I wonder if I can do it that way. I am beginning to doubt it.

A nurse bustles in, pulling me from my thoughts.

"Oh, Alistair," she says brightly. "You have company. How nice! Who is this?"

"This is my great-niece, Ella," he answers before I have the chance to manufacture anything. I watch the nurse's face but don't see a flicker. If Ella has ever been here, the nurse hasn't seen her. Nor does she look as though she felt I shouldn't be here. Maybe sign-in wasn't part of what she monitored. I allow myself to breathe.

"Well, nice to meet you, Ella," she says. She seems warm. Friendly. I get the feeling that she might be welcoming to any relative who chose to spend time with one of her charges. "I'm Jenny." And then kindly to Alistair, "It's near the end of visiting hours, Al. I'll leave you alone for a bit. But at quarter after, I'll have to come back and kick her out." She closes the door behind her quietly as she leaves the private room, and I realize I have a solid twenty minutes to do whatever needs to be done. My heart flutters towards panic, and I calm it with a breath. Calm it, also, with the thought that this is something I am required to do. I can walk away, sure. But the people responsible for giving me this assignment won't give me more if I do that, I'm certain of it. This is a single chance kind of thing. An audition, even. Anyway, if I don't do it, someone else will. There is always someone else. And if not someone, then time. Alistair is old. One way or another, he has used up all of his time.

I am moving before I realize I've made a decision. A pillow muffles the Bersa's already silenced bark and blocks Pattison's view of what is coming. Blocks *my* view of those sharp blue eyes. It is over almost before it began. Easy. Though an unseen part of me bleeds.

I flush the ricin before I leave the private hospital room. It all just seems kinder this way.

Back in my rented car, I text the number.

It is done.

There is no reply, but this time I didn't expect one.

CHAPTER NINE

There are more assignments after that. Slowly at first, then at a more consistent trickle. I figure it probably stems from their growing confidence in me as much as anything. And business, for them, is probably good. Apparently, there are a lot of people that need killing. Every day.

Of course, I do not do it every day. Not even close. But the work is lucrative, and I don't have to do a lot of it. My natural camouflage—an average woman of early middle years, neither beautiful nor ugly—stands me in good stead and I get a lot of jobs.

Life has a pattern. There is a trip, culminating in a job, followed by a period of quiet—spiritually and actually—when I use the money gained to try and rebuild something that looks like a life. It ends up being both easier and more difficult than I'd thought it would be.

A life.

What is that made of? A family. Mine is gone. A job? Mine has no watercooler, no office parties. Friends? I cut all ties with them after the fire. Directly after, I couldn't stand the pity I'd see in their faces. Later, I felt like an imposter when I'd see them. They would talk about things I found empty and inane. Or worse: meaningless. Not that my thoughts had so much meaning, but at least I did not pretend. I found I no longer had the capacity for it. Life. Death. Living. Dying. When your life is so basic, small talk doesn't really have a place, that's what I found.

And now? Well, now they don't even know where or who I am.

In my half-hearted quest to build a new life, I buy a house. I pay cash. It is very different from the house I'd had when I was part of a family. No Pebble Tec pool. It is little more than a cottage, really, this new-to-me house. And it is far enough from the nearest small town to be quiet, while really not being very far out at all: less than twenty minutes in a car.

The house has a living room, a kitchen with a little dining area in it, two bedrooms. I outfit one of the bedrooms as a guestroom, though I anticipate no guests. And there is a single bathroom. I can't imagine I would ever require more than one. The house is modest and old-fashioned, but with a sort of lost middle American charm. From the first moment, I feel very comfortable there. I feel like I am coming home.

It is private. A small acreage at the edge of a forest and no one around to see me come and go. I create a persona for myself, one with an indistinct name. Bland. Vanilla. I give the impression but do not actually say that I am a writer of some sort, likely of something uninteresting that nobody cares about anyway. Knitting in Hellenic times. Or the mating habits of baboons in captivity. Nothing anyone would ask about. Topics people would avoid asking about, for fear the answer would be lengthy. The profession goes along with the baggy housedresses I take to wearing out there alone and when I drive into town for supplies. The bulky sweaters. The outmoded glasses. The hair pulled back into a rough bun. I become an invisible resident in an already invisible demographic. I come and go, and nobody sees.

Invisible or no, I still need to fill my time. The time between. I take a stab at gardening, spending hours in the pale spring sun enriching a small, overgrown rectangle that looks as though it might have been a kitchen garden in the long-ago. A thick bunch of rhubarb starts sprouting of its own accord as soon as the weather begins to warm up. The enthusiasm of that volunteer rhubarb inspires me. If something can appear as though by magic with no effort on my part, what can happen if I add some muscle and intent?

And so, I set to work. But just as it looks like my new garden is about to flourish, I catch a job in the Far East that keeps me away for a number of weeks. By the time I get back, the poor baby plants I stuck in the ground before I left have withered and died. Even the rhubarb now looks as though it might pack it in. It ends gardening for me, and I don't have the heart to try again. It seems cruel to plant something in order to watch it die. There's been enough death in my life. There is enough death. I don't want it at home. Not anymore.

So gardening is out before it even really begins. I let the weeds reclaim the little bits of brown I'd unearthed and feel a dull satisfaction at the resilient green that results. I leave the rhubarb alone though. I'd never really acquired a taste for the stuff, and, in any case, it seems to manage better without me.

The jobs start slowly, then come with increasing regularity. There is a pattern to this. A rhythm. The quiet weeks and sometimes months at home, passing time at my house and rambling in the forest and making occasional trips into the nearby small town for supplies. And then work, of course. An assignment generally involves a few days or a week of traveling, stalking followed by a hit, and then—sometimes by circuitous methods—home, where it all begins again.

I devise systems to keep everything sorted. Everything tidy. I keep a packed suitcase and an empty gym bag in the trunk of the car that replaced the minivan. The suitcase holds the tools of my trade, including a darker twin of the Bersa I have with me always. I keep the second gun under a false bottom in my trunk, under and around the spare tire of the elderly tank-like Volvo I pick up and have customized several hundred miles from my little town. The car is invisible in my rural community. Like me. But solid enough to take whatever is coming. I hope that part is true for me, as well. I'm not always so sure.

I don't spend a lot of time thinking about fingerprints or DNA, but I do take basic precautions. Since I've never been arrested, I know I won't show up on any law enforcement lists, but I am aware that other databases exist in our society—such as murder databases. And so I keep nitrile gloves and disinfectant wipes in there, too. Just in case. I am careful.

All of this becomes my life. It is neither stimulating nor satisfying or even stifling. I am living. I am alive. I don't want for anything, except there is a sort of dull hunger in me that I seem never able to fill. And there are days I wake covered in sweat, and with my heart racing, like I've been chasing something; like something has been chasing me. Still, I know worse existences are possible. Worse outcomes. All things considered.

I am in stasis, in a way, though I can't imagine what I'm waiting for. Even though I have a home now, I am drifting, still. To be settled in my spirit, and to have a real life, that would not reflect the things I feel I deserve.

So I drift for a while. Time passes. This becomes my now. And I don't think about what my tomorrow will hold or even if it will develop at all.

CHAPTER TEN

THE DAY THAT everything changes, the only thing I see coming at me is lamb stew. I'd seen a recipe in a food magazine and, suddenly, nothing will do but that I drive into town to the butcher's for three pounds of lamb. I have the kind of life that allows self-indulgence of that nature. The drive, followed by the cooking, are the activities that will help pass this day.

Three pounds of meat is an extraordinary amount, really, considering it's only me eating and I never entertain. But it is what I want and, anyway, I have a freezer. If I end up eating defrosted lamb stew every few weeks for the next half year, that will work out fine, too.

The ingredients called for tell me the stew will be beyond good. It will have figs and dried apricots. Pomegranate molasses, masses of garlic, a full pound of mushrooms. Other things, as well. I imagine it will be super delicious. A stew worthy of the drive necessary to gather the ingredients.

Of all the things I *do* have in my new life, a television is not one of them. Not missing, but not wanted. For me, television had been a family activity in the life before. The three of us huddled around a pizza and watching some PG movie. Or my husband curled up with me on the couch, binge-watching some inane show, me folded into the protective curve of his shoulder, even when many of the other warmths we'd shared had passed away. There was this: physical connection in a puddle of evening calm, our shared life whispering all around us. Not stimulating, no. But comforting somehow. At least in memory. But that's not how it is now.

When I move into the house, I get a television right away just because one does. There is a wall in the living room that looks like the place where a television should be. But when I put it there, it leaves me feeling even more hollow and alone. The soulless voices in sitcoms and reality shows seemingly offering pale echoes of actual reality. The crime dramas all hollow and unreal. Family sagas are worse. They leave me weeping. And old movies bring back memories I have no place for. There is nothing I want to see. I keep trying, though. That's what people do: they watch TV. And so, every so often, I turn it on again.

And then it gets worse. I am watching the news; the coverage of the inexplicable killing of a prominent person I had seen die. Television brings me the keening widow. The grief-stricken children. Traces of a life I'd contributed to ending. I don't want to see that.

I can't see that.

As much as possible, I want—no, *need*—the people I hit to be nothing more than the scraps of information shared with me upon assignment. Then perhaps a few details I ferret out myself; just enough to get the job done. Anything additional makes those lives a little too real. Anything additional is surplus to requirement.

So I shut it down, half carrying, half dragging the huge television out to the garage, then immediately forgetting about it. Without the hollow black square of a television gaping at me from the living room, even significant news events have trouble trickling down to me. Everyone has to be talking about it, or else I will never hear. Sometimes not even then. This does not concern me. In the state I am in, I no longer have room for details that don't move my immediate concerns forward. The French president. The state of railroads in Italy. A heartbreaking car accident in Texas. None of this has meaning to me. It's not that it doesn't matter, no, that's not it. It's just that I don't care. It doesn't touch me. Nothing does.

And then one day that changes.

I go to the local butcher's for my lamb. That stew. There is a television playing in the back of the shop. And I hear something drift over from the TV that I cannot, at first, believe. The clerk helping me sees me stop and listen, right between ordering my lamb and a bit of chicken I'd intended to pop in the freezer. She sees my widened eyes and makes a sympathetic sound.

"I *know*," she says. "Another one. Can you believe it? How long will this go on?"

"Another? But how many have there been?"

"You really don't know?"

"I live under a rock. Never mind. How many?"

"This makes sixteen! Imagine. And they're sure it's the same guy. The MO is distinctive, that's what they said."

MO. Civilian talk learned from watching television. I know what it means though. *Modus operandi*. Method of operating. Whoever has done this heinous thing has done it frequently enough that his style can be determined by examination of what has occurred. A chilling thought.

I reposition myself so I can see the television better, and the clerk and I both turn our heads to see the screen where distraught-looking parents are being interviewed by a woman whose pale-blond hair seems to perch on her head like a hat. The body of the missing child has not yet been found, but there is little hope she is alive—that's what is under discussion. Everyone expects that she is dead. The child had been spotted getting into a van, driven by the man they knew had been taking these children. An item of clothing has been recovered. Things do not look good.

"Sixteen," I repeat. It's an impossible number.

"That they know of. They say there have been others they haven't been able to connect to the same guy. Not for sure."

Murder database. The phrase comes back to me again. In this context, it has a whole new meaning.

The camera is now showing a charming town. A bandstand. A high school football team. Oaks whose branches are heavy with Spanish moss sway over a golf course so green it makes you doubt the color balance of the set we are watching it on. Then a smash cut back to the grieving parents. The highlight of this hour. Something so raw in them. Animal grief. I recognize it. I feel it in my soul. They are my siblings. I am connected to them.

The reporter sticks a microphone in the mother's face.

"Do you have anything you'd like to share with my audience, Mrs. Webster?"

The eyes she turns on the camera are dead. Empty. She moves her mouth, but no sounds come out. It is like looking at the shell of a person. Like whoever usually lives inside has moved out. I recognize the expression, the emptiness. More than that, I hear the things she does not say, the tears she can't yet cry.

"My God," I say out loud, her tears running down my cheek.

"Yes," the clerk agrees, her voice bringing me back. I am in a butcher shop. For a heartbeat, I'd forgotten. "Unthinkable."

"Yes. Beyond thought," I say, as something hard locks inside me. It pushes the tears away. I complete my transaction, money and meat change hands, but my mind is elsewhere.

I go home with the three pounds of lamb I'd come for. The pomegranate molasses. Kosher salt. Figs. After a while, I start making the stew I'd been so excited about. But even following the recipe, my motions are automatic. Chopping, searing, deglazing; I am on autopilot. My mind is elsewhere.

I can't get the images out of my head. The dead eyes of the parents. The bleating newscasters. The trail of children lost. There is no room in my head, my heart for all of this grief. Mountains of it. Rivers. Even with my kitchen alive with the scent of onions, garlic, and spice, that grief wells up and overflows. More than I'd thought could be left in the world. And all of it had happened fifteen times before. At least. In some ways, I feel it more than I'd felt my own loss, even if only because, at that time, I'd been too numb to feel.

In desperation and like all the sheep around me, I pull out my laptop and look for the news. Finding it is maddeningly easy—the story is everywhere—though none of it is even really "new," simply constant rehashing of stories already told. There is only the occasional addition of some morbid detail, sometimes told in the breathless tones of someone craving and fishing for enthusiastic response.

Authorities know that the perpetrator—the monster—is a young man in San Pasado County in California. William Atwater, twenty-seven years old. The photos that are constantly being aired show pale blue eyes, a strong jaw and light hair that curls slightly. If he ever smiled, the total effect would be that of a surfer kid, though none of the photos show a smile.

Various newscasters are reporting that confirming that it had been Atwater had been surprisingly simple. After killing several of his young victims, he had posted photos to his Facebook page. He didn't have a lot of friends. Even so, several people had reported it instantly. And, the next time, several more. After a while, the officials had begun to believe and had looked into things. This alone, of course, had caused outrage. Had the authorities paid attention sooner, lives would have been saved, Atwater apprehended. And this is part of the reverberations that move through the news just as I tune in. Negligence of several sorts had been involved, various parties are saying. And the Facebook tie-in provides an Internet connection of the sort the media loves to crow about. Now it was an *Internet* killing, though from what I could see, that didn't reflect the actual picture at all.

But it is the local authorities who are being given the most grief. Those in charge had not paid attention and with that had not protected several young citizens who had come to horrid ends, that's what is being said. No one wanted to think about it, but there it was. The system had somehow broken down. Children had gone missing and had probably died. Children continued to die because, by the time the police and the powers that be put everything together, Atwater had fled.

I get up from my reading and watching. Move to the bathroom. Throw up tidily into the toilet. Wash my hands and then my face to redness with a rough washcloth. Go back to my computer. Continue reading. I don't know how much of what I read is true, but the stories are decisive and they're all over the map: Atwater's biological parents, both dead, had been second cousins. Bodies of two of the children he had killed early on had been recovered. Twin girls, aged eight. They had been found holding hands. An early teacher of Atwater's had come forward and said he had once found the murderer as a young man, in the schoolyard pulling the wings off flies. Any fact or almost-fact, it seems, is grist for the news mill: anything to keep the story alive. And with a story like this one? It doesn't take much.

By the time I've collected all of the available facts, it feels as though my heart is bleeding and there is nothing left inside me to throw up. And while I continue to learn everything I can, I weep. I weep as I haven't since my own child died. I weep for all of those mothers and fathers: I understand what this means to them all too well. I know mine is not a rational response: all this weeping to honor the death of other people's children. But still. I weep on.

After a while, I feel a shift inside myself. I feel the grief hardening; morphing into something different. I stop crying and feel something growing. It's an embryo at first. I lean into it. Embrace it. Feel it grow. I walk into a rage so pure and perfect, I have to sit back and taste it in my throat. This thing I feel is like love in its intensity. It fills my chest. Stops my breath. Fills me with need.

I look again at photos of the face of the killer. The man-child who has stopped the breath of at least sixteen rural California kids. I look at him and mark his face. Photos taken at the time of high school are the most common. His face would be more lined now and slightly more worn.

William Atwater. No violent history on record. Weedy. White. Maybe a little goofy looking, but nothing exceptional in his face. He looks neither super smart nor alarmingly dumb and, certainly, there is no hint in his face of the violence that will come. None I can see, at any rate, and I peer at the photos very closely. No hint of what, by the time these early photos were taken, may well already have begun, even if only in small ways.

He abducted these children, one by one. And other children perhaps, as well. He drove them into remote areas outside of town and he ultimately bled them, the way one does a cow at slaughter. That's what was learned from the bodies that had been recovered. The ones that hadn't been recovered, of course, no one knew for sure.

After reading all of this, digesting it as well as I can, I no longer feel anger. I have moved beyond it to a state that is unfamiliar to me. It feels like I'm stone, like I am altered. My feelings are so well defined and so pure, I can think of little else. I am consumed by it.

I understand that there are likely strong psychological reasons for all of the things Atwater has done. Behavior like this isn't born in a vacuum. Abusive father. Absent mother. Whatever the hell else: shit has happened to this guy and broken him in some important way. I know what I should probably be feeling is sympathy. Empathy. Pity, even. But that isn't what I feel. Maybe he could even be apprehended and repaired, but that isn't what I think about. And while the talking heads on the newsfeeds bleat on and on about what should be done, I come to understand one thing: I want William Atwater dead.

CHAPTER ELEVEN

THE WORLD IS fucked. And if not fucked, then at least it is broken. And it isn't only my world, though that part clearly is. But everything. Broken. People kill each other all the time, and for no reason and never mind all the people who get killed for big reasons. I have had a hand in some of those myself.

There are cops who kill innocent bystanders. Boom, boom, boom, boom: four in the chest for being born with a certain color skin. Or workers in a federal building. Or vacationers in an airport. Or a delicate line of kids whose big crime it was to breathe.

So the world is broken, and there is no way to fix it. At least, there is no way for you or me to fix it. Do you see? We can rage against a corrupt system. We can vent on our Facebook walls. Shake our fists or wave signs at politicians when we catch them unawares. We can tweet. But all of these things are acts of the powerless masses. Our hearts break with these things until we can't stand it anymore, then we weep until, finally, we get hard and move on. We don't do this because we are callous. We do it because we, quite simply, have no choice. We take the unthinkable and we grapple with it until, finally, we are forced to come to terms with the impossible. Sucks to be us. Yes, us. We make it thinkable and move on.

But what about me?

I can't stop thinking about William Atwater. Somehow, despite everything, he is alive. At least sixteen kids are dead with what seems like the very real possibility of more to come. I can't make all of these facts sit next to each other in my head.

Days go by and I think about this. Deeply and with no conclusions but, truly, there is little more for me to do. The plants have turned brown and have shriveled beyond life. The stew has been completed and divvied up into freezer bags and stored. I tramp around the forests some, but even the peaceful walks I usually enjoy don't give me much pleasure. I keep thinking about a world without justice. A world where angels die but monsters remain free, the threat of the possibility they represent an ever-present blight on the horizon.

Before I can ponder all of this too much, I get a job. For a little while, this commands all of my attention. In that way, it is a welcome break.

Now that I am established, a routine has emerged. Assignments come in e-mail. I check my account daily through my Tor browser on the DeepNet. The silence is always broken by a text to give me a heads-up to check my mail if they want me to get on something right away. The text is always the same, though the number is always different. I don't know if there are different phones, possibly burners, on their end. Or maybe it's different people all the time. Different places. Or the calls might be generated by some program that makes everything random and anonymous. I don't dwell on it, though. It's not like it really makes a difference in the outcome or like I'm ever going to find out.

"*Hey, sunshine! How's life treating you?*" will come the text.

And my response doesn't vary much.

"*I told you it was over. Stop bugging me or I'll block you.*" Or, "*I've moved on. Let's not do this anymore, okay?*" Or something else that indicates there will be no further response from my end. And then I go to my e-mail.

Since it comes from the DeepNet, theoretically the e-mail I am sent is untraceable. And it stays on the server; there's nothing downloaded to my computer. Still, it's a dangerous business. I don't take any chances. And neither do they, even though I still don't know who or where *they* are. Only that I get my instructions, execute the job—pardon the pun—then report back in when the job is complete. Within twenty-four hours, there is a deposit to my Bitcoin account. I now have more Bitcoins than I know what to do with. Not a lot of the things I desire can be bought. I keep doing the work anyway. At this stage, I wouldn't even know what else to do.

So I check my e-mail. And there isn't a message there every day, but there is one today. And it is cryptic. The nature of the beast. But by now I know what it all means.

49.256094 -123.132813 49.283847-123.093670 ASAP. AD.

And then a name.

The first two numbers are the target's home. The second two are the preferred location for the hit. And they want him taken out as soon as possible—ASAP—and he needs to die by accident. *AD*. Accidental Death. Not a lot of those come my way.

I plug the second set of coordinates into an app on my phone. It's an office building in downtown Vancouver, Canada.

I book my travel. Book a place to stay. Then get an early night's sleep. Tomorrow will be a difficult day no matter how well it goes. Assignments always equal difficult days.

I decide not to take the Bersa. Arrange instead to have another sent to me via a UPS store in the heart of the city. It will come to a name that is not mine, but I'll be able to pick it up. I pay a lot for this service, via a dark web connection, but I figure it will be worth it for the hassle to get an untraceable Bersa to Canada, where guns are much harder to lay your hands on.

There is nothing that cements me to my house. No man, no kids, not even a cat. Still, when I lock the door to go away even for a few days, there is a little pang that goes with me. Maybe missing something I don't have. Again. I try not to think about it. As time goes on, I'm getting better at that.

I take my car to long-term parking some distance from the airport. It is prudent to cover my tracks. Then a shuttle the last bit of the journey.

There are no direct flights from my local airport to Vancouver. I have to go through Phoenix, an airport I know well, because it's a hub. I change into more fashionable clothing. I'm going to a city; my baggy country housedress will stand out there and that won't do. I brush makeup onto my lashes, my cheeks. Sweep my hair up into something like a chignon. I feel ready for business. I feel nearly human again.

I have a lunch in the airport so good it is ridiculous. Airport food is not supposed to be excellent, but here we are. I savor it. Take my time between flights. Even order a glass of wine. I'm heading to a foreign country. One I've never been to before. I'm not certain there will be anything good to eat. Maple syrup and beavers. Possibly cheese. I can't even imagine what Canadians might eat.

I sleep much of the way to Vancouver. Why not? There is nothing else to do. But once there I have an awakening of the senses. It smells beautiful. Amazing. As soon as the plane is on the ground and we passengers are on an ill-protected walkway to the main terminal, I smell something rough and new. A bit of the mountains. A bit of the sea. My heart quickens with it.

In the terminal, one must deal with customs.

What is the purpose of your visit?

Why, pleasure. Of course. What else? To see this jewel. This well-designed city perched charmingly on the sea.

How long will you be here?

A few days. Perhaps a week. There is so much to enjoy!

Have a great visit!

Oh, yes. Yes. Of course. I shall.

I find Vancouver to be stunning. Beyond my expectations. City of glass. Of ocean. Of apparent racial harmony. It's a cool place.

I've arrived in the evening and it's raining. The taxi driver grunts at me when I mention the rain, and I'm not sure what language the grunt is in, but it's indecipherable to me.

It turns out the UPS store is on the way to the hotel, so I get the taxi to stop and wait for me while I run in to pick up my package. I breathe once it's done and we're underway again: there have been no obstacles, but one never knows.

My hotel is on English Bay facing the ocean. A venerated boutique hotel that is predicted not to last out the decade, but which has been here since the century before the one just past. A long time.

"Do you know Errol Flynn's dick fell off at this hotel?" Overheard as I stand in line, waiting to check in.

Response. "Who's Errol Flynn?"

"Wasn't he a Red Hot Chili Pepper?" I offer, deadpan. The two girls look at each other questioningly, then give me a wide berth as they head for the exit. I don't blame them. Theirs is probably the right call.

I'm not long in my room. I don't need time to think, but I've got time to kill and walking seems a better way to do that than fighting the hotel television system in my room. And I didn't bring a book.

I open the package containing my burner Bersa and a box of cartridges and tuck them into the safe in the room. I unpack my suitcase, then go back to the lobby. I get an umbrella from the concierge, then head out the front door and into a light and refreshing evening rain. It isn't cold.

There is a seawall in Vancouver. It snakes around the edge of the city for miles and miles, a little pedestrian highway at the edge of the sea. I walk this now. Not thinking about my destination or if I even really have one. I figure, in fact, I probably do not, just enjoying the feeling of being able to walk out at night. I tried it once in the country and it scared the hell out of me. Noises in the dark. Likely small harmless animals. Or deer, more frightened of me than I was of them. Still. I know all too well the danger that can lurk in the night. There are chances I choose not to take. Better safe than sorry, once again.

The city at night is vibrant, though. And I am in a safe area, populated by tourists and fashionable couples. I walk on the seawall in the direction of the city, not the big park near the hotel. I have an idea of where I am going. I let my feet take me there.

I force my mind blank, making the walk meditative. Healing. Trying to stay aware of the cool sea air filling my lungs and the soft kiss of moisture on my skin, welcome after the hours in airports and planes.

I walk along the seawall as far as I can, then up a few blocks to where tomorrow I will do what I've come to do. One way or another. I'm in front of a four-story building of tidy appearance, despite the crumbling brick. It has an aura of solidity, even though it is in a terrible part of town.

I stand there in the rain for a few minutes, looking at the building, thinking of what approach I will take when the time comes. I am so focused, and maybe so tired, that I am startled when the front door opens and a man pops out. He is energetic and more youthful than the photo I'd been sent had led me to think he would be, but I know that it is him.

Though I am a few feet from the entrance, to my surprise my usual invisibility shield of middle-aged woman doesn't hold. He crosses to me in a few strong steps, and does it so quickly, I have no time to collect myself and scurry away.

"Is everything all right?" he says when he reaches me. He is concerned. It is possible this is not the sort of neighborhood a woman can safely wander around in by herself. I hadn't known that.

"Well, sure," I reply reflexively. "I'm kind of a tourist. Out for an evening walk. I guess I got a bit turned around."

"I guess you did," he says, and I look at him quickly, but there is nothing but warmth in his voice and on his face. Nothing more than honest concern. "What's a bit of a tourist, anyway? Never mind. You can tell me while we walk. I'm heading home now myself. Walking. Will be no trouble for me to see you right. Where are you staying? What part of town?"

"I'm at the Sylvia. In the West End."

He nods approvingly and starts guiding me west. "Good choice. Charming. Not ostentatious. And all the right ghosts."

"Errol Flynn?" I say, pushing myself to keep up with his longer strides.

"Oh yeah. Him. Sure. I think. But others. Some apparition sits on the bed in one of the rooms on the sixth floor, if I remember correctly. Something I read. You're not on the sixth floor, are you?"

I shake my head.

"You should be all right then."

I laugh as we walk. "Well, *that's* a relief. Where are you walking me?"

"I live in Coal Harbour, which is not exactly where you're going, but it's quite close. I'm going to see you home."

"Ah," I say, trying not to think about how complicated this is getting. And then, after a while, not caring. We enjoy a companionable silence and, when we chat, words move easily between us.

As we walk, he talks about points of interest. He does it easily and well, and I can tell he is a man who is used to being treated like he has things worth saying. He asks what I do and something I'd read in the in-fight magazine provides the answer. I tell him I'm a civic planner, sent to Vancouver to evaluate local design.

"A lot of people are doing that now," he says. "I read about that somewhere. Apparently, we have a lot of civic design worth emulating in this city. Who knew?"

I wonder if we'd read the same article, but keep my yap shut.

"Well, this has been pleasant," he says once we reach the hotel. "For various reasons, I don't want to go back to my lonely abode quite yet. And I know the bar in this hotel is nice enough. Will you join me for a drink?"

"*Nice enough* doesn't sound like much of an endorsement. But sure. Why not?"

We sit at a table by the window, the three or four other patrons in the place far enough away that we can't hear their conversations, nor they ours. It's dark out, so not much can be seen from the window, but I know the ocean is waiting out there, just beyond my view. A gentler ocean here in Vancouver than I'd experienced in other places. Calmed by a large island that lies out there farther still, also out of view.

The wine we share is drinkable, not much more. As we sip and chat, a part of me dips down to darker places. Who wants this man dead? An ex-wife? A business partner? A jealous sibling? A business competitor? I seldom wonder. It's not part of my concern. And, except with prominent figures, I never have reason to know or find out. I try to stop myself from wondering now. It is not part of my business.

"Are you married?" I hear myself ask over our second glass of wine. I think about it a lot before asking. An innocuous enough question, considering our positions. It might even seem curious if I did *not* ask.

"I was," he says over his wine. "I'm not now. What about you?" And this is another thing I find myself liking in him: his directness. A simplicity to it, one that is rare. His eyes meet mine as he asks. They are a pleasant slatey color. Like stone warmed by sun.

"Same," I hear myself say. "Just the same." And we smile as we sip, almost as though we've shared a joke. Which I guess in a way we have.

CHAPTER TWELVE

It is not inevitable that he should end up in my bed on the not-haunted third floor of the Sylvia Hotel. There are other possibilities. When it happens, though, I do not contemplate the wisdom of the move. And I try hard not to think about the consequences of my actions.

As he slides inside me, I wonder at what I am feeling. It is as though I'd known it would happen from the moment he'd taken those few strong strides towards me as I stood outside his office building in the rain. Like nothing else had even been possible. If I wasn't certain of that before, it becomes clear in the elevator, the hard length of him pressed into me, his tongue exploring the delicate lines of my ear, my chin, my neck.

By the time our unclothed bodies join in the ancient bed, I know it solidly: this was meant to be. Human touch has become difficult for me. But not here now, with him. His warmth and laughter and maybe just the feel of his skin has melted whatever reserve there might have been.

Afterwards, there is this ethereal stillness. I am aware of street noise at some distance. I imagine I can sometimes hear the lap of a wave, though I know that cannot be the truth.

We call for room service. Our exertions have made him hungry, he says. And he wants something to drink. When room service comes, he answers the door with a towel wrapped around him. I admire the way the muscles move under his skin. He has ordered grilled squid and stuffed mushrooms, and a crab cake too big for its own good. We share the food, and the wine that arrives with it, with the abandon and comfort of long lovers. Feeding each other and laughing together, giddy with something too precious to hold.

I like the strong, hot feel of him. And the way laughter storms his face. And the intensity with which he watches me when I speak, meeting my eyes. Watching for signs of things not said. Watching. Ever watchful.

There is a time when we sleep, feet touching, his hand cupped gently into the curve between my legs. I don't know when wakefulness falls away, but it comes to both of us all at once. After a while, though, I wake. I pull the covers over us and extinguish the lights and try not to think about what I need to do. As I've said: human connections don't come easily to me anymore. And yet I feel something uncomplicated growing more quickly than I would have thought possible. Uncomplicated in feeling yet complicated by fact. I push that thought away. I think about the Bersa, snug in the room safe in the closet. I imagine myself going to her, loading. See myself, in my mind's eye, creeping towards him, holding the gun to the soft, flat spot just behind his left ear. Letting in the bullet that would find its way home.

His eyes fly open and he regards me levelly. I feel my color rise.

"Beautiful eyes," he says. "And what's behind them?"

"Hmmm," I say.

"What are you thinking?"

"I was thinking about how beautiful you are," I say without missing a beat. "When you sleep, I mean. You looked so very peaceful."

He smiles then. A real smile. His teeth are white and even. A movie star's smile. "You're lying," he says cheerfully. "But that's okay." I start to protest but he stops me. And he is right. It is okay. My thoughts are my own.

In the morning he leaves early with the air of a man who has places to go. He drops a kiss on my forehead before he bustles out the door. I realize we haven't made any plans and I don't mind. I have my own plans to consider. My own future. Because, at the moment, his doesn't look bright. I feel a pang at the place where comfort and satisfaction should be.

I stay in bed for a while after he leaves, luxuriating in the feel of the crisp hotel sheets and my own postcoital glow. I recline there, outwardly calm, while inside my brain is seething with all of these new permutations. I am processing.

I have a job to do. I've already been partly paid to do it. I've already cashed the check, as it were. And here is the reality: if I decline, he'll still end up just as dead. It might delay things by a week or so, maybe not even that. I'm not the only hired gun around. Thinking that makes me realize something: they'd brought me a long way and from another country to do this hit. There is a reason for that. Who *is* this guy?

Some simple Googling brings results right away, but none that answer the question. He'd designed a Sterling engine that purified water based on a proprietary system that utilized graphene. A by-product of the purification system had been a graphene-based fuel cell that was thinner and lighter by far than any other. That had been nearly a decade ago. He is now at the head of a company that develops and implements new solutions for both of those things: water purification and alternate fuel sources. The company has been successful enough that he also heads a large nonprofit that does good work in third-world countries cleaning water and providing power. He is a good and successful guy with a social conscience and the ability to do something about it. Nothing I read about him makes me like him less. And someone wants him dead.

On the surface, there is no one obvious who might be responsible. At least, it is not obvious to me. His is a private company, so no possible takeover plans could be afoot. No enemies that I am aware of. But experience has shown me that you can never tell what it looks like inside someone else's life.

I give some thought to sending a text, beginning a sequence, in order to find out who bought the hit, but I know even as I have this thought that it is a useless avenue. A network like the one I am part of didn't get and stay successful by giving up sensitive information like that. It strikes me that even asking about it might put both him and my livelihood in jeopardy. Maybe even my life.

I consider my options. I can do the job I have come to do. If I do that, I will know it is tidily and properly done and he didn't suffer. I will be humane. Not everyone in my business always is. Or I can feasibly not do the job without too much loss of face or reputation if I act quickly and bow out in a professional manner. "Something's come up." He'd still end up just as dead, but I wouldn't have had anything to do with it.

I don't love either of these options, so I toy briefly with the idea of telling him the truth, or something close to it. That there is danger here. For everyone concerned. It would expose me—and would he want to date a hit woman? Date and possibly more—it occurred to me that few would. And, in any case, his knowledge won't protect him. Possibly nothing can.

CHAPTER THIRTEEN

BY THE TIME I get to the seawall, the sun is shining. It seems transformed from the night before. A different place on a sunny midday than it had been on a rainy night. There are large ocean-going vessels at anchor in the protected water of the bay while sailing vessels bob around them like ponies playing in a field and kayakers paddle near the shore like merry little birds.

The seawall itself is packed with all manner of jovial traffic. Mothers and nannies pushing strollers and taking in the air. Kids on rollerblades and skateboards gearing up to inflict injuries they'll regret in a couple of decades. Couples holding hands and making memories to sustain them when love has died. Hairy youths followed by clouds of marijuana smoke flouting a law that is imprecise. All manner of humanity out to enjoy a rare day of Vancouver sunshine. I walk and walk and soak it in, enjoying the feeling of sunshine on my skin and the warmth that kisses the top of my head. It is a gorgeous day.

I am approaching his building when my phone rings. It is him.

"What does your day look like?" he asks.

"Looks like sunshine," I say in truth, still walking in his direction, though he has no idea. "What a gorgeous city."

"How would you like to see beyond it? I have to run up to Squamish to see a man about a dog. Wanna come? I figure after we could drive up to Whistler for dinner. Maybe stay the night. How does that sound?"

None of the place names have any meaning for me. It doesn't matter.

"Do you really have to see a man about a dog?"

"I do not. It's an expression. It's a meeting. Won't take long."

"Sure. Okay. If it's not an *actual* dog, that changes everything. I'm maybe half an hour, forty minutes from my hotel. So any time after that?"

"Perfect." I can hear the smile. "I'll pick you up from your hotel in an hour."

By the time we end the call, I am standing outside of his office building. It looks friendlier in the sunshine, all sand-colored cornices, sunlight glinting off original glass. I stay in the shadows of the building across the street, though there are few shadows on this bright day. With a plan to see him now in place, I'm not sure what I am doing here, though, in all fairness, I hadn't known why I was walking there in the first place. Thinking. Hard. Tossing around this and that. Knowing there are several possibilities, but really only one outcome I can see.

I trudge back to the hotel, day less bright now. Pull the Bersa out of the safe and put my belongings together. By the time he pulls up in a sleek, long car, I've checked out of the hotel and am sitting on a bench out front, enjoying the sunshine and waiting for him.

He tucks my suitcase into the trunk without comment. It is clear I'm not leaving anything behind. I think I catch the hint of a questioning look, but it is gone so quickly, I figure it is possible I am wrong.

We leave the city on a ribbon of highway he tells me is called the Sea-to-Sky. "It could also be called the sea-to-ski, I guess, but it's prettier this way."

And it *is* pretty. Raw young mountains, snow-kissed peaks, a picturesque sinewy oceanside that laps at the edges of the scene for what seems like a disproportionate amount of the way. Then the highway heads up into the mountains. A couple of times, my ears pop. It is lovely and I feel myself lulled, the feeling of being out of control, like a little kid, and the grown-ups are taking you on vacation; that is how I feel.

At Squamish, he has his meeting in a low office building with a nondescript façade. I find a café nearby and take my laptop with me and do some more research, trying the dark web this time and seeing if I can turn anything up that might shed some light. Still nothing. No matter how you slice it, this is a straight-up, straight-shooting, well-liked guy. He has, as he'd told me, an ex-wife. But that doesn't look complicated, either. From all accounts, they split amicably. Facebook photos indicate mutual respect and shared parenting of two teenaged daughters. Even the daughters look well adjusted and as though they are flourishing. It would have been maddening if it weren't all so lovely and perfect. Maybe it is both.

I am so focused on what I am doing, I don't see him come in. As promised, he has not been long, but I hadn't expected him quite so quickly.

"You looked *so* intense," he observes. "As though what you were contemplating was life and death."

I opt for candor of a sort. "I was Googling you."

"Me? Whatever for?"

"I just wondered if we had . . . I dunno? The right *stuff*." I let my voice trail off suggestively.

He drops into the chair opposite mine.

"Right for what?" he says with a credible air of innocence.

"Exactly," I say, deliberately obtuse.

"And what did you conclude?"

"No conclusion," I say tartly. "And here we both are."

"Exactly," he says in just the way I had moments before. And the smile he gives me goes right to his eyes. "And what would I find if I were to Google you?"

"Nothing," I say. "I am an enigma."

One eyebrow shoots up, but he doesn't say anything.

"A cipher," I add. "It might be that I don't exist at all."

"A cipher. An enigma. Those are interesting ways to describe oneself. And, if that is the case, how is it that this cipheric—"

"I don't think that's a word."

"—enigmatic woman should come into my life? What message does that bring?"

"That would be an arrogant way to frame things," I say, smiling brightly and hoping he doesn't see how close to the mark he's come.

To my relief, he laughs.

"It would, wouldn't it? Of course. Everything is about me!"

"But all our worlds are, aren't they?"

"I guess they are. Never mind. Let's get back on the road. We've still got nearly an hour of driving before dinner."

"That's okay," I say. "I'm not hungry at all."

"You could be by the time we get there, right?"

"It could happen."

The big black car slips along the highway soundlessly for a while before I chance the question I've been framing. It seems a risk worth taking.

"If someone were going to kill you, who would it be?" I say, as conversationally as I can manage.

He looks at me quickly before pulling his eyes back to the road. "That's a weird question."

"Right?"

He laughs. I'm not sure if I hear an uneasy note, though I listen closely for it.

"Okay," he says. "You first."

"Me first what?"

"Kill you. Who?"

"Me?" I say. He's taken me by surprise. He does that a lot. "Well . . . I'd have to think."

"That's what I'm doing. My turning it around was a stall tactic."

"Ah."

"But that doesn't mean I'm not interested. Go ahead and answer."

"Well . . . there might be too many to count," I say truthfully. "But they wouldn't know my name."

"Well, it would seem you are safe then."

"Yes, that's right. It would seem so."

"So no one in particular?" he asks. "Your ex?"

"No. He's dead."

"I'm sorry," he says quickly. "I didn't realize you were a widow."

"That's okay." My response is almost automatic. In this moment almost not remembering the man who had been my husband. Something about an accident. Something about a hospital bed. I put it from my mind. "Sometimes I barely remember myself."

"Children?"

"No," I say, turning my head quickly, something near my heart I don't want him to see. I watch the darkening scenery for a while. We are powering through a forest. The trees going by so fast, they are a solid blur of brown and green.

We are quiet for a while. A companionable enough silence. Though when he speaks, it is like there has been no interruption.

"Honestly, I don't think there is anyone who would want me dead. I've been thinking about it. I don't know if that means I've lived an exemplary life or if I'm just too vanilla."

I think before answering. And then, "Maybe neither. Maybe something entirely different is true."

"I think most people go through their whole lives without anyone ever trying to kill them," he says, deadpan.

"You say that based on what?"

He laughs. "I don't know. The number of people running around not dead?"

"So not your ex-wife?"

"We're still on the kill me thing?"

I grunt.

"Because that's a weird tack for a girlfriend to take."

I consider. And then, "I'm not your girlfriend."

"Okay then." he says, only slightly abashed. "But not my ex. No. We get along very well, and our arrangement suits both of us. And she's well compensated. It's possible she'd get less money if someone offed me."

"Well that's good. No one wants to sit around wondering if their ex is thinking about putting a knife in their back."

"Exactly. So do I pass?"

"Pass what?"

"Well, I don't know. It felt like some kind of courtship test. I wanted to know how I did."

"Anyone ever tell you you're too competitive?"

"All the bloody time." He pats the steering wheel. "How else do you think I ended up with the big Tesla?"

"You play to win." It's not a question.

"Always."

He is slowing, pulling into the village. We are months from ski season, but there are still scads of people around. At a glance, it's the sort of Alpine-village-meets-Rodeo-Drive motif that seems to have something for everyone year-round.

He checks us into a suite at a hotel that has "Chateau" in the name. The place is like a wintery castle: all grand height ceilings and old money finishing. Tapestries on the wall. Candelabras. All the comforts of home.

Our suite is like an elegant little house. The room we'd spent the night before in would fit into one corner with space for a yard.

"If this is how you usually roll, you must have thought the Sylvia was a dump."

"The Sylvia is not a dump. It's charming. A boutique hotel."

"Still."

"Yeah, this place is pretty sweet. I'm glad you provided me with the excuse to spend the night."

"I did?"

I am sitting on the edge of the bed, my legs dangling. He bends down, one hand on either side of where my butt meets the bed, and kisses me fully. "You did," he says when he comes up for air. "I would have had my meeting in Squamish and then gone back to the city." He collapses in an elegant heap next to me, touches my collarbone gently with his index finger. "But I wanted some of this."

I lean into him, and when he stands suddenly, I am disappointed. It is unexpected. I see him see that in my face and he smiles. "Look," he says, "we'd better go eat or we won't get out of here."

"They don't have room service in this dump?"

"They do. But I have someplace in mind."

Walking around the village, I see it is even more charming and unreal than I'd suspected from the car. Disney does a ski village. Everyone is wearing Lululemon with their Versace and there are quaint little shops, trendy bars, and lovely eateries in block after block. See and be seen. He leads me into one of these.

The food is exceptional yet somehow not memorable, though the wine is much better than what we'd had at the hotel bar the night before. Something from an extensive wine list that he ponders knowledgeably for several minutes before making his choice. Thankfully, conversation between us is as engaging as ever. It is easy to talk with him. No uncertain pauses or painful holes. I am easy with him. As close to myself as is possible for me. I'd forgotten this me existed.

We walk back to the hotel hand in hand, sharing jokes and easy conversation. In that walk, a shaft of pure happiness comes to me. I don't remember ever feeling anything quite like it. Just this moment filled with nothing but what is right here, in front of me. For the first time in my recollection, everything I have is enough. And maybe I am enough, too.

CHAPTER FOURTEEN

BACK AT THE hotel, we make love sweetly, then fall asleep in each other's arms. And here, too, there is this feeling of massive content. Other thoughts try to crowd in, but somehow, I keep them at bay.

Just a little longer, I plead with no one at all. *Just let me feel this a bit longer. I'll figure things out later, but right now let me have this.*

In the morning, he leads me to the bathroom. Somehow when I was sleeping, he had filled the tub with bubbles. They smell both exotic and expensive. They smell like you could lose yourself in there. Forever.

He scoops me off my feet so easily, it makes my head swim. Then he lowers me gently into the softly scented water. He doesn't speak, nor do I, but he drops to his knees next to the tub and begins to wash me. There are no words, just sensuous motions, but they are serious ones, as well. I can tell from how he approaches it that I'll be clean when he's done.

He washes my hair. No one outside of a salon has ever washed my hair before. He does it carefully, making sure none of the rich shampoo drips into my eyes or even down my forehead. Then he rinses me, head to toe, still silent. Drains the tub. Lifts me out and dries me with a huge, rough towel. He dries every piece of me, as one would a child, until I am standing there, my skin glowing from his efforts.

Now he lifts me again, carries me back to the bedroom, places me gently back on my spot on the bed, then snuggles his form next to mine, our curves joining as sweetly as though they have been designed that way.

"So what now?" he says, tracing the curve of my arm with his finger. It's the first time he has spoken in a while. Neither of us have. And the sound of the words seems almost musical in the silent hotel suite.

"I don't have a plan."

"You checked out of your hotel." It's not a question.

"Yes," I say.

"How long are you in town?"

"I'm not sure."

"You'll come and stay with me."

"All right."

We do the drive in reverse and it is just as beautiful as it was the day before, only now we are holding hands as we drive, or his right hand plays through my hair while I lightly touch his thigh or the back of his neck. We are never far from touching, like each of us is afraid the other will disappear if we lose contact for more than a few moments. It makes a difference.

His home is almost exactly as I'd expected. The top floor in a towering glass high-rise. There is a majestic view of English Bay on one side, Coal Harbour on the other. Whispers of ocean and far mountains beyond. Everything is as I'd seen it at sea level, but from here it is dwarfed to perfect miniature. It is beautiful.

"Do Vancouver views get any better than this?" I ask.

"Not much," he admits. "That's how I ended up here."

"It's all about the view?"

"Sure. And the jetted tub. Check it out." He leads me to three bathrooms, one after the other, each more exquisite than the last.

"Multiple bedrooms, as well." he says with a leer. "You can take your pick."

"I'll want one close to where you are," I quip back, a line he finds uproariously funny.

We have a lovely day, followed by a relaxed evening. He makes us dinner: some confection he calls his specialty that involves pasta and spinach. And cheese. He pours us glasses of twenty-year-old wine and we perch on stools at a counter in the kitchen that affords us a stunning view of the city. Sunset followed by nighttime cityscape. And all of it is breathtaking. All of it takes my breath away.

"So beautiful you could die."

He looks at me sharply. "What is it with you and dying all the time?" he says, and I can't read his voice.

"I . . . I don't know. I've . . . I've lost people. I guess that's what it is. It brings it closer. Makes it more real."

"Your husband," he says.

"Yes. Him . . . and others. Listen, I'm enjoying myself so much with you. I don't really want to talk about this now, okay?"

"Sometime maybe?"

"Yes. Okay. Sometime. Maybe."

We both know it is a lie.

CHAPTER FIFTEEN

IN THE MORNING I wake up alone. I'm disoriented momentarily, but it all comes back to me quickly. I am in a glamorous cave a quarter mile above downtown Vancouver, Canada.

I am in a large and comfortable bed. The sheets are impossibly luxurious: thick and soft at the same time. White. And covered with a white duvet. It is like resting inside a cloud.

I don't know right away what has woken me. When I realize, my stomach responds instantly. Coffee. Bacon. Onions. Other good things. I was not hungry, and then I am.

He has left his robe at the foot of the bed for me. Huge and white, a spa robe several sizes too large for me, and so I move towards the kitchen, now encased in yet another cloud.

"Good morning, beautiful." His face lights in a smile when he sees me. My heart flips a little in my chest in response to that light. One can wait a lifetime for a glance like that. "My robe looks good on you."

"Too big."

"Made for you," he says, pushing away from the stove quickly and enfolding me in his arms. "Made just for you."

We end up back in bed before we get around to breakfast. After a while, he gets up to go to the office. He eats cold food on his way out the door, but before he leaves, he drops a kiss on my forehead and a key fob on the bed.

"Make yourself at home. And if you feel like it this evening, there's a new restaurant I've been wanting to check out. You're a good excuse."

"Again, with the excuses. I don't know how I feel about that."

"Dork," he accuses.

"And the key," I say, ignoring his crack. "Aren't you afraid I'll rob you blind?"

"Not particularly. As far as I can see, you're the most precious of the contents of this apartment."

I just look at him, my heart in its own cloud. I don't know what to say and a part of me feels dangerously close to tears.

Without him in the space to warm it, the apartment is even more massive. I drink the coffee he left for me and nibble on the cold eggs and bacon, then roam around the space dwarfed by his bathrobe, looking at his stuff.

He has a sort of media room, and I imagine some overpriced decorator determining it should have a sports theme. I wonder if the signed balls under glass or the framed signed jerseys were his own acquisitions or some decorator's buy. It seems to me it matters. It speaks either of a personal passion or an urge to impress. I am curious which one it is.

Not that it will matter in the end—I remind myself of that. I have to keep reminding myself.

I turn on the television, then spend a quarter hour figuring out how to make the channels work, remembering a time when there was only on and off.

When I finally locate the channels, the first thing I see is his face. The other *him*. The one I'd briefly forgotten. William Atwater. It fills the sports-sized screen hanging on the wall above the baseballs trapped inside plexiglass. His face is so large and clear on the very good television. Too large and clear. High definition. I can see every pore.

He is beautiful, in his way. I think again how very normal he looks. How guy-next-door. Pale blue eyes, smooth skin marred only slightly by the acne he has yet to outgrow. There is a collar on his shirt and color in his cheeks and there appears to be nothing remarkable about him other than a sort of casual beauty. My stomach turns at the thought of it. How can this be? How can there be people who would do such things walking among us and there is nothing about them to set them apart? I feel as though there should be some visual marker, something off-kilter about his appearance. A scar on his forehead. A brand. Crossed eyes. Not quite a tail or horns, but something. But there is nothing like that. At all.

People would say that about me. The thought comes to me suddenly. There are those who would view me as a serial killer. When I sink into the plush sofa behind me, it feels out of my control, as though I have been pushed by the weight of the thought. I should have horns or a tail. There are those who would think I am of the same ilk. The same as *him*.

They would not be wrong, those people. I think about that now, too. I have killed serially: one after the other. I have taken lives. I don't know how many now. I don't count or keep a record or anything like that. It is more people than would fit on a bus, I know that. And none of them breathe. Not now.

I wonder if I have not considered it that way before because of the money. There is no emotion for me with killing. And certainly no pleasure. It is a job. And if the thought of taking a life for money might distress me, the fact that someone else would surely do it if I do not adds some comfort. These are not random, violent acts. And I am a professional. I put thought into what I do, and the deaths are always humane. Many times, the people I've been paid to hit transition from alive to dead with no awareness on their part. I've watched their faces at times, so I know.

I look again at the face on the screen.

No emotion, until now.

I think again of my lover, my host.

No emotion until now.

I close my eyes tightly. Push back the flood of feeling that threatens. I've held it off this long. So long. It has been years now. I know I can do it again.

I turn my attention back to the screen. The clipped Canadian accent is describing William Atwater's heinous acts. The announcer is mixing gun control into the conversation baldly, something that would let me know I'm not in the U.S. now, even if her accent had not. And the fact that she is passionless about it. Matter-of-fact. There are statistics that all add up to what she states as fact: gun deaths and the detail that people kill people with guns. She points out calmly that, in the United States, more people die by gun than dogs die in the street in other countries. Equating street dogs with human citizens seems like a stretch to me; still the point is driven home. And she has statistics, though the numbers are so horrendous one tunes them out. They are like random, unrelated numbers. They seem to make no sense.

"But these were not gun deaths," says another talking head. He is white. Apparently tall. Something paternal or maybe patronizing in his tone and delivery. His is the voice of reason. You can tell he feels that is the case; that he believes in his oh-so-reasonable voice and all that it intones.

"That's not the point, John," the original speaker says calmly. She is confident of her position. It is apparent in the arc of her back, the tilt of her head. "The point is violence. And a culture so steeped in it, senseless acts like this one are possible."

They go on in this vein, but now we are seeing images on the screen, as well; hearing the voices only. They are mostly images I have seen before. The thread of Atwater's victims, one by one. They make a tapestry of stilled voices. A small playground that will never be.

Now we see select parents, mostly so choked with emotion they are all but immobilized. Their faces are all different, as are their places in life, but I recognize them. It's like I'm looking in a mirror. They are me. Or, at least, they are the me that was. And I am them. She of the commuting. Of coffee in the morning. Of the Pebble Tec pool. She of the two dishwashers and the hopeful life that made sense.

The abductions and murders happened over time. The interviews we see now reflect that, and we are seeing these parents at different stages in their grief. The parents of the child lost most recently are so staggered by their anguish that they can barely walk—they are almost unable to stand erect. Wiped out. And there are deep shadows in their eyes and under them. I can't stop looking at their eyes.

But the killings have been going on for several years. The parents of earlier victims have moved on somewhat. They are able to stand. Because that is what we do, we humans. We stand. We move forward. We move on. Sometimes the movement nearly kills us for a while, but eventually, we move on. Make new lives. Lives without holes.

I think again of my dead garden, filled now with the green of hardy weeds. I close my eyes, put fingertips to my temples, blink back unexpected tears from a source I don't recognize. And then I take a deep breath. Open my eyes. Move on.

CHAPTER SIXTEEN

So deeply immersed am I in these thoughts that when my phone rings it causes a physical reaction in me. I jump, startled.

"What are you doing?" His voice is firm and warm. It sounds just as it does in my ear. I suddenly want him there. Very badly. To feel the firm, real length of him. To feel his strength. His warmth. And, yes, his desire and his humanity.

"I'm watching television, if you can believe it." I am surprised at how even my voice sounds. How *normal.* Like watching his TV is the most natural thing in the world.

"Good! You figured it out. Bright girl. I often have trouble with it myself."

"Why are you calling? Did you want to check to see what I've stolen so far?"

His laugh is deep and real. It is balm. I feel I could listen to it all day.

"Not at all. But if you *do* steal something, can you please take the sculpture by the ottoman in the living room?"

"The one shaped like the bottom of a horse?"

"Yes, that's it. I understand from my decorator that I paid a lot for it, but I really don't care for it much."

"What about the sports paraphernalia in the media room?"

"What about it?"

"Do you like it?"

"Sure." He sounds mystified. "I like it fine."

"But did your decorator buy it," I persist. "Or you?"

"Oh, that junk?" He sounds a little embarrassed. I like him for it. "I picked it up myself. Here and there, you know? I'm a bit of a sports nut. And I go to a lot of games."

We chat a bit more. To me, we sound like normal people and that wrenches at my heart. I had not thought I'd sound or feel like that—normal people—ever again.

And yet, of course, we aren't like normal people at all. The reality of that washes over me again like a dishwasher rinse cycle. It is inevitable. And required.

"You ever think about running away to a desert island?" The thought comes to me from nowhere.

"Let's do it. I'll peel grapes for you and fan you with coconut leaves."

"What sort of desert island has grapes?" I ask.

And so on. Because it is right there and because we can.

We agree: I'll meet him at the restaurant at six and then we'll come "home" together. The way that feels conflicts me so deeply I can't look at it. Not straight on. I have to look away.

Maybe in part to divert myself from the inevitable, I spend the rest of the morning snooping.

That's too gentle. What I do is more like a methodical search of the premises. Looking at me doing it, you'd think I was a cop. Naked beneath a man's bathrobe, so clearly out of uniform. But never mind.

As I search, I don't know what I am looking for, but I need to do something to dispel the restless energy. Plus, I have questions. And I feel some of the answers might be hidden here.

So I toss the place. Not truly toss, but I search deeply and carefully without leaving a discernible trace. I don't know what I am looking for. And when I find it—deep in a bathroom cabinet—I almost don't know what to do with what I learn. But I know this: there is nothing in my discovery that I want to know.

What I find is a stash of drugs. Prescription medications. And the stash is so deep and deadly-looking, I know it is something to see.

Zytiga. Rasburicase. CAPOX. Lenalidomide. Dexamethasone. Elotuzumab. Neupogen. And more still. The names are meaningless to me. Names from a spaceship. From a science fiction convention. From a gaggle of botanists. I have no idea what I'm looking at. And the dates aren't all current, but all of the prescriptions have been filled within the last twelve months. And they are all in his name.

I use my phone to photograph the bottles, then replace them as I found them before heading to find my laptop to hunker down and do a bit of googling. It doesn't take long for me to figure out that all of them are drugs used in the treatment of cancer and, coordinating the dates and the drugs, it doesn't take a PhD. to guess that the prognosis is not good.

CHAPTER SEVENTEEN

I DON'T REMEMBER the rest of the day. There was waking up in his arms. And there was my discovery. Then there was his potential explanation. And there was nothing I could put between that would have the balance of the day make sense for me.

I leave to meet him a good forty minutes before I need to, but by then I am ready to get outside and into the air. I'd begun to think about birds. And gilded cages. And the way the air feels when it flows through your wings.

The restaurant proves to be the kind Vancouver does very well. Elegance so understated it looks casual, until you glance at the prices and see a different story. And everything seems like traditional comfort foods, but with some exotic twist. And so hamburgers, but instead of bacon, the menu says you can add a "Soupçon of *lardon*" at an additional price. And the coleslaw isn't just chopped and dressed cabbage, but "a creamy ginger slaw with jicama and locally grown organic heritage carrots." It all seems a bit much.

"Isn't this place fun?" he says when he joins me.

I smile. He appears happy to be pleasing me, so I leave it be. What's a lardon or a slash of jicama between new friends?

I find myself watching him closely, a new layer now to how we interact. Are his hands stable or was that the ghost of a tremor? Does he look at all wan? How do his clothes fit his frame? But as I only know this version of him, I have nothing to compare. No before to hold against the after in front of me. And, as it has these last few days, the after looks just fine to me. More than fine.

I can't focus enough on the menu to decide what I want and I ask him to order for me. He lifts an eyebrow in my direction, but doesn't say anything, ordering vegetables that have been variously roasted and then put together with strong flavors—beets with harrisa, maybe. Cauliflower with chimichurri, and so on—and a chicken that has apparently been flame-broiled under a brick, which seems a horrid finish for a perfectly nice organic chicken, plus I can't imagine the possible advantage of the business with the brick, but I hold my tongue as I sip the cocktail he orders for us in advance of the meal.

"You're quiet tonight," he says before very long.

"Am I?"

"Yes. Even a little pensive. Is everything okay?"

"Not really," I say. "There's something I want to talk to you about, but I don't know where to begin."

"Sounds ominous." Another sip. But he doesn't look afraid. Not much scares him, that's what I've noticed. Not much knocks his natural balance away. It's one of the things that attracts me. He is solid. Whole, that's how he seems. Not many people are.

"It *is* ominous," I say. "I think so, anyway."

"You want to talk about it now or leave it until after dinner?"

"Are you sick?"

"So we're opting for now."

"I think it is possible you are unwell."

The levity falls off him then and he looks at me, suddenly exposed. I feel a moment of regret. Did I really have to do it now? I suddenly long for the façade of lightness that existed yesterday.

"Sorry?" And it seems to me he says the word in such a Canadian way.

"Yes," I say, ignoring the question.

He dips his eyes to his lap. Then raises them to a point just above and to the left of my face. I can see him searching for a reply, for something to say.

"How did you know?" he asks at length. He looks honestly concerned, like there might be some tell.

"I couldn't. I didn't. I found your stash."

He thinks about what I mean for a minute, but I quickly see a light dawn. "It wasn't out."

"I dug."

"Ah." He drops his eyes again. I can't imagine what he is thinking.

"How bad is it?" I ask when neither of us has said anything for a while. The remnants of cocktails are whisked away. Wine brought and approved and poured. We are sipping that, and largely ignoring the appetizers that arrive at the same time.

I see him consider my question, then appear to decide to give up and give. I have the feeling that whatever he tells me at this point will be the truth, though I don't know him well enough to be certain.

"As bad as you can imagine," he says. It's not what I want to hear.

"You don't look sick." The words escape before I can stop myself.

He laughs. A brittle sound.

"I even say that to myself. To my mirror self. It's foolish, right? Perfect health."

"And yet . . ."

"Exactly. I'm told it won't last, though."

"The appearance of health?"

"Right. I'm told from here it will get ugly."

"When?" I ask, but am not sure I really want to know.

"Weeks. Possibly months. Certainly no longer."

"And so, you ordered a hit." I am still and my voice is quiet. Not much more than a whisper. I see him lean forward; strain to hear. At my words, I can feel the tears stand in my eyes, but I will myself not to cry.

He looks at me sharply. Is he surprised? Or not surprised at all? I can't tell, but a part of me hopes he is surprised. That he hasn't known it was me all along.

"That's right. It seemed the most humane thing for all concerned."

"Under the circumstances."

"That's right," he repeats. Slightly defensive now, but who could blame him?

"What were the specifications?" I ask, though I thought I knew the answer. "How did you imagine it would be?"

"Well, obviously, I want it to be fast. Other than that, I'd rather not know."

"That makes sense." That's what I would want, too. To have it be a cessation of now. An unblurred transition. No time to ponder, reflect. No time to try and plead your way back. Just done and dusted.

The waiter arrives with our entrees. Having barely touched our appetizers, we wave the food away, soupçons of lardon and all. We sip some more at the wine and push the food already in front of us around on our plates.

"Where do I fit?" I ask when our quiet has resumed.

We look at each other deeply. Both knowing more than we are saying. Both unwilling to utter the words.

"Well, you were an unexpected element, weren't you?"

I don't think that is true, but I play along.

"Was I?"

"Well, yes," he says, reaching across the table. Takes my hand. I feel the trill of the excitement at his touch that I am beginning to get used to.

"Maybe not entirely," I say.

"Maybe not," he agrees. "But certainly aspects."

He runs two fingers up my arm and smiles, some of the dread off him now.

"I really am very sorry to learn all of this." I hesitate. Add, "I can't even tell you how sorry I am."

"Thanks. And I guess I know."

"I guess you do." I hesitate. And then: "So . . . now?"

"I don't want to know. Don't want to see it coming."

"But now is too soon," I protest, trying to keep my voice calm. And my heart. What was this?

"I just don't want to be one of those who goes out flailing." He says this calmly. Matter-of-fact. "I can't be."

"But you're so far from that. Look at you! It could be years."

He shakes his head. "Not years, no. Do you think I would do this lightly? Think of the stakes of getting it wrong. I've given it all a lot of thought. Thought through all of the angles, keeping in mind my kids, my insurance, the business, everything. This is the best time."

And suddenly I understand completely. “Things go better if you don’t die of the disease.”

He doesn’t answer me. Not directly. But he looks at me deeply and there is something in his eyes that tells me he appreciates that I have understood this on my own. That I didn’t make him say the words.

CHAPTER EIGHTEEN

So this is the thing that is. We know now where we stand. Both of us. We put it away for the time being. We have our dinner, though we don't eat every bite. It is delicious in addition to being both pretentious and expensive. Afterwards, we walk hand in hand down Robson Street, stopping to watch street musicians and performers. He asks if I want my fortune told by an old woman who is reading tarot at a card table she has set up outside Banana Republic. I decline. I feel comfortable that there is nothing in the future that I need or want to know.

That night we make love with a new ferocity. We are clinging to something that can't be held, that's how it feels. Afterwards, we collapse into each other's arms. I dream I am in the ocean, adrift. He is my life raft. I cling to him. If I let go of him, I know that I will drown.

I wake to strong sunlight and the call of gulls. I get up before he does and pull the pieces of myself together. Then I pack my things. It doesn't take long.

He wakes as I head for the door.

"Will I see you again?" he calls, his voice sounding weaker than I'd heard it before. Not from illness, I'm sure of that. But from something new. Something that grabs for my heart.

I don't answer. I leave his key on the sideboard in the hall. What is there, really, to say? I think about taking the sculpture. Something to remember him by, and I know he doesn't want it and additionally has no need of it where he is going. But I leave it, in the end. He has had enough taken from him, and it certainly would not go easily through customs and airport security.

I go to the airport. Get a rental, a tidy European job, small and expensive but all that was available on short notice. I only need it for a few hours.

I pack all of my stuff neatly in the trunk of the car, then park it deep in a neighborhood near his office, in a place where I'll be able to grab it quickly and go. I lock the rental car carefully and leave it behind, heading out on foot to find what I need.

It doesn't take long. I know it as soon as I see it. The car is longer and older than is usually available anymore and it is perfect for my needs. It is solid, like a tree, and the ignition is broken easily. From the time I put my eyes on the vintage car until I start it without a key is under five minutes and then I'm gliding down the street in a full-sized piece of Detroit steel that was old enough to vote long before I was.

I don't have long to wait outside his building. I know I've timed things pretty well. We haven't known each other long, but I have a handle on his routine.

When he emerges from the building, I try not to analyze the firmness of his step or the jut of his chin, the tilt of his head. I try not to think about how he is feeling. Is this a good day for him or bad? Is he in pain? Has he said all his goodbyes?

I follow him for three blocks before I see the right moment coming up. I wonder if he feels the shadow or the ghost of me, but I discard the thought. It is fanciful, and there is no place for that here.

I begin to accelerate as his feet leave the curb. I admire again the spring in his step, the length of his stride.

He is in the middle of the intersection when I hit him, full on. He slides under the car. I keep going, grimacing at the solid *bump bump* I feel under the tires. Between the impact and the follow-up, I feel as certain as I can be that he is gone.

I leave the old car running in an alley a few blocks away, slipping off in the other direction, the direction in which I've left my rental car. Slipping off unnoticed and unseen.

It all happens very fast.

CHAPTER NINETEEN

I GET THROUGH airport security in record time. In the age of racial and social profiling, I don't come up on any lists. I am someone's wife, perhaps. Someone's boss. Someone's mother/daughter/aunt. I am someone you need not fear. My pale face and gentle demeanor are practically a get-out-of-jail-free card, or so I've observed.

I get through security quickly and end up with time to kill before my flight. Despite my profession, that's never been something I'm very good at. Time is for holding. Cherishing. Time is for saving or even cutting. Killing time is just counterintuitive to me, as ironic as that may seem. But there is a wine bar near my gate and, with my nerves where they are, and some long flights ahead, a glass of wine does not seem like a bad idea.

I order what sounds like a serviceable enough Sauvignon blanc and settle down to watch one of the televisions perched at the corners of the bar space.

It is a local station and top of the hour is the story of a successful local businessman and philanthropist struck down by an unknown motorist. Beloved by his community, missed by his family, respected by his peers; his loss will be felt. It was a hit-

and-run and I learn that, though the car was found, the car's owner was nowhere to be seen. They are searching for him now.

I don't realize that I am holding my breath until they say the businessman died on impact. The pronouncement leaves me relieved and broken all in one breath. It's like a light going out. I want it to be true. I don't want it to be true. I don't know what to wish for anymore.

I keep my face stoic, but I taste what I am feeling and realize that I am gutted.

I send a text to my contact.

It is complete.

I know there will be a deposit in my Bitcoin account within hours. I do a bit of Googling and find a place that will accept donations in Bitcoin for cancer research. I donate the amount I know I will soon receive. I know it is not even a token gesture, but I do it anyway. It doesn't make me feel better, but it doesn't make me feel worse, either. That seems like a start.

CHAPTER TWENTY

About the time I am finishing donating money, Atwater is mentioned in the news again and my ears perk up. He is still near the top of the news cycle. The tone is different now than it was a few days ago. I sense it right away. More urgent. It is this urgency that catches my ear and it doesn't take long to determine what the talking heads are all chirping about.

When last I'd tuned in, Atwater's location was a big question mark. Extrapolations based on where he had last killed and the pattern from where he had killed before. Now there has been a sighting, not 100 percent confirmed but strongly suspected, at a beach community in the southern part of the county in which he normally lives.

The talking heads are happy now. Magpies on a fence. There is a lot of shiny stuff here to go over. Police have leads but also there is speculation that Atwater might not be alive. Dead by his own hand, and don't let the pearly gates hit you on the way out.

"It is not clear how William Atwater, who has now killed at least sixteen children in and around the San Pasado area, has thus far managed to elude custody." The county is roughly five thousand square miles, we are told. It incorporates miles of beaches, acre upon acre of rich and fertile farmland, a few lakes large enough to support boating and even fishing, a university town, some mountainous areas, and some densely forested regions.

The area under discussion is not huge, but it is varied enough to provide potential hiding places. And, after all, I remind myself, there is no reason I know of that will make him stay within the boundaries of the area in which he was born.

This brings to mind a picture of some feral creature, forced by nature to stay within a territorial area determined at his birth. Some pull of instinct. Something pure and primal.

Or maybe it's just all he knows.

The images wash over me. The ones I see on the screen. The ones I recall from the previous week. And then a bunch from my own personal library, supplemented by memory. Children. All of them. I almost can't bear it. Like the parents I see in the news, in that moment I feel as though I'd have trouble walking. Trouble standing erect.

I sip my wine. Outwardly calm, blinking away the feelings that surface.

The balance of the day of traveling and seething make things worse not better, and by the time I get home, I pad around the tiny rooms of my little cottage like a caged panther or some other cat too large to be constrained by the walls of a house. I'd expected coming home to soothe me, but it doesn't, and the walls seemed to reverberate with voices that aren't there. I feel awash in a sea of uselessness. Even the things that had previously given me some pleasure leave me feeling empty. It's as though I no longer have a place or purpose. Or maybe more like, I haven't had those things for such a long time, but something has now made it violently clear. I feel on the edge of something that is spiraling out of control.

I think of that pure column of happy I felt briefly in Vancouver. That tiny slice that felt like infinite possibility. Is it him that I miss? And what we'd shared in Vancouver? Or what had been possible—for a moment—for us? I found him, then I lost him. I want to howl at the moon.

If it were only that, it would be enough. But that is only a single facet of this diamond and each facet reflects on the others with a razor sharpness. Alone, one facet could cut. Together, they threaten to rip my insides to shreds. And each one is about loss. Loss of love. Loss of life. Loss of humanity. It feels like I could go on citing these facets, riding them down: a death spiral of loss leading to a sea of helplessness because, of course, there is nothing that can be done.

And then I realize that I'm wrong. Of course, there is something I can do. Something that both my profession and my background have combined to make me better equipped for than maybe anyone else on Earth. It is a ridiculous thought—I know that as soon as it hits. And beyond the rational, certainly. But even just the thought of it gives me purpose. And, with that, it gives me direction. I am in motion almost before I know what I'm doing. And *rational* hasn't had a lot to do with me for a long time, in any case.

I begin to research. Before long, I am more of an expert on William Atwater than the world probably needs. Like most people in the West in the 21st century, Atwater has left an electronic trace as long as he's been packing some sort of device, which has been his entire adult life. I come quickly to believe that somewhere, in all that electronic detritus, I will find a clue to where he is. And why do I need to find him? I'm not sure of that, but I know that I must and am equally certain that I will. Confident. I know he is somewhere. It is just a matter of narrowing down the where.

And so I settle in, at first searching for the electronic trail, then putting energy towards trying to read and understand it. There was a brief time when he had toyed with both Twitter and Instagram at the same time a lot of others had done so. Both feeds have long been neglected, but here one can see glimpses of forests and the occasional lunch. No real clues there, other than a location. For everything he'd tweeted or Instagrammed, perhaps five years before, he'd been in the north part of his county. This is a slim clue, hardly worth noting. I keep it anyway.

A plain old identity search on the major engines produces an equally thin stream. He played baseball in high school, but only for one year and that was early on and he didn't finish: he was notably absent from a team photo of the state champions at the end of the season, even though his name comes up on a team roster early in the year. The search also reveals some adjacent Atwaters who I don't figure have much to do with his family at all. They have better addresses in posher parts of the county. William Atwater's immediate family had definitely been from a poorer branch: a foreclosure notice to his childhood address in his sophomore year confirms this idea. There is more in this vein: things that are almost interesting but that together don't produce a very clear picture.

While I do this work, I don't think about what I will do if I encounter him. *When*. A part of me is certain that will take care of itself. It is locating him, that's the thing. Nor do I allow myself to dwell on the fact that platoons of professional hunters have thus far not turned him up. I have the feeling that part does not truly matter. At one point he will be found. And when he is, I'll be nearby and ready. And by then I'll know what to do—that's the one thing I know for sure. I don't know now, but I will. Then.

The search doesn't make me feel any better, but it makes me feel a little less empty. Like I am doing something. Moving something ahead.

To get things going in that direction, I read a book about a serial killer and discover the author had close contact with everyone close to him as she was doing the research and then writing the book. She'd had access to his family and friends and even, once he was incarcerated, with the killer himself.

I think about that for a while and realize that it is another—albeit low-tech—route to information. Apparently, for the author of the book I'd read, everyone was prepared to crawl all over each other in their enthusiasm to talk with her. Everyone has a story. Everyone wants to be heard. And, in our culture, authors are respected. So after a few days of trying to contact people and getting nowhere, I start saying I am writing a book. It's a lie, but it doesn't seem to matter. Everything changes. Doors start opening and suddenly no one will shut up.

With sudden access to the key people in his past as well as a lot of nearby bystanders, I begin to get a more complete picture of William Atwater. A loner, in school and as a young adult. Possibly abused by at least one of several stepfathers, according to a couple of his former classmates. That sophomore year appears to have been significant. Maybe things had been lost that can never be regained. But of course, at this stage, all of that is unverifiable. He is broken. Clearly. Beyond that, we don't know for sure.

His real father was dead or lost. Stories vary and it seems impossible to determine which is true. Maybe it doesn't matter anyway. His mother mostly raised him and is still alive. She had three other children, all with different dads, and it seems to me that she will have information to add.

Her phone number is listed. In all of this, that fact surprises me for some reason: How many people can still be reached on a landline? How many people still have a phone number that is on public record? Maybe that will change, I think, now that he is well known. Maybe these are the last days some of these phones will ring. It seems likely that the Atwater phone rings a lot. These days.

Though it might ring a lot, it doesn't ring long before it is picked up, and I can learn nothing from the single syllable used to answer the phone.

"Mary Atwater?" I begin.

"Yes." This time I can hear caution, or think I can. It doesn't surprise me. People have likely been calling her all day every day for weeks. Or more.

"I am calling about your son, William Atwater."

"Yes." And this time, there it is; for a second, I hear hope.

"I am writing a book about his life, Mary."

"Ah."

"If you could just answer a few questions . . ."

"Everyone is writing a goddamned book," she says mildly.

"Right. Well. Okay." I stammer a bit with it, not quite sure where to begin. "I'm trying to find him."

She laughs at that. A dry, unpleasant sound. "You and every goddamned one else," she informs me. There is a smokiness to her voice. Something illicit. I can't pin it down.

"Right," I say, "okay," wanting to keep the slim dialogue going and not sure how to do it. I feel like I'm holding a balloon by the most delicate of silken strings: I have a decent hold on it now, but it could drive upwards on a current, and the string could snap while I try to bring it home. "There is something in his face in the photos I've seen." I hesitate, grappling for the right words.

The words that will keep her talking. "Something . . . innocent. I don't know if that's quite right. But something that doesn't represent the things I've heard."

This is his mom, that's what I'm thinking. The person who gave him life. And I am pushing for the kindest version of the truth. That's all any of us can ever aspire to. There are worse goals.

"The boy . . ." she begins. Stops. Settles herself. Starts again. That smoky voice. ". . . the boy I knew would not have been capable of what he is accused of."

"He was not a mean child." I make sure it's not a question.

"No, no. That's just it. He was very kind. Very respectful." A pause between us. I let it be. And then, her voice drops. I can't hear the smokiness as I strain to listen. "But it's just that there was something on him." It's barely a whisper.

"Something."

"I don't know."

I'm straining to hear now, truly.

"Was he cruel?" I ask it as gently as I can.

"I . . . I don't think so." I let it ride. And then, "Maybe. Sometimes to me. There was something . . . other about him. He had big thoughts, I think." This last has been said with a kind of tragic hopefulness. Like you know what the outcome is, but you're still wishing. I have been a mother. I don't begrudge her the sentiment.

"How can I find him?" The words are there between us. They have no weight on their own. I can almost hear her ponder the question: decide how to answer.

"I don't know for sure," she says after a while. "I know he always loved Morning Bay. And the road there. Especially the golden road."

"I don't understand. The golden road—" But then I stop talking because I hear the click that means a landline has terminated connection.

The abrupt end of the call doesn't sit well with me at first. I think about it and ascribe meaning to the act. Then I realize it is probably just some self-protection. How often must that phone ring right now? How many times every day. And what if you have no answers? And what if your heart breaks every time the phone rings? Or lifts in fear. After a while, you hang up. And before very long, you probably stop picking it up at all.

I ponder the words she gave me, then check things out. Morning Bay is a beach community at the southernmost end of the county. I can't connect it to anything else I know about Atwater. It's just another place. I file it away.

I try to find the half-siblings; but they have all flown. Certainly, if there were any landlines there, they've all gotten rid of them by now.

I speak with former teachers. All of the ones I manage to reach feel there had been something wrong at home. However, considering the tenor of the news for the last weeks, it is difficult to tell if at least some of what they feel hasn't been tempered by seeing their former student's face plastered all over CNN. One thing comes through though: the causes are difficult to pin down. He'd always been one of many in an overburdened system, plus some sort of genetic boat had sailed, and maybe he'd been left too far behind.

Everybody knows that a William Atwater doesn't happen in isolation. I am shocked to find that, as I research, most of what I discover is cliché. It's like I'm reading about a Movie of the Week. And not a very good one, at that.

Paint a picture of a serial killer. The most popular of those paintings looks like this: born into poverty and abuse, predestined—or so it seems—for the life he ends up living. One can fill in the blanks without trouble. Neglect, pain, lack of love: the perfect recipe; the perfect storm. And self-esteem never existed, having been snubbed out like a snail close to the time of his birth. Snubbed out with alacrity and intent.

One imagines a little flower, reaching up for the sun; the cloud of his reality blocking the light for year after year. I think of my own plants, now dead. Without the right care, they wither. Maybe eventually die. But not before they become twisted in their efforts to survive. I saw that, in my garden.

And so here we are.

It is in the course of these telephone interviews with teachers, friends, and even a few distant relatives that I come to have a sort of dark sympathy for William Atwater. I can feel the painful paths that have led to wherever he is now. The things that have created the monster we all now see night after night and hour after hour on television. The sympathy is tainted, of course. And imperfect. Empathy twisted. But beyond all the hype the media machine is pushing, and even beyond the atrocious acts he has committed, there is a human. He is flawed beyond the usual and even broken and misshapen, but he is more like me than I would have at first thought. We have more in common than we do not. This thought could shock me to self-evaluation, but fortunately, I'm on a mission so I don't dwell on it.

On a practical level, the interviews help me to hone, not just Atwater's personality, but the way he thinks and the way he processes information. As I research, I start sticking electronic pins into a map on my computer. For every location mentioned by a former friend or classmate or teacher, I pop in another pin. I add a few for the ones I find on social media. After a while, a couple of areas are as thick with pins as the back end of a hedgehog.

"He is out there." This time the talking head is a forensic-psychologist-turned-mystery-novelist, and the expert du jour. He is over sixty, yet his face is weirdly unlined, and his thick dark hair is shorn close to his head. So close, you get the occasional flash of pink scalp. "He is hiding," he adds, exposing perfect white teeth while spreading his hands wide. An eloquent gesture. "But he will be found."

The statement is so fabulously obvious that the interviewer seems stunned. She has nothing to say to this. Then she recovers.

"Dr. Uxbridge, what can you tell us about the methods being used to locate William Atwater? Is there anything that, in your opinion, could be done that is not now being done? Are the powers that be really pulling all the stops?" The clichés emerge easily. They feel comfortable on the ear. They are effortless for her; for us.

"I don't think being critical of law enforcement agencies is at all the correct path at this point."

"That wasn't my intent . . ."

"The local police in that area are a particularly overburdened agency. I have it from very good sources that they are doing everything in their power."

"Dr. Uxbridge, you're on retainer with the San Pasado Police Department, are you not?" says the interviewer.

"Boom!" say I to the screen with a fist pump. Boom, indeed.

"That isn't really the point," says Uxbridge.

And I turn the television off.

For me, the time for data collection has passed. I know I've found everything I can by these methods and from a distance. Anything more will just be more words. It's time for motion.

CHAPTER TWENTY-ONE

The Earth is always moving. Quickly. I know it's childish, but that's a fact that's never really sat comfortably in my mind. Because of this discomfort, I've read a lot about it over the years: trying to comprehend what it all means. And what it all means to *me.*

For one thing, it's super hard to calculate how fast we're actually going. Taking into account the distance from the Earth's center, speed of rotation in every full day, and other things like that, some calculations indicate that, at the equator, the Earth is moving at about a thousand miles per hour. A *thousand.* That's L.A.–New York in two hours. I mean, we're really just hurtling along.

That's the part where we're spinning. The Earth is also hurtling around in orbit at the same time, this at an estimated 67,000 miles an hour. But things get even worse: apparently—because I haven't observed this with my own eyes—our galaxy whirls around the solar system at about 490,000 miles per hour. I can't even come up with comparisons for that one. It would mean, countrywide, that you'd arrive almost before you left.

So, think about it: you get out of bed in the middle of the night to pee. You walk a few feet to your bathroom. You come back to your still-warm bed, half asleep, and plunge back down into slumber. Meanwhile, all this high-speed racing is going on. If you stop to think about it—which I don't advise—it can make you nauseous.

But it's motion; that's the point. Do you see? Even with all of this going on, we still get up. Put one foot behind the other. Move forward.

Motion. It's what I will need to track William Atwater down. Even dropping through space at high speeds won't bring me closer. I have to get out and get on with it.

I look at the results of my research critically. It seems to me that the pins bristle most thickly out of a few spots in the Oro Valley, in the northeasternmost part of the county, nearly the opposite side from where Atwater had been born and where he grew up. It does not escape me that, in Spanish, *Oro* translates to "gold." That's not a lead, but it seems too strong a connection to be full coincidence. I start to move.

Before I do, I look over the system I have devised, realizing that it is imperfect and possibly even fatally flawed. Based on my system, there is no strong reason to think my method will yield results. It doesn't matter. At this stage, I have nothing left other than a dead garden and rage. When I decide to head out, I'm not even aware that I've made a decision. What, after all, is there to lose? And it isn't as though anyone will even care that I am gone.

I try not to feel pathetic with this thought.

Getting in motion means another shuttle, another flight out, another rental car when I arrive. None of that bothers me, even though this is not a paying gig.

Pro bono, I laugh to myself. A dark laugh. *Pro bono* like a lawyer who takes someone on for free, just because they need representation. Only in this case, it is society that will be better off, not the client. That's what I tell myself. That's what I need to feel in this hour. I decide to ignore the voice that questions the correctness of my saddling up as both judge and jury.

In the last few years, San Pasado has been labeled one of the happiest places in America. It isn't happy now, though. Now it's a small city pushed to the edge of its seat in mortification and worry. A hamlet that seems about to consume itself with concern over a product of its loins. A son no one would ever want to claim. It wasn't supposed to be this way.

Even as the small commuter jet circles into the rural airport, I see flags flying at half mast, something I see more of when I pick up my rental car and drive the short distance to town. San Pasado is mourning and uncertain. Rocks and hard places. The small city scuttles on the edge. Used to being peaceful and beautiful, it doesn't know what to do with the pall of sadness and silence that floats over it or the armada of newsies winging in from all over the world. It doesn't know what to do with the feeling of being imperfect. Fatally flawed. You can see it even in the townsfolk, or so I imagine. The perfect streets. The carefully wrought civic architecture. This is a town not used to dealing with imperfection. And now here we are. No small imperfection: a mark so large it is beyond blight. A mark so intense it blemishes the spirit.

San Pasado is a hamlet, everything charming. Easy. Even the city streets seem half in the country. It is the sort of place where you imagine people smile a lot, and some of them even go to church on Sundays. They have barbecues and go to high school football games. They lean against fences and talk amicably with neighbors. Life is easy and sweet. There is a mall, but there is also a well-manicured town square with a bandstand and a lot of stores that don't belong to franchises. People walk around the town and visit quaint shops featuring signs admonishing visitors to "shop local" in enough windows that you understand it's some kind of cheerful conspiracy.

In short, San Pasado is the kind of place people in big cities all over America dream of moving to; raising their families. And some of them do. But mostly they do not. Mostly they dream and wish they could be here or someplace like here. And now the dream is tainted, a rotten core at the gooey center. At the moment, it feels like nothing will ever be the same.

I park my rented car, intending to walk around town, assessing before I settle in somewhere, now not sure what will be available. The level of media circus is a variable I hadn't counted on before my arrival. At noon, it looks like rush hour in a town that usually has no reason to be anything but sleepy. But now, everything is jammed with media types and their various gear and entourages. I fear there will be no room at the inn.

Despite the emotional calamity currently in San Pasado, the weather is untouched. It is a perfect Central Coast day. Just sweet sun in a clear blue sky and you swim through it like Eve in the garden or a fish in the sea.

It is difficult, with the sun touching your shoulder, to imagine a town like this producing a William Atwater. This is small town America with a Central California kiss. You can't see the ocean from town, and yet you know the sea is only a half hour run from that bandstand. The little hamlet looks like a place where nothing bad could ever happen. And yet. Here we are.

With no other starting point in mind, I begin at what feels like the beginning and drive my rental to Atwater's last known address. It is maybe fifteen minutes east of the charming downtown core. And it is light-years away.

My first impression is of gray. Gray house, shutters sagging, paint weeping. A gray cracked driveway, valiant weeds trying to push up between the cracks; reclaiming the ground. A gray chain-link fence, sagging in places. A mangy-looking gray dog, patches of brown. The dog is chained to a sun-damaged Honda. Red. The car is the one spot of color in the scene, and taken all together, what it really looks like is squalor. You can taste the hopelessness and desperation on your tongue. It's worse than expected somehow. It is worse than should be allowed.

I debate going to the front door, knocking. Questioning whoever answers. Sticking to my authorial cover story. Beyond having already been hung up on by the mother, what stops me are the other watchers. A couple of media trucks, associated with local affiliates of large networks, are encamped not far from the driveway and a small horde of various media types lounge around in front of the house, just out of reach of the dog. They make me feel oddly self-conscious. Like they'll be able to tell things about me I don't want to share. I avoid looking directly at them.

The trucks look like maybe they've been sent from other planets; high-tech gear perched on roofs, ready to send and receive signals. It's as though we are in a war zone. As though we are at the front.

I sit for a while and assess. I don't recall now what I'd been imagining, ensconced and planning from the safety of my house at the edge of a forest. But whatever I was thinking then, it wasn't this. And now I understand how naive I've been. I am surrounded here by expert hunters, attending now in their full stalking regalia, satellite dishes and all. They are bloodhounds. And me? I'm the pampered house pet spaniel who has lost her forever home. We have all the same equipment, those bloodhounds and I, but their tools have been honed with hard use. I feel like a child among them. I feel distressingly ill-prepared.

Still. I bolster myself. I've come all this way. There is nothing to deter me from the broad stroke plan I'd come up with back at my cottage and then on the flight out. It might be a naive plan, and half-baked, I concede that. But it's really all I've got and I'm here now, after all. I try to remember the rage; hold it, fan it. I know it will sustain me.

When I leave the car and walk to the front door of what I know to be one of Atwater's childhood homes, I am aware of my pulse. I don't know if this is an elevated heart rate or an excessively brisk rushing of my blood. All I know for sure is I feel a little lightheaded. I hunch my shoulders; press on.

As I make my way to the door, I am lightly afraid that the dog will rush out and attack me and I can't tell who is more scared: me or him. We both keep our distance, eyeing each other warily. He doesn't take his eyes off me while he backs off his chain, and he doesn't growl or meet my eyes.

The walk is cracked, and plants grow up through them, stunted weed babies, stretching for light. So much all around me is cliché.

A curtain is drawn over the dirty front window I walk past to reach the door. The doorbell is broken, so I don't bother pressing it, opting instead to knock, picking up a splinter when I do.

I feel rather than see motion on the other side of the door and, for a heartbeat, I feel like it will open. I brace myself for what I might see then. It doesn't happen though. Instead, the curtain pulls back, so quickly that later I will ask myself if it was real. I have the impression of a thin, pale face, and wide, alarmed eyes. Then the curtain drops and nothing happens and I question my impression.

I hover there foolishly for a few long minutes then retrace my steps because I can't think what else to do. I'm still cautious when I pass the dog, but we're both a little less skittish this time.

I head towards the safety of my car, but a man gets out of one of the media vans, blocking my path. He would have startled me, but he is just so pretty I figure he's an on-air personality, and though he's come upon me quickly, there isn't anything menacing in his bearing.

"Nothing, huh?" he asks, and I understand he was hoping my visit would meet with success. He doesn't know who I am, but he's prepared for me to be his next segment of the story and he's hoping that I'll do something he can report on. I can read all of that in his smile.

"Nada. Zilch."

"Sucks," he says with regret. I know he means it. "Been camped out here a few days now, hoping for a break. Nothing much doing." He puts out one big hand. "Curtis Diamond, WBCC Los Angeles," he says. I can tell he figures I will know who he is.

"Hey," I say in a way that I hope is admiring. It's clear it's what he's used to, so it seems prudent to deliver. "I'm working on a book on Atwater," I say, sticking to my story. "I talked with the mom briefly before. On the phone. It seemed worth a try to take a run at getting in."

Curtis nods. "Nothing ventured, nothing gained. Can I interview you for my afternoon segment?" he asks. "I got a lot of nothing, and at least you'd be a talking head."

I feel my eyes widen at the suggestion and panic clutch at my breast. For so many reasons, getting interviewed wouldn't do at all. Me on TV. Thinking of it makes me want to duck for cover. I try to show none of that.

"It's a work in progress," I say, trying to think fast. "And, honestly, I don't think it would serve my purpose to put my face up there ahead of my book." Whatever that means, but he seems to understand the words better than I do because he gives in without a struggle.

"I see your point, I guess," he says. "No sense getting the publicity machine working before there's an actual book to promote."

I feel myself sag with relief. There are nearly two hundred thousand words in the English language. Against all odds, I appear to have chosen the right ones.

"This case, though, you know. It's an awful business."

I nod. Nothing more is required of me. I am in agreement. It is an awful business, no matter how you look at it. We are here, far from our homes, because we imagine that we can get something done.

"Did you hear about the psychic?"

I shake my head: no.

"She went to the police here, before things got real rough."

"Went to the police for what?"

"A police source told me: she approached them with information about Atwater's whereabouts, but they wouldn't listen."

"You did a story?"

"Naw. I thought I might, but my news director nixed it. Said there were enough crackpots running around out there without us encouraging them."

"Fair enough."

"I guess." Curtis seems a bit wistful. "I think it might have made good TV."

I laugh, though I agree. It seems to me I have seen a good range of crackpots on television since all of this began. And I can't, of course, judge good TV from any other kind though keeping the crackpot quotient to a minimum strikes me as a good idea.

We laugh together briefly, then I say goodbye and head for my car.

He stops me. "Here, take my card," he says, pressing it into my hand. The stock is thick and creamy, the letters raised. There is a network logo emblazoned on it, and his name in stark letters: CURTIS DIAMOND, REPORTER. "Call me if you want to talk. I'm thinking I'll get to interview you before long." He flashes me a smile so white I fight the instinct to cover my eyes while I push the card into my bag without really looking at it.

"See you at the next stop," I say, hoping that, too, will have meaning beyond my understanding. I don't wait for his response, though. I walk straight-legged back to my rental car, outwardly calm, but feeling anything but. I know I wasn't nearly exposed as a fraud, but I feel that way just the same. Maybe we all do, really. That's the thing. Maybe we all always do whether we are lying or not.

I start the car and pull away gently, even though I feel like hitting the gas and getting out of there so quickly that the pea gravel under the car sprays the media van. I don't want to punish ol' Curtis; I just want to put distance between his practiced steely gaze and me.

The crappy neighborhood gives way rapidly to a better one, and with the media van out of my rearview, I pull the car up at the end of a cul-de-sac and go over my plan and my notes. Now that I am here in the real world, with actual reporters and an at-large bad guy, when I go over said notes I feel abashed and ever so slightly ashamed. What had I been thinking in coming out here? It's all I've got, though, so I go over the rather broad plan in my head once again.

I know I want a full day to do my exploration of the northern part of the county. It is over an hour's drive, and there are several stops I want to make along the way. And now I revise my mental picture. Before my arrival, I'd imagined peaceful semi-wilderness settings. Now I sketch media teams and trucks equipped with space gear into that image.

The platoons of media have altered the picture in other ways, too. The small town is full. I manage to book a hotel just outside the downtown core and only because I catch a break, walking in on a cancelation. The little inn is on the tidy side of modest. No hint of squalor, but far from the four-star places I generally stay when I am on a job. It has been my experience that getting in and out of hotels undetected is best done at a place with a large staff. Hotels so professional it's possible to remain anonymous. Small places tend to be understaffed. Or worse, run by the owner. In either case, being remembered by someone is more likely in smaller places. And I pretty much never want that.

San Pasado is small enough, however, that there aren't a lot of options, especially under the circumstances. The hotel I end up in is two brick stories and not far from one of the main streets. Austere but unremarkable. No room service and probably no ghosts.

Once in my room, I drop my bag on the floor and flop on the bed, grabbing the remote as I fall. Nothing much has changed in television land. Though no one has seen any sign of Atwater, the fever pitch has grown. I let the anxious voices lull me into fitful sleep, traveling and fretting having taken their toll. I wake at the sound of a vaguely familiar voice, noticing as I gain consciousness that, since the time I put my head down, the light has gone out of the day. I don't know how long I've been asleep, but it was long enough for me to have missed a West Coast sunset.

On the television, though, is a familiar face to go with the familiar voice. Curtis is standing not far from where I left him, and it must have been filmed around that time, too, because he is standing in sunlight, so it was apparently hours ago.

"Things have continued to be quietly tense here outside William Atwater's childhood home."

Quietly tense. I wonder what that even means.

"We had a recent visit from an author, who says she is working on a book about Atwater."

My blood chills as I see a figure that is clearly me hunched behind the wheel of the rental car. I will myself to breathe. It was a very brief glimpse and the plate of the car was not shown. There is no way I could be recognized from what was revealed on-screen. Still. It feels like a close call. It feels like the possibility of endings.

"Though she said it was early days, this reporter was left with the impression that it would be a work of merit."

"Curtis, can you share the author's name?"

"I'm not at liberty to say, Jennifer," he says blithely, and I find myself looking quizzically at the screen, head cocked, a smile forming. "But I recognized her as a leader in the world of true crime."

And with that, my smile is full. No one is looking for me. No one *knows* to look for me. They are looking for someone sorta famous, and I am not that.

"Thanks, Curtis," I mumble, knowing as I do so that the half-lie was for his benefit, not mine.

I get myself up and together and walk the few blocks into the heart of town. I am hungry and restless and I walk into both of those feelings.

The town is as charming as promised. I prowl around, looking for both food and inspiration. I keep to the shadows and see what I can see. That man over there—might he know something? That woman pushing a pram—had she recently seen someone suspicious? I wonder if this is how it is with small towns in general; when it's possible to know everyone, everyone is both suspect and safe.

I settle on a couple of slices of pizza in a cobbled square, and sit in a courtyard while I nibble, watching people go past while I wonder and consider. At this moment, the task I have set myself seems larger than I am. This thought nearly paralyzes me.

There comes a time, after I've eaten, when I am no longer hungry and I feel there is no more for me to learn just by hanging out and watching. I take the long way through the town and back to my hotel.

Once there, I do it right this time: slip out of my clothes, leave them in a pile on the floor, turn off the television and the endless bleating of earnest and alarmed voices. And, finally, I pull the curtains shut and turn off the light. And then I sleep, sleep, sleep.

CHAPTER TWENTY-TWO

When I wake, I discover I have been asleep for a freakishly long time. It was maybe ten when I lay down, and now, it is ten again: I have slept an entire half of a twenty-four-hour cycle away.

I get ready for the day, thinking I will grab breakfast on the road on the way to the Valley de Oro, but then I realize I am hungry *now.* And it's not like anyone is expecting me. Once I shower and get myself ready for the day, it is after eleven and never mind breakfast, I'm ready for lunch.

Wandering through the streets I'd walked the night before, I am hit again with the double-barreled charm of this place. It doesn't take long for me to find an eatery that is charming, as well.

I sit on a patio at the back of the restaurant at a wrought-iron table right next to an actual bubbling brook. The servers all have the clean look of the college students they probably are, and all the staff have names like Kelsey and Madison.

My server is a lanky blond who identifies herself as MacKenzie. I stop myself from saying "of course it is" when she tells me that's her name.

The place is a microbrew, so I order beer in a tall glass. When it comes, it is pale and fruity. A grapefruit honey amber ale or something else that doesn't generally belong in beer. I order it, because it is today's special brew, but I don't really pay attention. And, since it's first thing in the morning for me, I get a coffee on the side.

The food on the menu looks very good, but I'm not hungry anymore. I was before, but now I can't make it happen. After considering what healthy thing I should order to tempt myself, I tell MacKenzie I'd like some fries to go with the beer and coffee and call it a day.

The thing that keeps going through my mind—as I walk, as I sit, as I nibble: What am I doing here? Not in the restaurant, but in the town. On this chase. What do I hope to accomplish? What do I bring? I am no super sleuth and I have no extraordinary finding skills that I am aware of. I have finally gotten good at not losing my keys, but that took some doing. I find my keys only by practice and rote. I don't think any of that will help in this situation. It is one thing for me to take out a target: someone at a known location when I have received instructions, sometimes down to fine details. But this is something else again. I think about badgers in holes or other even smaller animals, that's what this feels like. Atwater has gone to ground. It is all too far out of my control and, in any case, the professionals have gotten here ahead of me. Journalistic professionals like Curtis Diamond and even actual police and FBI types. Surely, with all their experience, they will find him first. This has been a lark. Possibly even a diversion. But probably I should just pack up my shit and get out of Dodge.

I am sitting, sipping at the final mouthful of beer, nibbling at the last of the perfect French fries, when I feel the buzz and energy of the restaurant shift. It is almost a physical thing.

"What is it?" I ask MacKenzie as she passes. I can see that the hands on the tray she is carrying are not quite steady. "What's going on?"

"Arden's daughter is missing," she says, indicating a petite red-head with a stricken expression just inside the doors. The red-head is talking to a small group and wringing her hands. I can see that decisions are being made.

"Missing," I repeat.

"She disappeared from her day care." MacKenzie's voice has risen an octave. The fear she is expressing is real. "Arden just got a call."

"How old? The child, I mean."

"She's just five. The whole town is spooked right now, right? It could be anything. It's not necessarily . . ."

"She's thinking Atwater?"

The girl nods. Drops her voice. "I mean, Ashley wouldn't have just wandered away. She's just this little kid, you know?"

MacKenzie bustles off and I sit and consider. As I do, it comes to me: fate or kismet or dumb blind luck has led me to the hottest point in the search. And I am here before everyone else: before the police or the occupants of the media trucks or the experts from the media circus's front lines. It seems crass to try and speak with the upset mother, but I don't have anything to lose. I figure maybe she doesn't, either.

"Hey, Arden," I say as I approach her.

The young woman turns saucer-like eyes to me.

"Yes?" Whatever else is true, she is scared as hell. I can practically smell it on her.

"MacKenzie just told me. About your daughter. I'm . . . I'm working on a book . . ."

"A book?"

"On . . ." I find myself reluctant to say the name.

"On *him*?"

"Yes. And I have discovered things about him. I know some things. Maybe I could help."

"Help find Ashley?"

"Maybe. I mean . . . I'm here, right? Maybe for a reason. I could try."

She turns wild eyes on me and looks me up and down. She looks at me like I'm speaking a foreign language or like I'm a freak, and in the shadow of her glance, that's exactly how I feel.

"My daughter is missing," she says. And there is dignity and fear and contempt in her tone. And I feel all of that, too. "I'm not interested in helping with your *book*."

Maybe something else was said. I'm not sure, because I slink back to my table, with my head down, keep my eyes to my computer. Address again the last of my beer; my fries. The dregs of my coffee are long gone, but I suddenly wish for at least the solid hit of a caffeine buzz.

For the balance of my time in the restaurant, I try to continue the research I'd been doing online, and think about where I will go now, where I will aim the rental. After a while, my mortification eases, and I get into balancing out places on the map with Google street views and local images and other things that help me build a picture of the place I'm about to go.

"She disappeared from day care." The voice at my elbow startles me. It is unexpected. I try not to show it.

"That's what MacKenzie told me," I say. "That's terrible." I say it with compassion, and I don't have to work hard at it; it's right there.

"Yuh." She surprises me by swinging down into the seat opposite mine. I give her my complete attention. Now that she is sitting across from me, I can see she has remarkable eyes. They are slate gray and rimmed with brown-gold. Just now her pupils are dilated, most likely with fear. Fight or flight. She wouldn't have to say anything for me to know that, whatever else is true, she is scared as hell.

"Ashley's day care called me," she says in a whisper that feels like a scream. There isn't much sound, but the reverberation from the words takes a long time to die. And she's desperate, I can see that, too. I figure that's the reason she is now sitting across from me. "I'm trying to decide what I should do." And then, "I mean, I have to *do* something, right?"

"Have the police been called?"

She nods. "Yeah. They told me they called the cops even before they called me."

Something in that tells me that the day care thinks the situation is serious. You call the cops *and* you call the mom? That probably means they've already checked under all the rocks in the playground. I'm not sure but I'm imagining: losing kids is probably crappy for business.

"What'd the cops say?"

"They're on their way."

I nod. "So you've done what you can," I say.

"Yes, that's right," she says, "but I don't want to just sit here. Pick up tips. I feel there's something I should do."

"Take me there," I say before I can think about it and shut myself up.

"What?" she says.

"To the day care. That way you won't have to be alone."

"But I don't know you," she says. Her nails are painted. One of them is chipped. There's something touching in that.

"Does it matter?"

She meets my eyes with that gray-gold look again and I can see the answer to the question. Does it matter that I don't know her or her daughter? In this case, no. It does not. So we head out.

While we drive, Arden fills me in: she doesn't have a car. She tells me the whole story, but I only retain a small percentage of the details. Something about her mother and a trip to the coast and a bunch of other things I'm certain at first hearing won't concern me. The upshot is, Arden doesn't have a car and I do, so I end up driving the rental to places I would have never found on my own. I just follow Arden's voice. Left here. Right there. Seventeen miles down this highway. I hesitate at that. Why is she taking me so far afield? She sees my hesitation and understands.

"Yuh. It's weirdly far out, I know. In North County. But day care is cheaper out here and my ex got me a deal."'

"Ashley's dad?"

"Yeah."

We don't say what we're maybe both thinking: cheaper isn't always better. And some things arrive with a cost.

When we get to the final turn, I am taken aback. A huge sign swings ranch-style over a wide driveway: "Valley de Oro Day Care."

"This is Valley de Oro?" I ask from between lips that are suddenly parched.

Arden looks at me quickly. "I thought you weren't from around here."

"I'm not."

"Then how do you know about the Valley? No one who's not from here knows about it."

"Long story. Let's go in and talk to them, okay?"

Arden nods and gets in motion. She doesn't need to be asked twice.

Inside, the little-kid smells nearly kicks me off my feet. I did not prepare myself for it. The smell of innocence. Of senseless joy. My heart quivers under it. I am briefly undone.

The day care is in a former house, but now the place is dedicated to very young children. I stand just inside the front door. In every direction, I see tiny furniture and brightly colored bits of learning and fun. It looks like a fairy tale. The place is more quiet than I would have expected. Subdued. You can taste the sense of hush. Something has gone terribly wrong.

We are met at the door by a young woman. She is in her late twenties, the kind of open-faced girl who gravitates to working with kids. I suspect that on a different day she would be beautiful. Tall and slender like a flower, with hair the color of the far edge of sunset. But now her face is gray, her brow furrowed, eyes rimmed in red. She has been crying. She looks like hell.

"Ohmigawd, Arden," she wails as soon as she sees my companion. "Ohmigawd. I'm so sorry. I don't know what to say."

Arden's lips are stretched so tightly across her teeth, I imagine I can hear them squeak. She cuts the apologies off in mid-wail.

"Please. Don't. Just . . . the police?"

"They just left." Her breathing is returning to normal, but one gets the sense that tears are not far. On this day.

"And . . ." Arden prompts.

An empty look. A voice so low, we have to strain to hear. "They took our statements. Searched the premises . . ." She lets her voice trail off, and we understand: they searched and did not find. And now here we are.

"What happened, Jenn?" Arden's voice is low and deadly.

"I'm not . . . that is, we're not . . . well, we're not really sure. She's just" —tears advertised by the red-rimmed eyes start again— "gone. I told the police that all we can think is, we had a repairman in for the air-conditioning at nap time." The girl looks even more stricken. Her voice drops to just above a whisper. I have to strain to hear. "Afterwards, we looked. We looked, Arden. We really did. And Ashley was gone. When we couldn't find her, we called the police. And then we called you."

Arden's face fell at this. Her expression is mostly not there. What is the correct order, I wonder? The parent, the police. Who do you call? And you can see all of this on Arden: a part of her wants to blame, to lash out. To her credit, she doesn't do it. She just wants her child back. I get that. I get that a lot.

"Where are the other kids?" I ask. The girl looks at me for the first time. "No other kids missing?"

"This is my friend," Arden says, answering Jenn's unasked question. "She drove me here."

Jenn looks me over but not that carefully. She's got other things on her mind.

"Stephen and Loret have the kids in the big playroom. They're doing a quiet time. It just seemed best to keep everyone in one place while we looked for Ashley. And, yes"—she manages to look even more stricken—"just Ashley. I'm so sorry, Arden. I don't know what to say."

"She didn't just wander off?" Me again.

Jenn shakes her head. "We'd hoped so, even though it's not like Ashley to do something like that. But we've looked everywhere."

Clearly not everywhere, I thought. But I didn't say it out loud.

"That's true," Arden agrees. "Ashley would never just go off by herself. She knows better."

"I'm guessing the police will be calling you," Jenn says. "I gave them your number."

Arden nods, but we all know the drill. It will be form: eliminating all possibilities. Did the child's father take her? Some other relative? Was it Arden herself? And they'll hope that. And we'll hope that, too. Because any of those things is better than what we suspect.

"So the air-conditioning went, you said. Someone came to fix it. What was the repairperson driving?"

"I didn't look," Jenn says, sounding sheepish. "He just came in and we were so glad to see him. It was so hot. The kids were whining and stuff."

"When did it stop working?"

"The air-conditioning? Just this morning." She stops and looks at me fully, her face full of thunder. Like a cloud. "Wait. You think maybe this wasn't a coincidence?"

I shrug. I don't know what to think. "It's possible, I guess. What did he look like? The guy that came?"

"Maybe six feet. Heavyset. Not fat, you know. But he was a big guy. Hipster beard. Ball cap."

I try not to say what immediately comes to mind. Saying instead, "He looked like a lot of people."

"Exactly."

So there is an obvious conclusion, but I don't want to go there, not without eliminating every other possibility.

"Is it all right if I have a look around outside?"

Jenn nods that it's okay. "I'm sure you won't find anything. Like I said, we looked everywhere. The cops looked, too. But, yeah: you're welcome to have a poke around. And I'll ask Loret if she saw what he was driving. I'm pretty sure he was already here when she arrived today."

I start to head outside, and Arden looks like she's not sure what to do with herself. In the end, she tramps down into the garden after me. I ignore her. I just want to focus my senses on what is all around me. I'm sure that Ashley is not here, but I want to look anyway.

And, of course, once in the garden, there is nothing, really, to see. The yard itself is a currently empty outdoor play area, fenced off as though for small dogs, which is quite sufficient for keeping little kids corralled. In addition to a well-used jungle gym and a swing set, there is a playhouse. Empty. And many of the kinds of nooks and crannies kids love to play hide-and-seek in. We check them. They are empty, as well.

"Ashley," I hear Arden say at one point. It is not a shout, more like a plaintive statement of fact. Like she just wanted to put the name into the air. "Ashley."

I check the fence for holes, or other places a small child might have crawled under or climbed out. Nothing. Valley de Oro Day Care had done a good job on the fencing. There is no way they would have lost any kids this way, which probably leaves only one other possibility and it's not a good one.

"Arden, you stay here, okay? I'm going to take a drive around the area."

I start towards the car, but she follows me.

"No," she says firmly when I indicate she should stay behind. "You have something in mind. I can see it on your face. I'm coming with you."

One look tells me I won't be able to dissuade her. And I realize maybe I don't fully want to. Maybe a part of me understands that, as far as stakes go, hers are the highest. And what am I asking her to do? Sit at the day care and wring her hands?

"Okay," I tell her. "But you have to do everything I tell you, all right?"

Arden gets into the passenger seat of the rental car without another word. She is nearly beside herself with fear and grief. It has a metallic smell. But I am the best game in town, at least from where she is sitting. We both understand this.

Just as we're about to pull out, Jenn puts her head out the door.

"You coming back?" she asks Arden, but I answer.

"Yeah. We're just going to explore."

"Okay. Well, see you in a while," she starts to retreat, then catches herself. "Oh, Loret says she saw the vehicle, but it's not very helpful."

She has our complete attention now.

"She said it was a white van. Some kind of lettering on the side. She doesn't remember what it said."

And she's right, as far as vehicle descriptions go, there's not much less helpful. How many white vans on every road, in every community? I'd hoped for an identifier, but this isn't that. I feel myself sag in disappointment as I start the car.

CHAPTER TWENTY-THREE

"WHERE ARE WE going?" Arden asks as I point the rental out of the driveway. It is a valid question. I just really have no idea. Or maybe I do, but that idea is not yet fully formed.

"I'm just going to look around at first," I say honestly. "I did some research before I got here. But I don't know the area at all."

"There's a park not far from here. Might be worth a peek."

"Show me," I say.

Arriba Park is a ten-minute run from the day care, further down Highway 46. There's not much to it. A stand of trees, a dog park, a baseball diamond. A single glance at the parking lot tells us we've struck out. The thing about a purely urban setting: it is both easier and more difficult to go to ground. In a small town, it is possible to keep your eyes out for a certain vehicle or a distinctive type of person, unlike in a city, where every street might be bristling with people and white vans. But in the country, there are barns and forests and other natural landscapes; places to hide. Atwater is the needle, the countryside the haystack. We roll on.

We take a run through the sweet and tiny hamlet at the northernmost point of the county. A sign swings on the roadside as we head into town: SANCTUARY, POPULATION 7674.

There is a grain elevator at the feed store, a gas station, a donut shop, a town square, a barbecue place, and several country bars, all on a couple of main streets. In all of that, we see one white van. It is stopped at the gas station. I feel my heart jump to my throat as I pull up and then get out of my car, leaving Arden behind.

My hands are almost shaking by the time I reach the driver's side, lean in. But the van is filled with electronic equipment, and the driver is a fresh-faced kid with a skinny ponytail and wispy facial hair.

"Can you . . . can you tell me how to get to the freeway?" I don't know what else to say.

He directs me politely, looking slightly curious. There are, after all, signs indicating the freeway is this way or that every few feet.

"Nothing," I say with a sigh when I get back into the car.

"Do you know about Hoyo Lago?" Arden asks, like she's been thinking while I was otherwise occupied.

"I don't. Tell me."

"It was a gravel pit. Hoyo. Long ago. Now it's sort of a weird little lake. Dried out half the year. More than that. More like a pond most of the other time. But it seems like . . . like a place . . ."

I look at Arden for several seconds that stretch into a minute. I think about strength and fortitude and the things mothers are sometimes called upon to deal with. Things beyond normal human endurance and certainly expectation. And I hope that, whatever the outcome we have here and despite the evidence of my own search to the contrary, the child has merely wandered off and is even now being discovered waking from an innocent nap in the day care garden, dirt on her face, a leaf in her hair, hungry and maybe afraid and looking for her mom.

But I don't really think so.

"Okay. Hoyo Lago sounds like a good next step. And it is consistent with what I've been thinking. Tell me which way to go."

I send the car in the direction Arden shows me, making turns along the way as she instructs. "Here," she says finally, indicating a driveway so lightly used, I would have missed it without her keeping watch for it. I say as much.

"Yuh," she says, coloring slightly. "You pretty much have to have grown up around here to know about this place."

Unspoken: parking with boys. Fast cars. Torrid summer romances. Crickets in the dark and the smell of cum on upholstered seats. Memories I don't possess anymore, if I'd ever had them at all.

The road is bumpy and overgrown, but nowhere near impassable. It's not ideal, but I push the rental down it, beyond the place where rental cars are meant to go.

Here, further off the road, there are indications of forgotten activity. Old road signs with bullet holes in them; someone's long-ago weekend target practice. Faded fast-food wrappers. Discarded cans, some with still more bullet holes. After a while, the overgrown road thins out and the old gravel pit comes into view, looking more like a small, dried out lake than the center of the beginning of urban growth it had been a hundred years before.

"Not much to see," I say.

Arden's eyes scan the area closely. She is familiar with this place. She knows better what to look for. She gets out of the car and I let her go, watching closely as she looks at the ground and the immediate vicinity, a mother animal on the hunt. She looks frightened and dangerous in the same moment, though maybe heavier on the side of dangerous. She seems calmer than she did at the day care. We are hunting now and we are hopeful, but I feel she has resigned herself for the worst; whatever small hope she'd had having been squashed by miles and time.

"Someone has been here," she says, getting back into the car.

"Are you sure?"

"No," she says. "But I feel it." It doesn't occur to me to disagree.

"Where does the road go?"

"More of the same, just like how we got in here. And then it just stops after a while. Or it used to. But it will be harder going. And there's not really anything up there to see."

I start to turn the car around. "Wait. What was that?" The urgency in her voice brings me to full alert.

"What?"

"A flash of . . . never mind. It's gone."

"Say it." My voice is quiet, but insistent. There is nothing. And there is everything. The sense of something that matters.

"Well, I thought I saw a flash of white," she says. "Like metal? But then it was gone."

I strain in the direction she's looking. I can't see anything. But her face—tense and certain and urgent—tells me she isn't making it up.

"Like a car maybe?"

"Maybe," she says hesitantly, not like she's afraid I won't believe her, but like she doesn't dare believe it herself.

"Look, Arden, I believe you and I want to go in and investigate, but I don't want to endanger you. Please take the car back to the day care and call the police. If it *is* him and he's here, we're going to need help."

"No," she says. Firm and solid. Nothing of movement in her voice. Or weakness.

I look at her in surprise. "No" hadn't been on the table. I hadn't thought she had it in her.

"I'm not arguing this, Arden."

She crosses her arms. "Whatever. I'm going with you. If Ashley is here . . . with *him* . . . you'll need me."

I regard her. Think it through. She actually has a point.

"Okay. Fuck. Okay. Stay close, all right?"

She nods silently. She is pale. Barely there. But the hope that had been nearly dead minutes before has been flamed slightly. She has everything at stake. I can see that in the profile she's turned to me; the firmly set jaw, the tilt of her little chin. And I get it. If it were me, I would be the same. I don't have the words in me to make her do what I've asked. Instead, I move to the trunk of the rental, open my suitcase. Arden has followed me and her eyes go wide when I pull the Bersa out of the place where I used to keep my underwear.

"Holy," she says quietly. "Are you some kind of cop?"

I laugh. It sounds humorless, even to me. "I am no kind of cop, for sure." I pop a magazine into the gun and rack the slide. Get her ready for business. "But I *do* know how to use this." The reflection in her eyes makes me feel like an action hero. It's an odd feeling, but I don't hate it.

I put the gun carefully into my purse and we follow the trail. It is not much more than deer might have made. We are silent, like the leaves. We move slowly. Carefully. Feeling the dense oaks all around us. Feeling, also, every disturbance, every crack of every branch beneath our feet. Every sound ahead. We haven't been moving like this for very long when we hear a sound that stops us both cold. The cry of a child, more shocking in the quiet of the oak forest than it would otherwise have been. I look at Arden and see a bouquet of emotions in her eyes: hope, anticipation, fear. I don't need to motion at her to be quiet. We both understand what is at stake.

Everything.

Our eyes meet and neither of us breathe, let alone speak, but we don't doubt it is Ashley. Arden has recognized the sound of her daughter's cry. Something primal come home to roost.

I blink at Arden. I can almost see her thoughts. Her daughter is alive, when minutes ago she feared she might be dead. But, if we find her, will she be hurt or damaged in some way?

I nod, reassuring and silent. Her child is crying. I can see her gathering up her energy, as though she might bolt towards the sound. It might even be pure instinct. I restrain her with a look, almost a wish. The wrong move right now can change outcomes. She understands this; I see that, too. See her settle into what must be done. Her expression becomes stoic.

The cry comes again. The cry of a child who is frightened, but not in pain. I can see Arden have this thought, as well. It is all we have, in any case. We inch ahead on hope.

The oaks thin. The trail widens. The source of the flash of white Arden saw in the first place becomes apparent: a van tucked amid the trees. Magnetic signs on the side advertise Liam's Air Conditioning. I feel a surge of anger so pure I can almost touch it. Liam. A short form of William. He is so bold! And he feels so superior, so smart, he thinks he can flaunt such a thing and get away with it.

I calm myself. Focus on breaths in. Breaths out. Anger won't serve me here. In any case, he'd been right: he'd sailed in there and taken a child from right under their noses. And now here we all are.

I do a fast calculation. We have moved quickly. The child was taken less than three hours ago, and we have heard her, albeit briefly. She is alive and she seems unscathed. I say a prayer to someone's unseen god and move forward, inch by careful inch, and then—suddenly—there they are, across a clearing from us. A tarp is spread on the ground next to the van. I try not to think about its purpose, why a child on a tarp. A naked child. She is spread-eagled. She is tied down. I try not to ask myself about any of those things, in part because I am so relieved about the final piece: she looks unhurt. I breathe, but not much. We're not there yet.

Atwater's presence commands my attention, but I notice other things about the scene. This is not a random stopping place. There are signs of frequent usage, even something that looks like a rough garden at the edge of the clearing.

I don't have time to look around or ask myself questions. Atwater stands over the child. I don't recognize him at first, but I know who he is. The small paleness of her makes him look even larger. He looms. There is a knife in his hand. Something long and deadly looking, as though it might be used for fighting. Or gutting a deer. I want to close my eyes, but I know that won't make it go away.

I feel rather than hear Arden gasp. I feel it in my gut. Atwater is too far away to feel it, but he hears it and my heart sinks. The advantage of surprise was all we had. His head comes up and swivels around like a dog's.

I want to kill him then. It would have been the simplest thing. Instead, I hear myself say in a loud, clear voice, "Stand back from the child." A ridiculous thing to say, maybe. But it's all that comes to me in the moment. And it's the only thing I really want.

He doesn't, though. He doesn't stand back. Maybe I'd known all along he would not. To my surprise, he looks at me—straight at me—and smiles.

"I've been waiting for you," he says. There is a madness in his face, in his voice. I know he is insane. Truly, I knew that going in. But the words chill me nonetheless. Who am I, that he should be waiting?

"Stand back from the child, William. Stand away from her." The Bersa is in my hand and leveled at his chest. And Arden. I can't hear her anymore, can't hear the mother heart in her chest beating. It seems possible she has stopped breathing.

"Fuck you," he says, quietly. Almost sweetly. He moves towards Ashley. Raises the knife. The child sees or senses the shift and starts to scream.

And scream.

I know I can take him out easily, but I also know there is more here at stake than the life of a single dog. And I am thinking that, whatever happens here, the killing time will come before long. But for now, he is better to me alive than dead. It is the chance I take.

Knowing the risk—knowing that missing this poisonous target might mean I'd kill him anyway—I calculate and aim for the shoulder of the arm that holds the knife. I always underestimate the severity of the Bersa's kick. There's a price you have to pay for her small size. The shot is true, but the gun bucks in my hand. I have to hold on tightly so I don't lose my grip. It's a good thing another shot isn't required. I don't even really have time to think about anything, but I know in my heart I've hit my target.

Atwater is on the ground screaming, in that moment not realizing how lucky he is that my aim is accurate.

"You crazy bitch! Look what you did to my arm!"

I motion for Arden to follow me. There is relief on her face now, washed in with the fear. Her ordeal might be nearly over but she fears that, maybe, it has still just begun. Perspective is everything, yes. And luck rides a white horse.

"Get Ashley," I say to her quietly beneath the din as we move forward. "I'll just shut him up."

I don't have to tell her again.

While she springs instantly towards her daughter, I move in the direction of the van and recoil at first from what I see. Inside, it looks a torture chamber. If I had time to think about what I'm looking at, I would weep. But I don't have time, so I close my mind and grab the first thing that will suit my purpose: a rubber mallet. The handle fits neatly into my hand. I go to the screaming man and hit him on the head with it. A solid whap, stronger than a tap. I know I risk killing him with the blow, but it is yet another calculated risk. And, as I'd hoped, for better or worse, it shuts him up. He's out for now. I know we don't have long, but we have priorities. And, in truth, his death would not be the worst thing in the world. Not the worst thing, at all.

Now Arden has her daughter untied. I see joy on the woman's face, but also fear; like something might happen that turns the whole thing south again. She can't believe her good fortune, that's what I see.

I wonder how close by the police are. Wonder if they are within easy calling distance. Wonder even if I want them to show up or stay away.

Along with all the other stuff in the van, I find a blanket. I toss it to Ashley so she can wrap the child in it. The rough material envelopes the tiny form. With the warmth and proximity of her mother, Ashley's cries subside. They are no longer screams of terror, just the hiccuppy burbles left behind after your body has forgotten for the moment how to do anything other than articulate distress.

"She's okay?"

Arden nods, visibly sagging with her relief. "She's perfect. Nothing broken." And then, just above a whisper, a thought she is almost afraid to articulate: "I think we got here just in time."

"I think so, too. Listen, pop her into the passenger seat of the van, okay? Then come help me."

A fledgling plan is beginning to form. Atwater's van has everything I need. I find rope, several knives, handcuffs, leg irons, bedsheets. I work quickly, trying hard not to think about what this vehicle has seen. I know we don't have much time.

I find a couple of T-shirts in the van and tear them into strips to bind his shoulder. It is going to hurt like hell when he wakes, but I don't care about that. Maybe something even less than care. Compassion is not the reason I want to stop the bleeding. Having him bleed out will not suit my purpose.

I stop the bleeding with an efficiency that surprises me. Once that happens, I bind his hands and feet then ask Arden to help me move him into the van. It is easier said than done. Atwater is probably two hundred pounds, and, at the moment, he is dead weight. At one point as we work, he gets a little restless and I think he might wake up, so I give him another knock on the head. Gentle-like, though, not a full-on bash. Just enough to send him back over. Again, the risk to him is real, but it is necessary. Even damaged, he is dangerous to the two of us: we are much smaller creatures. We have to do everything we can to even the odds.

When we are done, when he is once again out cold and has been secured in the back of the van, I indicate that Arden should join Ashley on the passenger seat. She clutches the child to her in a relieved-mother's death grip, and we bump back through the forest to my rental car.

I look at Arden and hope I can trust her with this next part, realizing that I have no choice and maybe it doesn't matter anyway. From here, the success of the plan that is forming will be a matter of timing and fate.

I meet her eyes. "I need you to help me get him into the trunk of my car," I say, glad that the car rental company had upgraded me to a full-sized vehicle at the airport, not the compact I'd initially ordered.

She looks startled for a second, regards me with big, questioning eyes, which, on this day, have seen too much. But when she speaks, all she says is, "Okay."

Her agreement is one thing. Actually pulling it off is another. It takes us a long time; longer than it should. He seems to start to rouse again, but when he hits his head on the hard metal around the edge of the trunk, I don't save him from the bump. The knock on his skull this time is loud enough that even I, who don't wish him well, cringe. But the hit of his head on the edge of the trunk seems to send him back over, saving me from having to give him another bonk with the mallet.

As we work, I am aware of a certain ambivalence growing inside me. I have a goal and a plan. If Atwater dies before I achieve it, I would be perfectly comfortable shunting him to the forest floor and leaving him for the vultures. I know I would do so without real regret. There are things I need him alive for, but if he dies in the course of getting him there, well, maybe that's okay, too.

When it is done, and Atwater is neatly tucked into the trunk of the car with the lid closed, I grab everything I think I'll need from the back of the van. I move quickly while I do it. He's taken a few good bonks to the head, but I don't know how long he'll be out.

"Now take the van and Ashley to the police. If you could give me an hour's head start, that would be perfect."

"What'll I tell them?"

"Just . . . everything, I guess." I hadn't really thought that part through. "I mean, if you forgot the color of this car, that would be a bit of a help, but they'll need to know everything else that happened so that they can deal with it all in the best possible way. That van is full of evidence—more than we can see, I'm sure. And some of it might help other parents know what happened to their kids." I blanch a bit thinking about it. Meet her eyes. So much that doesn't need to be said. "There'll be DNA, etcetera." Thinking of that reminds me that I'll need to be careful to leave none of my own.

"Are you going to kill him?" There is nothing beyond mild interest as she asks this. She will not fight me either way on the outcome. She has her daughter back, so she cares less now what happens to the monster. She has her daughter back and she is looking cool and under control, but there is a wildness at the edge of her eyes, a sort of surprised joy that she is containing. The ordeal is not over yet, but her daughter is alive. Once they are both in a safe place, I think she might collapse with the pure post-shock of it, but for now, adrenalin keeps her moving forward.

"I'm not sure yet," I reply. Even I am surprised by this answer. I keep thinking the correct outcome will present itself. But right now, I am not sure what that is. "I'm going to try and get information out of him. But I guess it could happen that he ends up dead."

"Good," she says. Something hard and unexpected glitters in her eyes. "Good."

She gives me a quick hug, then secures Ashley in the passenger seat of the van. She hops into the van and drives away. I imagine she doesn't look over her shoulder. I wouldn't. The future is waiting for both of them.

I have a lot to do. I watch the van's taillights fade to distant red specks and then disappear. After a couple of minutes thinking, I get into my now heavily laden rental car and do the same.

CHAPTER TWENTY-FOUR

THERE ARE MOMENTS in all of our lives that we understand to be pivotal. Not a lot of them. That is, we mostly don't recognize them while they occur. You can spot them looking back over your shoulder. Sure, that's easy. But while they are happening? I think maybe each of us gets less than six of those in our lifetimes. Of course, I'm making the number up. It feels right, though. It's how it seems to me.

Leaving the nearly hidden driveway at Hoyo Lago, and pointing my rented car west, towards the ocean, I get one of those moments. I have the sense that nothing will ever be the same again. And I'm not even really sure why.

I take Highway 46 towards the coast. Before long, I hear furtive noises from the trunk and pull the car over at a wide vista point. I am at the top of the world. The hills roll out and over towards the ocean. The sun is falling fast in a darkening sky. It is as though the gold and blue are bathed in blood. It is beautiful.

I watch the sun set and the darkness grow, not certain I've ever seen a more beautiful end of day. Before full dark, though, while the sky is still shot through with indigo and red, I open the trunk and meet angry eyes. Before I silence him again, I see a hatred in those eyes so thorough I almost think it can kill me. But it doesn't kill me. Maybe it even makes me stronger.

I shut the trunk. Toss the mallet onto the back seat. Keep driving.

When I get to the coast, I head the car and my precious cargo north. I'm not sure why. I just keep following the Pacific Coast Highway while dark falls properly. I am driving into a darkening sky.

I think a lot while driving. I think about what to do. I have done all of this with no real plan in mind, so now I think about what needs doing: what is going to be required of me in this special situation. All of the steps.

And I have a sense of standing up. There would have been easy things to do in this situation. Killing him. Leaving him for the police. And then there is what I am doing now. This is the hard way. I am certain of it. But it is also the right way. I am doing what has to be done. There is something good in that. Noble, almost. I have a sense of things coming together in the right order. Contrary to some of the details, there is a rightness in all of this.

When I see the sign for camping at a large state park on the ocean, I pull up. I have arrived at something like a plan. I tell the park ranger at the entrance I am coming back to camp later, but could I please drive up now and pick a spot then pay for it? I am told that will be fine; that there is a map right there showing what spots are available. That she is leaving in the next few minutes, but she tells me the procedure for selecting a spot and leaving my money and the parking spot number I choose in a metal contraption that looks like a mailbox but that she calls the Iron Ranger.

I choose the high camping area, farthest from the ocean, figuring that will be less busy on a weekday in a shoulder season. I drive around until I find a spot that backs onto an area of tall trees and high grass. It is full dark now, but I am imagining a beautiful vista, looking away from the sea. And it is private, making it perfect for what I have in mind. As I figured, the campground is nearly deserted and at the spot I choose there is no one around. It is a state park, but it might as well be the middle of nowhere and I have a strong feeling it will stay that way.

I back the car into the spot. There is no one around and darkness is now complete. I spend the next hour getting William Atwater's prone form out of the trunk of the car. It is much more difficult on my own than I'd imagined it would be, but there is no alternative. I have to stop several times to catch my breath. By the time I finally manage to pull, push, and leverage him out and into the tall grass at the edge of my camping spot, my clothes stick to me damply and I feel sweat running in smooth rivulets down my forehead and between my breasts. But I am pleased with the results of my labor. Atwater is out of the car; the tall grass and the tree shield him from casual viewing.

I check him over with some distaste. It has been the most difficult part of all of this: the necessity to touch him. His wound has started bleeding again, but not strongly enough that I need to do anything. I figure it will stop on its own after a while. His breathing seems normal and is not ragged. I'm not a nurse, but he looks healthy enough to me. It seems likely he is in pain, but I'm certain none of it will kill him.

He feels warm, slightly feverish, but considering what he's been through, that seems normal to me, as well.

I do a good job of tying him up. And I gag him so that, if he does wake, no one will hear him hollering. Then I drop the tarp over him and leave him there. I know there is a small chance that someone might find him before I get back, but I have to risk that possibility. A calculated risk. If he is discovered, it won't be the end of the world, but I'd prefer it not happen. And the park is so quiet, he seems more at risk from a wild animal than unwanted human discovery but, just to be on the safe side, I pay for the spot I've taken and the ones on either side, feeling confident that Atwater will be left alone to ferment in his own misery.

I drive back to San Pasado with the aid of the light of a nearly full moon. I drop the keys in the after-hours box as I leave the rental car behind, then take a cab to my hotel where I drop onto the bed fully clothed and sleep for six solid hours. The sleep of the righteous. The sleep of the damned. I'm not sure which, but six solid is a rarity for me so I don't ask any questions, just sleep until I can't anymore.

CHAPTER TWENTY-FIVE

IN THE MORNING, I am more clearheaded than I have been for what feels like weeks. I stand in the shower and let hot water pummel me so hard it is almost painful, but it feels good, too. Painfully good. I know it will help me get through what promises to be a full day.

After the shower, it doesn't take long for me to get myself together, and I am packed and standing in the hotel lobby ready for my Uber within a half hour of waking.

The address I give the driver is just a few minutes from my hotel and on the main road out of town. After the car drops me off, it feels a little awkward wheeling my suitcase into the sales office at the RV dealership, but at least they can tell I mean business.

"I'm looking for an RV."

"You've come to the right place." The salesman is my age, even though his hair is retreating from his forehead and the middle of his body shows the signs of decades of riding a desk. When he grins at me, I get a glimpse of an almost imperceptible hole in his smile, at the corner of his mouth, near the back. He points to a sign above his head: "Renfrew RV," the sign says. "Used. New. In Between. We've got what you need."

"I'm Jack Renfrew," he says after he follows my glance. "How can I help you?"

"I want something small but roomy. An RV. Not flashy. It should be used, but in good enough condition that it doesn't stand out."

"Stand out from what?"

"It shouldn't be trashed. Or trashy," I add, almost as an afterthought. "It shouldn't draw attention to itself in any way."

"How many does it need to sleep?"

"Two. Tops. Maybe not even that."

He arches an eyebrow in my direction but chooses not to comment, taking things, instead, to a different, more neutral place.

"All of our used vehicles are in good condition," he says, a hint of defensiveness in his tone. I ignore it.

"Good," I say. "Then we won't have a problem. Show me."

He indicates the suitcase. "I gather you're planning on making a deal today."

"I am."

"You've got cash."

"That's right."

"Okay," he says, echoing my tone. "Good. Then we won't have a problem." I know from all of that, that he is someone I can do business with.

He shows me three vehicles. I like the second. It is more like a van than an RV. And small enough that I know I'll have no trouble handling it on my own. At the same time, it is large enough to have room inside for two people to move. Just. Also, it has a bathroom with a full shower. It is old and worn-looking enough that, had I been heading onto a long journey I wouldn't have touched it. But the trip I have in mind is shorter than that and there won't be a lot of miles involved.

The price is fifteen thousand. I offer him twenty. I let the number sink in before I explain.

"There's a catch," I say.

"There's always a catch," he says with no change in his expression.

I see him sit up to pay closer attention when I shut his office door.

"I want you to lose the paperwork on the transfer."

"Come again?"

"I want the vehicle to stay in your name. It won't be for long."

"I can't possibly do that," but the way his eyes shift around, I know we aren't far from a deal.

"Twenty-five."

He blinks. Says nothing for ten, maybe fifteen seconds. Then: "How long?"

"If you keep the paperwork in your desk for a week, that will be enough."

I can see the avarice in his eyes, so I push for home.

"You'll probably get the vehicle back in any case."

His head goes up at that. Then the blink again.

"In that case," he says, "maybe I don't even transfer it."

"What are you thinking?"

"Maybe I hold the paper for a week, then report the vehicle stolen."

I look at him evenly. "That would be best for me. If it were to happen that way, and without any ID from me today, another five thousand would show up for you within the month. Plain envelope. Unmarked bills."

"We're talking thirty grand, all in?"

"Yes," I say without hesitation.

He extends his hand. "Deal," he says when he lets go. I suppress the urge to wash my hands.

We shake, then he helps me load my suitcase before giving me a tour of the van's features. A solar panel. A generator. A refrigerator. A microwave. Where to fill the propane. Where to plug it in to fill the water. Where to plug it in to empty it out. And so on. I only half pay attention. I know that I won't be around long enough to use most of these features.

I stop at a Walmart on the way out of town: home away from home for RVers everywhere. Inside, I shop, pushing my cart with purpose and direction. I get a first aid kit, Polysporin, hydrogen peroxide, and a big bottle of ibuprofen. I get a lot of small bottles of water and a plastic jug of vodka. The vodka is not for drinking so I am more interested in quantity than quality and there's a lot in that jug.

I get tins of soup and some fresh fruit and a cheap camping kit that has plates and cutlery and even a little multipurpose cooking pot and a can opener. A few pre-made sandwiches. Towels. A stack of single sheets and a couple of blankets. Toilet paper. Garbage bags. Battery acid.

I have already unloaded my shopping cart before I realize—too late!—that the person in line in front of me is none other than L.A. news reporter Curtis Diamond. His purchases look exactly right for the situation: toothpaste, a three-pack of men's briefs, a six-pack of Gatorade, and a couple of chocolate bars: nice quality, I notice. Probably the best they have. It's obviously the purchases of someone who is going to be away from home longer than expected. As I take note of what he is buying, I also consider how what *I* am buying will look. I think to start packing my purchases back into the cart and heading to another register—or even just abandoning the stuff I'd accumulated and starting again—but before I can organize my thoughts enough to get in motion, he looks over at me. Any hope I have of him having forgotten me is banished instantly.

"Oh, hullo!" he says in a loud and friendly voice. "Written any good books lately?"

"Oh, yuh. Heh, heh," I say, aiming to sound just as cordial. Likely failing miserably.

I see him move his open smile from my face to my waiting purchases and I cringe inwardly. He takes in the huge vodka. The piles of sheets. The battery acid. The giant bottle of ibuprofen. Garbage bags. His eyes rove on.

"Looks like you're heading to an interesting party," he says in a tone that's intended to be light, like he's making a joke, but that I can tell is covering up genuine curiosity. And maybe something more than that.

I search my brain but there's just no good explanation for what I've got there. So I decide not to try.

"You don't wanna know," I say honestly, but also finally. He can tell I'm not going to say any more, and so maybe he's curious? But he decides not to press. He has a pretty good idea I'm not going to say.

He makes his purchases but turns again to me before he heads out the door.

"Remember what I said yesterday: call me any time." He lets his eyes roll back to my purchases, now beginning to be rung in. "I figure you've got a story for me."

I nod and wave while I wish him away.

After that, the sailing is clear. I finish buying my load of crap, then I drag it all out to the RV, pack up, then head on my way.

When I get on the road, it's a funny adjustment, driving something so big. I've never done it before. I underestimate how wide I am and nearly wipe out the pumps when I stop to fill up. But then I kind of get the hang of it. The sheer size of the thing. The sway on the road and the way every little breeze seems telegraphed from outside the vehicle right into my hands on the wheel.

After a while, I settle in. It's sort of like driving a watermelon. And while it's kind of exhausting and I wouldn't want to have to do it for long, I know I'll manage easily with the relatively short distance ahead of me.

I wonder, briefly, if Atwater will be as I left him. Then I chide myself: it seems to me virtually impossible that he won't be. Unless some animal has killed him, which I wouldn't count as a loss at all.

The road ahead. That's all there is. What else does anyone need?

CHAPTER TWENTY-SIX

AT THE PARK, I pull the RV into the spot I'd selected, aware that the sheer bulk of the vehicle will hide the place where I dumped Atwater from any kind of casual view. And the spot is well sheltered from a distance by trees and bushes. And it is dark. It has been more than ten hours since I left him and I have mixed feelings about what I might find. Will he still be breathing? Do I even really care? Sure, I have a plan and I'm fairly certain I have the fortitude to pull it off. But is it the right course, really? Or am I, at some strange level, playing the part of an exceedingly cruel god?

I ignore those voices and push on. I am aware it is a chance I have to take.

He is awake when I pull the tarp off him. His eyes fix mine with a blend of fear and loathing.

I can smell piss and shit and feel heat roll off him—the fever of infection. There is drool and maybe a bit of puke at the edge of the binding I used on his mouth and his eyes have a kind of yellowish tinge. When I pull the tarp back, he regards me with the wary expression of a cornered dog. I take care to stay clear of his teeth.

I pull the Bersa out of my bag and take some small pleasure when his eyes widen at its appearance. Good. It means he still cares about staying alive. Which means I still have a chance to do what I intend.

I pull the gag out of his mouth carefully. The last thing I want is a bite, and I keep that cornered dog image firmly in my mind. It is not inaccurate. A dangerous dog. He's probably been that his whole adult life. Or longer.

"Bitch," he spits when he can. But the voice and the energy are weak. He's cursing me, but he's on autopilot.

"Now, now, William," I say. "You'd better be nice to me. I'm the one with food and water."

"What makes you think I give a fuck about your food and water?"

"You'd rather die." It's not a question.

"This is bullshit. You can't keep me here like this. I know my rights."

I laugh. The kind of laugh that feels good because it is so honest and pure. He looks at me like I'm crazy, but I see the fear grow in his eyes. It feels good to be on the receiving end of that look. It is the best gift he could give me. And in that moment, he is not wrong: I am crazy and fear is his best response.

"Your *rights*? You think that's the conversation? Do I look like a cop, William?"

"I guess you kinda do, yeah."

I reflect briefly. He's right, of course. I probably do. But still.

"I am not."

"What do you want with me?" There is a helplessness in his tone. Something childlike. I almost feel sorry for him. Almost. Plus, I don't really have a fully formed answer. Not yet.

"You're lying there in your own shit. I'm going to cut you loose and get you cleaned up. We'll talk later."

He doesn't say anything. He just looks up at me from under hooded eyes. I'm not sure what to say either, so I get down to business.

"I'm going to toss you the knife," I say. "You're going to cut yourself loose, then let the knife fall. Make any funny moves, and I will drop you right where you are. The reason you are still alive has nothing to do with any reluctance on my part to kill you. Are you clear on that?"

He nods yes, but I can tell he doesn't fully believe. I decide to move forward with my plan anyway. His opinion is not high on my list of priorities.

He cuts himself loose, tosses the knife where I've indicated, then stands in front of me, shoulders slumped, hands at his sides, waiting. He seems beaten. For now. It surprises me that I have no feeling about that, one way or the other.

"Strip," I say.

He hesitates.

"Trust me," I say, "this is not for my pleasure. You smell like shit and piss. We need to get you cleaned up. Throw your clothes into the bushes, over there."

"But I got no other clothes." His voice is weak, and with the edge of a whine to it, he sounds like a child who has almost been pushed too far.

"Don't worry about it for now. I've seen a naked man before. I'm not expecting you'll offer up any surprises."

"I'm thirsty." It is a snivel. A better person would feel badly about how good that makes them feel. I don't go there. It just seems better not to.

"Yuh. I guess you would be thirsty by now." And I've anticipated this and am ready. I toss him a plastic bottle of water. "This should help."

He opens the bottle, dropping the cap to the ground, then turns it up to his face so quickly, a third of the water splashes down his front uselessly. It is like watching a dog drink, if dogs had opposable thumbs. But watching him I think that a dog would be more efficient.

"You're going to take a shower." I hook a thumb at the RV behind me. "And don't get any ideas. I rigged a camera in there. I'm going to watch you."

"But my rights . . ." he says again, though he sounds less sure this time. I can see that he is wondering if, just maybe, he might not get any rights, after all.

"You don't have rights, asshole." My voice is flat. I don't recognize it. "Not out here. The only ones you'll have are the ones I'll give you. Now go shower up." I use the muzzle of the Bersa to point the way, feeling tougher than I intended. And also feeling less so.

I've left a bar of soap for him in the tiny bathroom, a towel and a couple of sheets, and, as I told him, I rigged a small camera in there, as well. I managed to hide the camera neatly in the molding and I am proud of my work. Unless he really goes hunting for it, he is unlikely to see it at all.

He does as I directed. I'd been counting on him being hungry enough and in so much pain that he wouldn't put up much of a fight. That had been part of my plan, as well. Because a real fight between us with him at full strength would see me losing handily, and that's not conjecture. So I don't take any chances, and I use every advantage I have.

When he emerges from the bathroom, his skin is pink and rosy and he's fashioned one of the sheets around himself into a sort of crude toga. It will do.

The injured shoulder is open to the air and I can see the beginning of an angry infection there. I have to work quickly. I don't need to be a doctor to tell me that, without care and antibiotics, Atwater won't be much good to me or anyone after a couple more days.

I am standing at the front of the RV and toss him one of the Walmart sandwiches, indicating he should sit at the table. He snatches the ham-on-rye out of the air and barely takes the time to pull the plastic off before wolfing it hungrily. I am glad that he is well enough that he still feels like eating.

I keep my distance, the gun in one hand, and I'm starting to realize the magnitude of the task I've taken on. It dawns on me that it is possible that watching him could be a full-time gig for a few days. I have acted on impulse and, to a certain degree, on instinct. And now I am fully committed, but at what price? And where does this road lead?

I give him time to eat the sandwich and drink a couple of bottles of water before I get down to business.

"There's pen and paper just to your right there," I say. "See it?"

He nods.

"I've got a list of missing children here. We're going to go through this list together. You're going to tell me about those missing kids and where they are. Or use the paper to write things up if it helps the process."

He looks at me with an expression so incredulous it shifts towards the comical. I want to knock the look off his sick, smiling mug. I want that so badly I can taste it. So badly it makes me question my own wellness, but only for a beat.

"Why would I do that?" It comes out over a sneer. Like a teenager questioning bedtime, but even less endearing.

It is a valid question, though. I've thought that part through and am ready with an answer.

"Because I'm going to hurt you, William. If you don't tell me. I'm going to hurt you in ways you can't even imagine." I drop my voice to a whisper. I can see him strain to hear me. "The things you did to those kids? Those things will pale in comparison to the hurt I'm going to rain on you."

He shrugs. He doesn't care. I have ways to make him care, but I know instinctively that's not the place to start. So instead, I ignore the shrug. I ignore the insult implied by his carelessness. I ignore it and begin as though he hasn't responded at all.

"Kandra Smithe," I say, reading from the top of my list.

"The name doesn't mean anything to me," he says right away. He's looking in the other direction and his voice is flat. Distant. I can't determine anything from the tone.

I look at him. I'd put her at the top of the list because, of the kids that are still unaccounted for, little Kandra had been the one with the strongest clear connection to Atwater. She was four when she disappeared three years ago. The daughter of one of Atwater's former babysitters, the little girl and her mother had lived down the block from him in a trailer at the back of a neighbor's property. There had been lots of clean lines between Atwater and the missing girl. And her body had never been recovered. But I look at his face now. There is nothing. It's like looking down an empty well.

"I don't believe you."

He shrugs.

"Maybe you don't get how this is going to go." I am containing a column of rage. I feel as though I am doing it admirably. I don't think anyone would be able to tell what I'm holding back. Or maybe they would, but I know it doesn't matter. Not now.

When he speaks, I can see he has missed the rage in me. Or he does not understand yet that it is going to make a difference to his future. He is used to being impervious. In charge. He is used to choosing his victims in a way that leaves him in complete control. He is not in control now, but he doesn't know it yet, not completely. I can tell from his body language and his face. He doesn't yet fully understand. His next words solidify that idea.

"How is it you think you can tell me how to be, what to say?" There is an arrogance in his tone. A self-righteousness. Clearly, in this scenario, he is the injured party.

He is feeling more comfortable now than he was a while ago. He has been recently fed. His most basic needs have been seen to, though I figure by now his shoulder is giving him hell. Still, everything is relative. He feels clean, not hungry, not thirsty. He is no longer under a tarp in his own shit. He no longer feels as vulnerable as he did then. What could possibly go wrong?

He settles more comfortably into the narrow bench seat at the RV's dining table and shoots a belligerent grin in my direction. Whatever else is happening, he figures he is in control.

I hold onto my quiet rage. Fan it a bit. Focus my energy. Ask again.

"Kandra Smithe. Please."

He smirks and then I've had enough.

"Don't be an asshole," I say. My voice surprises me. It is low, close to the bone. There is a growl in it. It's not like my voice at all, and he looks at me like he is taking my measure. I don't know what he sees.

"What kind of stick do you have?" The words surprise me.

"Excuse me?"

"Like with a pony," he says. There is a taunt in his voice. "To move him forward. Maybe you hit him with a stick. The way you're talking, I guess you figure you've got one. What's the stick you reckon you can hit me with? What's the stick you think you'll use on me?" And he is confident. I can hear that, too. He can't imagine a stick exists that will work on him. He is confident, also, that he is a superior creature. A superior pony. Superior to me in every way.

I don't answer his question off the hop. He has surprised me. I think for a little bit before I answer.

"A stick. I don't need one. You tried to guess before what I do for a living. But you guessed wrong. No social work. And I'm no cop. I kill people. That's my job."

There is probably no one else on Earth I would have said it to in just that way. Matter-of-fact. With most people, I would have found some other, gentler way to say it. A euphemism or an intentional misdirect. Or, more likely, I would not have said anything like that at all. But this is a different conversation. Another sort of man. And my goal is different from anything I could ever have imagined.

I know that I should be concerned that once he is arrested—and I know that, if he lives, he will be—he'll tell the police everything I've told him. On the other hand, though, are they likely to believe him? And, if they do, will they connect this inexplicable admission with me? I don't think so. Plus, honestly, in this moment, I don't care.

Whatever reaction I expected from my revelation, though, I don't anticipate the one I get. He laughs. Full throat. It's a mirthless sound.

"You're, like, what? A hit man?" More laughter.

"Yes," I say. "That's right." He quiets some, but not much.

"Someone put a hit on me? That's rich."

"No, actually," I say matter-of-factly, and maybe with more malice than I thought I had around it. "No client. This is a freebie. I just want to see you dead."

He looks at me a bit before speaking. I can see his Adam's apple jump in his throat. I can't tell what he's thinking, but he doesn't look afraid. "So you're going to kill me?"

"Oh, probably." I reflect. Then, "Yes. I would think so."

I am gratified to see him sit back and blink. It is apparently not the answer he'd been expecting.

"But there are variables," he says finally. "That's what you're implying."

I think quickly. "Well, death, right? That's boring. Everybody dies. All of our stories end the same way. Death was always in your future. Yours more than many. The trick, William, is how."

"How?"

"That's right."

"Are you trying to scare me?" He doesn't look afraid, but he's not laughing anymore. That's something.

"Am I?" I consider. "I guess maybe I am. It's real enough though. Listen, I don't have to tell you that there are good and bad deaths. You and I? We've seen both kinds."

He nods in agreement. Clearly, I've struck a chord. "Yes," he says. "That's so." I try not to think about the pictures he's seeing. Nothing good comes of thinking about that.

"Now me," I say, "I'm paid to do it, so generally I make an effort that it be painless." He kind of snickers. "But I could make an exception in your case if the situation demanded it."

"Are you threatening me?" The belligerence is back. It is a light in his eye.

"I don't think that's the right word," I say, thinking it through. "I'm probably going to kill you, though that's not a foregone conclusion. But if you make things difficult, it will go worse." I hesitate. Letting it all sink in. Hoping it matters. And then, "So Kandra Smithe . . ."

I let my words fall into a void, resisting the urge to chase them with more words. Letting them flutter and sink under their own weight. Nothing happens for a while, but I coach myself to be silent. There are words in him for me. I can feel them coming. And so I wait. After a while, he starts to talk.

"She was the first one." His voice is low. I have to strain to hear. It is not shyness. I can identify what it isn't, but not what it is. He says the words, and then I regard him silently. Without judgment, at least not on the surface. I know he has more to say.

"She was just so very tiny. And perfect. And she looked so soft. And her hair. These beautiful gold ringlets. And that softness. I really just wanted to pet her skin."

I feel an eruption of tears pulling together inside me. A harvest of tears. A valley of regrets. And I know I don't want to hear more. Not of this. Though there are things I do want and need to hear. And I'm not even sure why he's telling me. I'm certain he was not afraid of my threats, even though he knows they weren't empty. My fear is that he has recognized, at some level, a kindred spirit. He understands I have seen some of what he has seen. I don't want to be connected with him in that way. My heart strains against it. But I don't want to lose the ground I've gained.

"Where is she, William?" My voice is ragged, though as tender as I can manage. I am the hunter now. And I need to be gentle. I know I am close to getting what I need.

He is quiet for so long; I think maybe he's not going to answer. And then he does.

"But she's there, don't you see?"

"Where?" I don't quite understand, though a part of me does in an instant. Part of me understands and backs away.

"There in my garden, by the lake."

"Garden." I repeat the word. Think back to the rough plot near where I found him with Ashley and my heart sinks. I'm not even sure exactly why, but it plummets down, somewhere in the region of my feet, though I struggle to keep my face expressionless. "Garden. What do you grow there?"

"Flowers." He laughs again. A small, soft laugh, devoid of mirth.

I imagine the feeling of the Bersa in my hand. The cold heat of her. I imagine the weight of Atwater dying, right here, right now. Imagine the weight of it on my soul. It is not a troublesome thought. I know it is a weight I could bear.

"More than one," I say. It isn't a question. The way he said it, I know I don't need to ask. A single perfect flower does not a garden make. I ask it anyway, though I'm fairly certain I don't want the answer.

"Yes. They're all there. The ones that haven't been found. So soft. All of them. Brittle." There is a harsh accent on the last syllable. I suppress the shudder this invites.

He meets my eyes as he says this. He knows what he is doing. It is not for nothing he has been studying human emotion this closely. He has not come all these miles without learning a thing or two. He can see, or at least guess, the effect of these particular words on me.

"Why did you tell me?"

He doesn't answer for so long, I think he isn't going to. And, when he does, his words take me by surprise. "You're going to set me free."

"I am?"

He lifts his index finger. Points at me. Indicates a shooting.

"Yes. Free."

It would be so easy. I can imagine all of the actions. Imagine, even, the release I would feel. I haven't really wanted anything else since I first heard of William Atwater. It is almost like lust. I haven't wanted anything beyond a world that doesn't include him.

I raise the Bersa. At this close range, both the noise and the mess would be terrible. I can feel it in my gut, just thinking about it. And the force of the kick of the gun. But there is a terrible hunger on me. A force unseen. It would be almost like orgasm to kill him. To watch his face disintegrate under the force. To stand by while the world is cleansed of his presence. What arrogance on my part! But I know this. I feel the arrogance. And it doesn't slow me down.

I tilt my head. Tilt the gun. Look at him. Feel the result of the muscle memory I have for this action.

It would have been *so* easy. Too easy. That is the answer. Too easy. Not the right course. It takes a force of will, but I lower the gun.

"No. That's not how it's going to be."

Without taking my eyes off him, I grab the leg irons from where I'd left them on the passenger seat. The same ones I'd taken from his van and secured him with in the trunk of the car. While he'd been asleep in the grass, I had taken the time to remove part of the overhead storage so that the frame rail would be exposed. Now I instruct him to attach the leg irons to this frame. I knew that, having done as I instructed, there was no way he'd be able to get out of the RV without a key or tools.

"What are you going to do with me?" Is his voice weaker? Less sure? I'm not certain, but I let myself think it is true.

"Honestly, I don't know yet. But I'm working on something."

It is only partly a lie.

He is still dressed in his makeshift toga, and I wait for him to settle down on the bed in the RV and for his breathing to grow regular before I feel comfortable enough that he won't try anything. It takes a while. But until the breathing changes, there is no part of me that feels I can relax at all.

The driver's seat swivels so it can face the cabin where Atwater sleeps. I do that now so I can keep an eye on him while I think. But I have to stay awake: I don't want to sleep in his presence. He is as dangerous a creature as I've ever encountered. He is capable of anything. More. I keep an eye on him as I sit and think and watch. It feels like meditation.

I have a lot to think about.

CHAPTER TWENTY-SEVEN

By three in the morning, Atwater has been sleeping for several hours. Sleeping soundly, too. I thought he would. The physical trauma he's endured combined with the small amount of comfort he's been given have taken their toll. He is entirely out. I figure he is down until first light, at least.

One of the things that has come to me while I sit in the dark listening to him breathe is that I've gotten everything I came for. Sadly, it was easier than I thought it would be. He was able to clear the list with just a few words. Sadly, because I would have liked a different answer. One with a happier ending; better outcomes for some of those missing. With that realization, my next move comes clear.

I leave a few of the plastic bottles of water and the bananas within his reach. If somehow no one gets to him for a couple of days, he'll survive. And if he doesn't? Well, that is a different conversation, but the thought doesn't perplex me too much, either.

I pull my suitcase out of the RV as quietly as possible, then lock the door behind me. Next, I spend some time looking around for a rock to leave the key under. I need something distinctive. Something big enough to be remarkable. With that accomplished, I wheel my suitcase down the deserted campground road, feeling ridiculous but unobserved. It is off-season and a weeknight and there are no late-night partiers around. I've gotten lucky with a pale moon, and after a while my eyes adjust to the almost-total-darkness, and I'm not forced to use the flashlight on my phone. I want to be as invisible as possible. I want to be unseen.

Not a lot of the camping spaces are taken, but after a while, I spot a big land yacht with Arizona plates and a Jeep parked next to it. The Jeep is probably a tow vehicle, but it is loose now, and it looks like it will suit me fine. For one thing, I know I can boost a classic Jeep easily, but before I try to do that, I check the visor and, sure enough, the keys are there. I get lucky again because they'd parked the Jeep at the top of a little hill. I pop my case gently onto the passenger-side floor, closing the door quietly. Then I put the truck in neutral and push it forward, gratified when it moves and grateful the vehicle has a standard transmission and I can drive a stick. So many things to be grateful for. A car with automatic wouldn't have budged, but it doesn't take much pushing before the Jeep is bumping silently down the campground road. I swing into the driver's seat and pop the clutch. With the RV well behind me, the Jeep comes to life, though I wait until I hit the highway to turn on the lights. And then I head north.

I drive until I see a gas station. There are enough cars parked there that I feel some shuffling might not be noticed if I am careful.

I park the Jeep close to a dark green minivan that looks as though it would not be out of place next to a soccer field. I use my slim jim to open the passenger door, relieved when there is no alarm.

As I transfer vehicles, I hesitate, thinking about fingerprints. I know that my fingerprints have never been recorded; at least not in relation to me. It's not something I usually actively worry about. Still. I know I need to be careful. Mindful. I use one of the disinfectant wipes I always carry to wipe the Jeep down quickly as I leave it: conscious of where I have touched and where I have not. This, too, has gotten to be as easy to me as breathing.

In the driver's seat of the minivan, I jam my OBD tool into the dataport. On-board diagnostic tools are little miracles. You can use one to prevent a thief from ever stealing your car. Most people don't do that, though. In fact, they pretty much freak out when it hits home that basically anyone can take over your car's computer and override all security functions with the right OBD tool. Which is what I have. It takes about thirty seconds before the car starts. I slide back onto the highway before anyone even notices.

Near Monterey, I pull into an all-night diner for a bite and a quiet place to think about what has to happen next.

I pick a corner booth where my laptop and I will be mostly unnoticed. I order a cheeseburger and a beer for the same reason: it is not an order that will draw attention in this place. I munch excellent fries and a passable cheeseburger while I think about what I'm going to do now. I don't relish it, but I need to be done—complete—and I am now far enough away and with well enough covered tracks for it to happen.

I use my Tor browser to get the general information e-mail address on the San Pasado Police Department website. I figure that the general address will get it scattered out to several department heads, and feet will start moving quickly, one way or the other. Time, it seems to me, is of the essence.

I begin:

William Atwater is chained up inside a small RV in space 204 of the San Simeon State Park upper campground.

I'm saddened beyond words to report that, under duress, he confessed to me that he created what he described as a garden composed of the corpses of many of the children he has abducted. Sorry because I would have liked it to be better news. The garden is at Hoyo Lago in the north part of the county. This is based only on what he told me. I don't know for certain it is true.

A young woman named Arden will have contacted you with the coordinates of this garden, as this is where we found her daughter, Ashley (alive!), along with Atwater and his van, which you probably already have by now.

My identity is unimportant but I'm happy to have been able to help in delivering him to you. I don't need to tell you to handle him with care. He should never be put in a position where he is a danger to society again.

I look at the letter for a long time before sending. It sounds a little trite to me, but there's no help for it: it is my truth and also my shield. In reality, the police could have an awful lot on me if they manage to put it all together. I hope I've been careful enough to avoid that happening, but this moment was what it was all about: delivering Atwater to police alive so he could be made to spill whatever additional things he knew. There are parents out there who will be able to sleep for the first time in years with this knowledge. Parents who can finally begin to grieve. Their possible final relief was the only thing that had kept him alive. With Atwater in custody and details on the whereabouts of his garden, the police will be able to pull further needed details out of him. And as long as he is in custody, he won't be able to hurt anyone again, and I can't imagine a world where anyone would release him.

I sit in the restaurant and consider the unsent note on my laptop. Consider the end of one of my fries. Consider the gentle froth at the top of my beer. The cold, amber liquid in the glass.

I consider.

I could go back. Right now, I could go back and finish him off. My whole body craves that solution. The only thing that holds me back is the thought of the parents. If I leave him alive—bring the law to him and allow justice to take its course—there is the chance that some of these parents will be able to rest. Finally. They will get to watch the course of justice. I am imagining clenched hands held in courtrooms. Reassuring grips on perspiring arms. Long-held breaths releasing. There is a chance that can happen for those parents. Completion. I don't want to be what takes away that possibility.

The story, as written, is as close to a happy ending as it can be under the circumstances. I read my note back one last time before I hit Send. It will do.

CHAPTER TWENTY-EIGHT

I CONSIDER THE personal implications of what I've done. It is the closest I've ever come to breaking cover, and yet I think I am safe. I've been careful. Even though people have seen me, and I've interacted with them, I am so very average. I can't imagine anyone connecting me to my actual identity. And if they do? It would not be the end of the world. Some things are larger than we are, as individuals. Sometimes you just have to jump in and see which way the wind pushes you. Me? I hope somewhere in there to find flight.

I sent the message using my DeepNet mail program. It is untraceable. Now that it has been sent, I can feel the fullness of my actions and I know there is no going back. What's done is done. I lean into this feeling. Savor it while I can.

Just as I leave the restaurant, a couple park their Chevy Silverado in the deep shadows right next to the green minivan. The truck would not have been my first choice, but a combination of factors make it the obvious candidate for my next ride. It is easy. It is invisible in this area of many trucks. It is one of the easiest cars to steal. And it is right there.

Once on the road, the big truck swallows the miles. I get to the Embarcadero at two in the afternoon and park the truck at a meter, plugging it dutifully so that it will be a few hours before it is ticketed. Then I jump on the BART train and head for the airport.

While I sit on the train, I locate the next available flight back to my own rural airport. It is not a direct flight from San Francisco, but everything meshes well enough that I don't expect it will be a difficult trip.

And my assumptions prove to be correct. From the time I book the flight until the time I touch down near my home, I go into a kind of autopilot fugue state. I am dog tired. I am emotionally dead. All I want is to drop into my own little bed and sleep.

And sleep.

And even more sleep.

CHAPTER TWENTY-NINE

THERE ARE NO immediate expectations of me. There is nowhere I need to be. As a result of this, once I get home, I am able to sleep for three solid days. I get up only occasionally to deal with the functions of my body. There is a vague recollection of occasional food and hits of cool water from a vacuum flask at my bedside.

On the fourth day, I stir myself and look around. I don't feel better, but I feel as though I've accomplished something. Like I've gotten something right. I have not yet confirmed that Atwater is in custody, but considering the way things were set up, I don't even consider any other possibility. And the world is not necessarily a better place with William Atwater out of circulation and some of his secrets spilled, but at least it is safer. There is some satisfaction for me in knowing I've been instrumental in making that happen.

Beyond that, home is soft corners, dull edges. Home reminds me, again, of other homes at different times. Other lives. It makes me think for a time about Vancouver, too. About what had and hadn't happened there. About desert islands and peeled grapes and different outcomes. And for a single morning, I am choked with a regret so detailed it is like a spider living in my heart.

I ramble the forest. I wander scant trails probably made by deer. Wander also country roads. It passes the time. More than that, it gives me a point from which to begin to process many things. To place them in context. The walking begins to have a meditative quality, letting me see the continuity of life and how the more things are stretched in different directions, the more some aspects of them come to be the same.

I go out to the garage and unearth the television I'd packed away. I dust it off and settle in to watch the twenty-four-hour cycle of news about William Atwater. For once, I have an interest in the outcome. I want to know what the police did with the tidbits they'd been given, and I wonder if they will be able to extract everything from him that they need.

Watching the news is as distressing now as it was before. Talking head after talking head, expert after expert opining in onerous, knowing tones, dredging up endless details, as though they believe that the smallest thing will be relevant to the larger story. It seems to me a form of brainwashing, and yet for what are our brains being washed? What outcome is being shared in which we need to believe?

On the television, psychiatrists opine on Atwater's mental condition, even though they have not been anywhere near him. On the screen, a well-known news personality talks with Atwater's aunt about what he was like as a child. The presenter is a celebrity, as well known—or better—than the notorious subject under discussion. It's hard not to be diverted by his familiar and beautiful profile; the helmet-like smoothness of his hair. We cut to a different news personality; less well known. She talks with the arresting officer. Both are giving us their opinion on Atwater's state of mind. From what I hear and from what I know, neither are particularly close.

My ears perk up when the officer says Atwater had been found and apprehended in an RV parked in a state park on California's Central Coast. There is no mention of a phantom woman vigilante who had captured Atwater, then tipped the police off. And I am relieved about that, of course. But a part of me is also disappointed in ways I don't truly understand. It's not that I want acknowledgement. Not really. It is potentially disastrous for any sort of finger to be pointed at me. But I would have thought some aspect of the true story would come out. The fact that it has been totally suppressed makes me think there is a reason for that. And I wonder at the nature of that. And I wonder what it means.

After a while there is a press conference. Here the police mention Hoyo Lago. Camera crews are dispatched and the tone of the story changes again.

Finally, action—though now it is of the most horrific kind. The bodies of children, some of them ten years dead, are brought back to the light. Tents are set up over excavations. I can see this from a distance on television, the familiar locale rendered unfamiliar again by all of this activity. It looks like an archaeological dig. I stop myself. Realize. That is, of course, what it is.

Forensics goes in, as well as more traditional branches of the detective arts. After a while, news trickles back to us, the waiting public. Bits and pieces over time and all of it is reported in breathless tones and accompanying still photos.

And so many horrid details. Too many. They had discovered that the decomposed corpse found at the furthest edge of the space wore the outfit little Sally Lund had been wearing when she disappeared. Or still more exacting forensic and detective work: the little boy found near the base of a huge and twisty oak had his femur broken in just the same place as had little Riley

Rajagopal, gone missing some eight years before. Dental work. Jewelry. Recovered toys. DNA. Pieces of a gruesome puzzle come together piece by painful piece. It is impossible to watch. Difficult, also, to look away.

The garden theme has been adhered to beyond metaphor. It is horrible to see the story unravel; watch the pieces being put together. A twisted jigsaw that makes my heart weep. Every moment.

A carefully lettered "headstone" was buried just beneath the earth that covered each child. This discovery produces an almost physical reaction. It is beyond horrible. It is unthinkable. And yet it provides the information needed to know how all of these pieces fit and who all of these children were. And with their identities, we also learn Atwater's impressions of each victim.

We learn, for instance, that little Contessa MacDonald had been a "clinging vine." So she had needed to be planted in shade and near others of her kind. Exhumation has disclosed wounds less severe than on some of the others, as though Atwater had felt the need to be more gentle with this little vine than some of the others. On the other hand, little Daniel Croft had been "willful and in need of discipline," and not all of the results of those words are shared with the public. And yet we know.

And all of it is horrifying. All of it is beyond thought. The idea of a garden. Of growth. Combined with the end of so many little lives, and none of them came to a good end. There is such a thing, in case you have wondered. An end that is good. I have seen it myself, on more than one occasion. But none of these is that. It is almost more than I can take.

Then it becomes more than I can take. And just when I think I will break with the saturation of it all, the coverage begins to wane. There has been no further activity, so some other story jumps to the top of the news cycle and it seems as though Atwater's five minutes have expired. Again.

For a few days, I am unexpectedly bereft. Watching everything about the story and surfing news channels for mentions of him and his poor lost garden had become my life for a short time. And now it is over. There is suddenly nothing left to do.

I make the trek into town and go to a garden center, buy half a dozen healthy little lavender plants and a few medium-sized rosemary bushes. I've done some research. They would survive when nothing else would. They are drought and deer resistant. They should be safe, even from me.

Touching the earth. Planting. Growing towards healing. As I pat the earth around the last plant, I start to weep. What was this now? Soon sitting, hands laced around knees, allowing a torrent to overtake me. Allowing myself to be swept away by it. An overcast day, wisps of sun fighting through clouds, a feeling in my chest of complete and utter despair and surrender.

I can't imagine anything that is more than this. I can't imagine, even, a reason to lift my head.

After a while, the crying falls out of me and I lie down next to my plantings and just breathe. I press my cheek to the soil and inhale, trying not to think of Atwater's garden. Focusing instead on my own newly broken soil. *Garden*. I want to reclaim the thought of that word from the dark. It is difficult. For now, anyway. The word is tainted. Stolen.

Another part of me wants to join those poor children. For the first time, maybe in my life, the fight has been leached out of me and I think about what it would be to die right here, on my own little patch of earth. Lavender growing on one side. Rosemary taking root on the other. To die and let the sun rise higher in the sky. To warm me after I could no longer be made warm, sun kissing my stiffening limbs and blood cooling in my veins. I can almost feel it.

As time passes, mercifully, the thinking stops. I lie there still. I am listening to the sound of the wind in the trees. The faint "whirr, whirr, whirr" of a distant helicopter, nothing to do with me. Infrequently, I hear the sound of a car on the country road that snakes past the house. I feel a bug walking over my arm. I let it walk there, undisturbed. It is likely harmless. And if it is not? What then? Something interesting to take beyond. A closing door to end my time here.

Time passes. The pale sun sinks. Dusk and then darkness come, night falling, like a corpse. I remain with my cheek pressed to the earth, the scent of newly turned soil rich in my nostrils. I am feeling something like ennui, but more. Feeling for a while that there could be nothing beyond this. What more, in any case, is required?

When it starts to rain, I don't go in right away, though the irony of water falling from the sky, the sheer unlikely ridiculousness of it, does not escape me. Rain when I hadn't seen any here for weeks. I lie here still, in the darkness, the soil now turning to mud. It isn't long before I can't take it anymore—the muddy wet. I laugh as I pick myself up. Not a heartfelt laugh, but still. It is perfectly nice to be dramatic on a fine summer's evening, that's what I'm thinking. Quite something else to do it when the rain comes. "Fair weather ennui," I chide myself as I go inside, step into a hot shower intended to wash off the mud, and perhaps something else. Wash away something unseeable. Unknowable. Wanting to wash things away.

I don't remember getting into bed. I am only aware of waking and finding myself naked on top of my covers, as though I'd collapsed into bed in a sodden heap after the shower. Drunk on pain and soaked with emotion. And all of it was enough.

More than enough.

Something has ended. I don't know if that's good.

CHAPTER THIRTY

ALMOST THE FIRST thing I do when I get out of bed is check my phone. There is a text. I regret the impulse that made looking at it a priority.

"Fuck," I say out loud as I thumb-type the required reply. The last thing I want is to catch a job right now. Really, all I want is to sleep some more. I don't feel like crying anymore. That, at least, has stopped. All I want is to be left alone.

Still.

It turns out the job is in New York City. That represents enough of a change of venue that I think it might be solid diversion. I realize that maybe I can use one of those right now. Too many more sodden nights in the dark and I'll perish; that's what I'm thinking. I need to get away from possible sodden nights in the dark.

And then my thinking changes as I grapple with what is real.

I toy for a ridiculous moment with the idea of taking in a show while in the City, but discard it in favor of a nice hotel room in midtown where I can recline in posh anonymity while recovering from the trigger I am required to pull, and never mind whatever I'd been putting myself through on the Central Coast and before that in Vancouver.

I can tell from first glance that the job itself will be unremarkable. Routine, if such a thing can be said about an assignment in my particular line of work. But once I get there, the City energizes me, as it always does. So many people, and all so beautifully, stridently, vitally alive. It is all I can do, sometimes, not to smile at people as I walk around. I control the urge though. People sometimes remember people who smile.

I feel those people inside me, though. Waking some nearly dead part of me. Making me feel a part of something instead of separate. Or more a part of it, anyway. Walking around that singular city, I feel alive in ways I haven't for some time.

I am in this sort of lighthearted, people-loving mood when I get to Times Square. The job has gone well, textbook after the last one, and I have a solid day before my flight is due to leave from La Guardia.

In Times Square, I buy a brightly colored shawl from an old woman, thinking the color will bring out my eyes, plus she looks hungry, as though she needs to sell as many shawls as she can. That seems reason enough to buy.

She is set up next to a newsbox, and I let my eyes run over a headline, then feel my heart move down.

"William Atwater Escapes Custody," reads the headline. "Serial Killer Loose Again," reads the subheadline.

I buy a paper. Find a bench, the shawl forgotten in my hand. I sit down and start to read. As bad as the headline had seemed, things are worse, even, than that.

The paper reports that he had disguised himself as another prisoner, then faked his way out on a work detail. No one had realized the switch until they found the corpse of the prisoner he had impersonated. This sounds simplistic to me. I suspect the truth is somewhat more complicated than what the news is reporting, but I also know that the details won't change the outcome. Alarms had been sounded, but it was too late: Atwater was nowhere to be found.

I sit there for several minutes, just letting the information penetrate and thinking about what, if anything, I can do. What, if anything, I even want to do.

I am aware of the blood forcing its way through my veins, making an echo through my mind. For a short time, I am aware of a sort of absolute stillness in my brain where all of the shouting should be. I hold things together in this way—careful of thought, of sound—while it all sinks in. After that, I don't know quite how I feel. I only know it is terrible.

Somehow, I find my way back to my posh hotel room. Once there, I forget about the relaxing I'd intended to do and turn on the television. The media circus has returned. Though now I wonder: Were they ever really far away? Whatever the case, once again it is all Atwater, all the time. It hasn't taken long at all and there is a sort of dull satisfaction in my gut at its return. This time, the networks already have a pile of file footage in the can. I'd seen it in the newspaper, after all. It is no surprise that it is already streaming on every station.

Through the magical lens of television, I see again the charming town of San Pasado. It feels like a homecoming. And then the most endearing photos of past victims, the most heartbreaking stories from parents, the most hair-raising stories from people who had experienced near misses with Atwater or thought they had. It's the same material that was aired a few weeks ago, but this time dramatic twists have been added. It's like in the time between, teams of artists have been working on all this material, just in case. And now here it all is: ready to make us feel more frightened and afraid and apprehensive, if any of that was even possible. And it seems that it was.

And now again there are the talking heads. Those with opinions on Atwater himself. Those with opinions on what his condition might be and what can be done about it. A psychiatrist who looks as though he has been summoned from Central Casting grabs my attention. He is slender to the point of thinness—his hair, his face, his hands. Even his voice is thin. His words stick with me despite that.

"What we are discussing here is the very nature of good and evil."

"Are we?" The host has flat blue eyes and a helmet of close blond hair. This is already not going as she'd thought it would.

"Well, of course. It's not as though we're talking about someone who can be captured and neutralized and then remediated. We are not discussing here the aberrations of a petty thief or a crooked stockbroker. Nor are we discussing someone who has fallen off the rails of civilization because he is having trouble making his mortgage payments and so has poked his hand into the till. No!" The thin glass table in front of him is slammed so severely, even on television we can see it shimmer and shake as though in fear for its life. "What we are discussing here is something else entirely."

"Well, these are different issues, certainly." Helmet Head is trying hard here. I can see it on the glisten of sweat on her brow. And she's not even treading water while her makeup assistant sweats it out offstage. Helmet Head's goal is to keep her interview in check and under her control. I can see she doesn't really care that much about what her guest is saying, one way or the other. She's just concerned that he doesn't come across as a loon or, worse, that she herself comes over as an asshole. It's image to her, nothing more. Another day at the office. The doctor, meanwhile, is just warming to his topic.

"Different issues!" The five syllables come out on a snort. "These are like different *planets*."

"Well, I wouldn't go so far as to say . . ." but Helmet Head doesn't get to finish. The doctor is a horse galloping downhill. The thin reins she is holding will not stop him.

"But yes, they are! Don't you see? Even Sigmund Freud understood—at the very *infancy* of psychoanalysis—that we are *not* all created equal. The reparation of a brain such as William Atwater's is beyond the capabilities of psychiatry."

"You are suggesting then that he can't be rehabilitated? That he can't be cured?"

"That's right!" The response is an explosion. "As Freud maintained, for psychoanalysis to have a hope of working, it is essential for the subject to be of good character. We are talking about the true nature of Evil." I hear the capital on "Evil." It's in the way he pronounces the word. And then a further and even more dire pronouncement. "For what is wrong with William Atwater, there is no cure."

There is more, including a sort of mildly horrified backpedaling from the interviewer. What the doctor had said was so outside of Western thought and also how we think about doctors answering. Weren't they meant to help everyone? That was part of what she said and also part of what I thought. And yet he had said that he felt that, for someone like William Atwater, there was no hope.

That he is beyond hope.

Though the faces on the screen have changed, I am still thinking about what the doctor said—and about the nature of evil—

when a familiar face startles me. I sit up and pay attention even though the crawl has told me the story at a glance. "Atwater accomplice stole RV at knifepoint."

At knifepoint? That was quite the innovation. And the frightened face of the sales guy I'd dealt with fills the screen. It is horrible in HD.

"At first you thought she was like any other customer," prompts the trim blond reporter. She might have been the younger, less confident sister of the helmet-haired one I'd just seen. The microphone she is holding in front of the RV salesman's face is quivering faintly with her excitement. This can be career-making. We can smell that in the zealous way she licks her top lip, flips back her shellacked hair. She is almost overcome with the excitement of it all. She has caught a prized peach. She is going to squeeze all the juice out of him that she can.

"That's right. She even had a suitcase. She wheeled it into my office."

The best and most solid lies are built on a well-created foundation of truths. Every liar knows this. I watch the screen carefully to see where the lies kick in. It is seamless. The guy is good.

"At what point did you know you were in danger?"

I snort at the TV. The interview keeps rolling.

"Like I said, at first I thought she was just like any other customer. The suitcase made me wonder a bit, but that didn't seem impossible. I sell RVs, after all. But then when we sat down to make a deal and she pulled the weapon on me. Demanded the keys. That was really when I knew."

"Did she mention Atwater?"

"No, she didn't. But the RV she took from me was the one they found him in, so it stands to reason."

Actually, he is right enough about that, which would explain the seamless lying. But for the knife, he thought it was the truth. I retract my scorn. He is pretty much going with the script I'd fed him. All systems go.

"But you haven't come forward until now, nearly a week later. Why?"

"She had my home address." This is a lie, of course. Though still seamless. "I don't know how she got it. But she threatened my family."

"And you've come to us now."

"She asked me to keep it to myself for a week. But then the RV was returned to me by the police."

The tidy blond ends the segment by turning to the camera. "The possibility of Atwater having an accomplice has not been floated before now. Dana, we don't know if this person is a lover, relative, friend . . . or something else entirely. But learning of her existence has raised many questions. And with William Atwater at large, it might be some time before we have acceptable answers. This is Sebring Mahoney reporting from San Pasado. Back to you, Dana."

CHAPTER THIRTY-ONE

THE POSSIBILITY OF an accomplice spreads quickly through the media circus. In a culture dominated by the news cycle, new fodder is candy and this is all of that. All news sources in all mediums and medias jump on it instantly. It is like watching a worm wriggle under the sand. You can follow the shape of the thing, but you can't quite see what it is.

It is something new to chew on while I watch. Really, while the whole country watches. Maybe the world. There are implications here. For one thing, it seems possible to me that the laser-like attention being leveled on Atwater and San Pasado might bring some negative responses. Not just people resentful that their charming little town is now notorious: the center of attention in a heinous crime. Beyond that, though, the news cycle is a monstrously hungry beast. Spit it up and move on. There needs to be some new aspect to the story constantly in order for it to stay fresh and on top. But, of course, real life just doesn't work that way: new things don't appear just so that the story currently under the microscope stays daisy fresh. So sometimes, in apparent desperation to keep their stories going, some of the connections offered up are pretty thin. That's how it seems to me anyway. And it strikes me that it is possible that this RV angle—and with it the presence of an "accomplice"—is one of those: a thin connection only polished and then milked in order to keep the story flowing.

This thought is confirmed once I flip stations and word of Atwater's "accomplice" has spread through the circus. Everyone is reporting it, everywhere. Following the lead. It seems possible to me that all this attention aimed in my direction cannot ultimately be a good thing. That it might, in the end, lead to a weakness in the armor of invisibility I've worked so hard to surround myself in, though I've been careful with details. I make a mental note to be extra careful in my motions and activities. Renfrew, the RV salesman, appears to be playing ball and sticking to the vague story we concocted, but he is far from a sure thing. I think of the oiliness in him. The avarice. Anything is possible.

And then the screen pulls my attention back. The whirling logo of *The Renton Report* has caught my attention. As the intro music eases back, we can see Grady Renton readying himself to opine. From the look of his serious expression, what he's about to say will be well thought out and considered, though it always is. That's his style: the stuff he says is generally worth listening to, that's why he gets the colorful logo and the big chair. Renton is a good-looking East Coast blueblood who has spent the last couple decades at the top of the news chain. He adds opinion and a bit of poetry to the run-of-the-mill reportage he shares. I watch him now with mixed emotions. I don't know what to expect.

"An accomplice for Atwater is a frightening thought. Does that mean we are now looking for another Gardener? Is this *accomplice* someone who has shared in the planting of his crops? The thought terrifies me. And it should terrify *you.*"

It even terrifies *me* until I remember that Grady is potentially talking about me. That makes me blink and reconsider. After all, what do we really know about anyone? In a world where Atwater has wreaked havoc on a small community, everything seems possible. It's not a heartening thought.

A few channels over, on *The Blair Donner Show*, they have gone so far as to hire a sketch artist to sit with Renfrew, the RV salesman, and they've come up with a drawing of a woman who, fortunately, looks so little like me it is comical. The woman in the drawing has wide-set, startled-looking eyes and a feral mouth. She is perfectly coifed and sharply attired. I am pleased to see that Renfrew has taken a few liberties and not been completely honest with the artist. At least, that's how it seems because no one would ever recognize me from what is being presented. I feel certain that was his intent: it could not be so far off otherwise. It puts my mind at rest. Slightly.

But it is all so diverting, it is troublesome. Had the topic not been so dire, it would also have been funny: watching the contortions the media presenters are going through in order to keep the spotlight not only on the story, but on themselves. And is the story served by these actions? And will it help justice ultimately be served? Well, that isn't really the point, is it? The point is to grab more eyeballs for their stats. Sell more soap and this-year's-model cars. It's not easy. As a result, you can almost smell them sweat. It is a difficult road. In a world of dwindling viewership, it's often the oiliest presenter who wins. The coverage offered up illustrates it. I'm sickened by it. And I can't look away.

I don't leave my hotel room for two days. I live on room service and the twenty-four-hour news cycle. Inhaling it. It is as though I am possessed. The smallest tidbit of news from the front could change the whole trajectory of the reportage. This fact worries me. How did things like this ultimately impact the case? And it didn't seem to me even a question that it would.

Rather, I wonder: How could it not? Bombarded with "facts," it becomes impossible to not form an opinion. And the opinion has to be based on partially seen truths and weighted opinions.

When I finally decide to leave the safe nest of my hotel room, the circus follows me home. In the cab on my way to the airport, I see his face. In the first-class lounge waiting for my flight, I hear his name, hear the anxiety rising. Overheard on other people's computers, spied on headlines, whispered in lineups. It is everywhere.

It is *everywhere.*

William Atwater's name has reached mythic proportions, his deviancy amplified by constant exposure and total saturation. We as a culture are as enthralled by him as we are frightened. And it is awful. I can't get away from it. And even if I could, I can't *look* away.

I get home before my new plants have completely dried up. I get home in time to save them. Standing in the twilight, increasing the pressure of the hose and the distance the water will travel by holding my thumb over the opening. Vowing again to get a nozzle for the sprayer the next time I'm in town, while feeling the pleasure of using innovation and my body to solve a problem. From ethereal to real. There's something that pleases me in that.

And I don't miss a beat. I get quickly back into the pattern I'd created the first time around, settling down in front of newsfeed into my laptop, outwardly calm. Passive. Inwardly seething, twisting, writhing.

I spend weeks like this and I don't remember anything of that time that isn't media watching. I know I must have done other things. There must have been food consumed, walks taken, books read and considered. But I don't remember any of that. I remember only the vile passing of hours while I consider his face and his actions, his childhood, and his future. I consider everything that is offered to me.

I am beyond saving, or so it seems, until I am shaken loose by the only thing that could have saved me. A text comes in, and I prepare to phase back into the land of the living for a little while, at least. The land of the living and the nearly dead.

CHAPTER THIRTY-TWO

MY FIRST THOUGHT is an inward groan. Reflexive. Then I realize an assignment might be just what I need. I am growing pale in my inactivity. If nothing else, an assignment will get me out of the house and away from newscasts for a little while. I try not to think about the irony of that: a phase in my life when I consider leaving the house in order to kill someone for money to be an expedition that at least gets me into the fresh air.

Unusually, it is not an overnight assignment. A few hours' drive to the major center nearest me. It looks easy peasy. Straight in and out. I opt to take my own car as far as the suburbs, then jump on light rapid transit for the move into the core of the city.

LRT is always a good move for me and I take it when I can. I like that it's the most environmentally friendly choice. Also, I think there is even less risk of detection or observation when I'm just another face in a sea of commuters.

Being anonymous gives me room to breathe. Allows me to focus on the job at hand. I can't afford to get things wrong. In my line of work, there can be no mistake.

So I take the LRT downtown. Living in the sticks has gotten me sensitized again to the sights and sounds and even smells of the city. Once I'm there, it is like I am a child again. The buildings so tall, towering above me. I think about the birds up there, among the tallest buildings, silently winging their way above the symphony of human sound below. Even that's not correct. Living in the country, I have learned that birds don't fly silently at all. In the quiet of the forest or the stillness of an open field, you can hear the wind move through their wings. It's a gentle "whoosh, whoosh, whoosh," which startled me the first time I heard it: made me crane my head up to see what could be making the sound, endlessly surprised to find it synchronized with the flight of a bird.

Now in the city, though, I don't hear that sound. Endless noise drowns it out and the smells overwhelm me, too. Sun on concrete. Restaurant grease at full heat. A salad of flowers beneath a dressing of motor oil. Nothing smells quite like a city in full sun.

I find my target easily enough. The instructions I was given are good. He is younger and better looking than my targets tend to be. Maybe close to thirty, but not yet there. It will be a shame, though it mostly always is. You can't think about that part. It just makes it worse.

He is beautifully dressed: pressed trousers, trim sports coat, loafers shined. In general, there is the look and air of Ivy League and old East Coast money about him. I wonder vaguely, as I mostly never do, about who might want this splendid young creature taken out, but the possibilities are too numerous, and it's a fool's errand in any case. Jealous sibling, angry stepfather, jilted lover: whoever paid for this hit has their reasons. Thinking about it only makes one despair for the fate of the world. It's possible my heart could have held that at one point. But not anymore. Not today.

As a target, he proves to be as easy as he looks. From his office at a blue-chip investment firm downtown, I follow him to a tidy apartment building on the west side. There is no doorman so it is easy to watch for a while and wait for an opportunity.

It doesn't take long. It is early evening and I follow a pizza delivery person into the building. When the pizza goes left, I go right and set off on the coordinates I've been given. The target's apartment is on the top floor of a modest but well-kept older building, and all of that is in keeping with the old money vibe I've had from him since the beginning.

Aware of the peephole, the Bersa is behind my back when I knock. I can stand up to that: I'm not at all scary-looking. Even if I were trying to be scary looking, I wouldn't be. He swings the door open right away, meets my eyes, friendly but not overly curious. He likely thinks I am here on some neighborly call—a cup of sugar, an open house—or that maybe I'm a political canvasser who sneaked into the building and will be easily sent away. I just have that look.

With him standing and smiling in front of me—"Can I help you?"—I step out of my own way, bring the silenced gun up without hesitation, and plug him solidly between the eyes. I note as he collapses that my shot has been eerily accurate. If he'd had a solid red "X" marked on his forehead, I could not have gotten it more dead on. With that shot, I figure he is dead before he hits the ground, and so I know it is impossible to believe in the questioning look I think I detect on his face. A sort of partly formed "Why?" If he'd articulated the question, I wouldn't have been able to answer. But, of course, he is beyond articulation.

The door opened inwards and he has fallen backwards, into his apartment. There was a spray of blood, but what has flown into the walls of the hallway has only been a spattering. Anyone passing this way would be unlikely to notice.

I pick up my spent cartridges, then move his leg a few inches and am about to close the door with him entirely on the inside of his apartment when I hear a whimper. I cast my eyes heavenward, though I'm not sure why, then bring them back to focus beyond the door and into the apartment to the outline of a very small dog. At first, I think it is some sort of miniature canine—a bichon frise or a yorkie or something else permanently tiny—then I realize it is a puppy and he is wearing a collar attached to a leash. It is as though they had been just about to head out for a walk.

The creature is small and fair and I figure it is a golden retriever puppy—another blueblood, like his late master. He has a black nose that glistens wetly and earnest eyes of a color that harmonizes eerily with his coat. Those eyes regard me calmly, though I can tell he is afraid. The smell of the gun, I suppose. And also, the collapse of his master. To the dog I probably don't look particularly scary, but scary things have happened and he's smart enough to know that requires some caution.

I am about to close the door, leave them both behind, but as I move to do so, I realize that I simply cannot. It is one thing to leave a dog alone. Or to leave a corpse alone. But leaving a dog—especially a puppy—alone with the corpse of his master apparently is the line I cannot cross. Funny how there can be a line you don't recognize until you're standing right over it.

I grab the leash, hoping the dog will cooperate, grateful when he does. He moves forward with caution and then with more enthusiasm as he realizes we are on a mission that will take him outside.

He relieves himself as soon as we get out of the building, and I figure he's been waiting for this all day, while his owner was at the office. He produces a fast number one a couple of times and then an epic number two. I feel guilty not picking it up, but push myself over the guilt. In the picture I have been painting this afternoon, not scooping is not my greatest crime.

With the dog in tow, I retrace my steps: a few blocks to the LRT. I worry for a minute about the status of dogs on trains, then realize I will just have to chance it and hope for the best. Human nature being what it is, people are more likely to "tut tut" than actually say anything, and I determine that, if they say anything directly, I will ask them to call a cop, the sort of passive-aggressive move it pleases me to even think about.

The dog and I take the LRT to the suburbs and back to the park-and-ride lot where I left my car. I worry for a second that the dog won't cooperate, but he likes the car. He jumps right in and sits happily in the back, clearly not aware that I have killed his master, or not connecting this current turn of events—this miraculous and unexpected ride—with the scary, life-changing events of an hour before. As I drive, I wonder idly about the genetic mutation that has occurred to make dogs such big fans of rides in cars.

The dog and I take the car directly to the safety of my house. Do not pass go, do not collect two hundred dollars. Except for the necessary purchase of a tank of gas, we don't stop at all.

CHAPTER THIRTY-THREE

BACK AT MY forest home, it is quiet. So quiet. Quiet beyond what I've ever noticed before, despite the company of the dog. I can barely move beyond the stillness. And it's odd: I should be hungry. I should by now need food. But I have, for the moment, lost my appetite. Or something. I keep seeing the questioning look in the splendid eyes as he fell. The thick shock of dark chestnut hair. The blood spattering onto the walls of his hallway. I try to shake it off, but I can't quite. That look. There was nothing particularly remarkable about this engagement, and there has been no change in me. And yet, somehow, I feel changed.

The dog is an easy addition. It is like he has always been here, a part of me. He is happy eating the food I offer him from my refrigerator and freezer. It appears he enjoys steak, lightly cooked. And steamed carrots. And chicken breasts, grilled. Thawed lamb stew. I determine I'll have to find dog food someplace, but in the meantime, since I nibble around the edges of the food I prepare for the dog, I figure both of us are eating better than we might have done before. Though, in fairness, the young Ivy Leaguer—looking gentleman had appeared to be the sort that would have stocked his pantry with high-quality dog food for his baby best friend. I chastise myself for not checking what the dog was being fed before I took him out of the apartment, then realize the foolishness of the thought. After what I'd done, I couldn't really hang around taking notes and grabbing supplies.

With the dog fed and resting, I try to move beyond the feeling of change. I try to get back to something more comfortable to me. Try to think what had so engaged me before the assignment. What had most pulled my concern and given me that feeling of complete and total immersion, to the exclusion of all else. William Atwater. At large. Back in the world. But even that can't move me now. And it isn't only me that has lost their fascination for Atwater, nor simply is it just my own ennui. Things have been quiet from the West. Even the endless nattering of the media has slowed to almost a complete stop. The news cycle hasn't had any food in this direction for a while and it is possible to sit in front of a television and slip from station to station without a single mention of Atwater. He is loose somewhere, but he has gone quiet. Maybe he'll hide forever. But there is nothing to see here, and the newsies have moved on.

I lean into that. Begin to get my mind around it. Begin thinking about plants and maybe cooking; puttering. Pushing away thoughts of splendid, questioning eyes. Lost children.

There are several days of this, but not enough of them to make up weeks. I am in a sort of stasis, but I apply myself. Tell myself to snap out of it. I take forest walks with my new pal. Make excursions into town for dog food and other supplies. Spend time in the garden. More time at the stove. Time to pass and fill. And just as I feel myself begin to relax into a sort of rhythm, the news trickles to me: a little girl has gone missing. And as I wake, the world wakes up again, too. And both of us—the world and I—

we sit up and pay attention again. It's like someone has turned a light switch on. Or maybe, shut it off.

Her name is Emma Schwartz and she is six years old, forty-two inches tall, and forty-eight pounds. We are told clearly that she is an average six-year-old, and she has been poached from a house just outside the city, while the babysitter sat in the other room. The parents had returned from an evening out to find that their little girl was gone. No signs of a struggle. Nothing broken in the entry or exit. It was possible a door had been left unlocked—and in—and then out—he had gone.

One can imagine Atwater with the child over one arm. Perhaps placating her, "It'll be okay. I'm taking you to your mommy." It's a horrible picture and I force it away.

I see the distraught babysitter on the screen. She is a pale teenager with watery blue eyes and pale hair. The newsies capture her beside herself with remorse and, yes, even grief. The seriousness of this has not escaped her. There is a very good possibility that this loss will be complete.

"I was so sure I had locked the door," she explains to the reporter. The words are smooth, the sides worn down. This is not her first interview and the words are beginning to feel dog-eared from use.

"And you didn't hear a sound? You weren't alerted by a knock or a cry from the child, or . . ."

"No," the babysitter says, breaking into this litany. Her voice is still calm, but there is a wild look in her eyes. She wishes things were otherwise. You can see it. But they are not. "I'm sure of it. There was nothing."

"Are you absolutely sure you locked the door?"

The hesitation is deep. "No," she says after a pause that feels like twenty minutes but that had to have been less than fifteen seconds. And then again, "No. I'm not sure." Eyes downcast, remorse thick on her like fuzz coating a tongue.

I hear all of this in increasingly alarmed tones on the various channels I search. Once again, experts are brought in and friends. We see the missing child's tearful parents. The father has the studious air of a college professor, which I suppose is possible as San Pasado is a college town. He has glasses and a long chin. Today, his face is void of expression. But the lines on his face indicate this is not his usual look.

The missing child's mother herself appears to be little more than a child. She has a waiflike face under so much hair, there would seem to be danger of it bending her neck from the sheer weight of it all. Together they are an attractive if slightly eccentric-looking couple. And they are beautiful in their grief. You can feel that anguish come in waves over the television.

At first it is not conclusive that Atwater is involved in this disappearance. I know in my heart that this is his work, even while I hold my breath in hope that it is not. I don't want it to be Atwater. I want him to have fallen under a bus somewhere. Or, better still, gotten some sort of awful virus and drowned in a puddle of his own phlegm. Even though that feels very specific, the sentiment is clear: I want it to be anything that would remove him from the picture. Out of any picture. Forever. But the markers are right. After a few hours it is conclusive. It is Atwater, the police tell us. Or maybe it is more correct to say that the markers are wrong.

I sit in front of the television and watch and listen, but I don't truly hear. My mind sees again little Ashley at the edge of Atwater's garden. Ready for planting. Arden's pale face drawn in on itself in fear for her daughter's life. And though the timbre of his voice has faded in my mind, and I can't quite remember his tone, I see us both in the dimly lit RV and the words I hear are painfully clear.

She was just so very tiny. And perfect. And she looked so soft. I really just wanted to pet her skin.

I shudder with all of it and try to shake it off like a wet dog, though I find to my distress that it is impossible to do that. The marks he has left have rooted too deeply.

I find myself wondering how much time we have. Last time we managed to bring little Ashley home, if not perfectly intact, then at least alive. How long would it have been? She'd been missing maybe four hours at most before we found her. I'd had the sense that things had been about to get worse just as we intervened. But I also knew that, in the past, there were those among his victims he had kept alive for days. I'd been keeping track of the numbers the talking heads had thrown around when endless newscasters talked about each of the children. One of the things that had been estimated with many of them was how long between capture and time of death. Time of addition to the garden. The estimates had varied widely. And what would have determined the variation? What would have been the contributing factors? I realized that some of it might even have been a bit random. By comparison, I thought about me taking a crack at his skull with that mallet while he was in the trunk of my rental car. A light and calculated crack, to be sure. But still, any one of those could have killed him. An inch to the left. A few pounds more pressure. Anything a little different and he could have been dead. I reason that it's been like that with his victims, as well. In the course of the type of torture he would have subjected them to, some would have expired before others. It all makes a sort of terrible sense.

Even while I think it through, I try not to observe too closely. There is a world of guilt in those thoughts. There had been an opportunity. Several, really. What if it was something that my inside knowledge could have helped control? And on the tail of that thought comes another: I had the opportunity and did not take it. It would have been so easy to stop him there in the campground. Stop him forever and right in his tracks. And then all of this would have been over. This latest missing child? This is my fault, that is clear.

I had felt compassion for the parents of lost children, not for him. It was my sympathy for the parents that had stopped me from killing him right there. And I had let him live. And now? Now yet another child would pay the price. It is hard to think about.

The dog sits on my feet while I'm at my desk trying to book a flight. My feet are warm, but the flight booking is unsuccessful. I want to leave right now—this instant!—but I will be unable to book anything that will get me there in under two days. Two days is too many. I know that driving there will not in the end offer much of a time saving, but it will at least get me on the road. Plus, of course, I have a new consideration. Bringing the dog with me is ridiculous, but I feel I don't really have a choice. I want action and I need it now.

Within the hour, I am back out the door, but first I water the baby plants and pack up some water, dog food, and dishes for the consumption of both. A small part of me is acting like a mom again. I am uncertain about how that makes me feel.

Once again, and even on this longer trip, the dog is a good traveler. I fashion an old blanket into a little bed on the back seat and he settles into it quite nicely. I barely hear any peeps from him at all.

I spend my time on the road trying to cool my brain. Not an easy task. I try to remember the traveling games I played as a child and then later with my own child, but it seems those times of innocence are so far behind me, there are only vestiges left. Little wisps of colorful memories, but distant and faded, as though viewed through a sepia filter. Something about colors: a purple car, a purple roof, a purple jacket on a child crossing the street. Something about Volkswagens—and why that particular brand?—and then punching someone in the arm. I see one and punch myself in the thigh and with enough force that it will leave a bruise. The dog jumps when I do it, but otherwise the punch does not have the desired effect, whatever that was. I give up on the road games. They aren't meant to be played alone in any case. Or even with a dog.

In my twelfth hour on the road, I pull off the freeway and into a Walmart parking lot. I stash my car between a couple of RVs, not unlike the one I had purchased recently, then left behind.

I kill the motor and, after I empty the dog, I sit in the car and lock the doors, but I can't rest my brain as easily. I know my body needs downtime, but I can't turn it off and I sit there counting the stitches on the steering wheel and the slats in the air vents until finally I give up, go into the store, buy an energy drink, a box of Milk-Bones, and a bag of cheese puffs from a bleary-eyed cashier. Then we get back on the road.

It is another six-hour drive to my destination. Not that I know the exact location of my destination. But my research into Atwater had paid out before. I've turned into the most deadly kind of stalker: a potential author. Maybe my big inside knowledge will pay out again.

Before I get to San Pasado, I pull into a diner to think and recharge. I park in the deep shade of an ancient oak. The dog seems unbothered by all this activity. I take him on a quick tour of the parking lot where he takes care of some business of his own. When I open the back door of the car, he jumps in and settles happily back onto his blanket. I have a little pang at this ease of transition on the dog's behalf. I think again of the shock of hair; the questioning eyes. It's possible, I reason quickly, that the life of the dog has been improved. His position is better now. Ivy League financial guys spend long hours at the office. The puppy would have been alone a lot. I've saved him from that.

I've saved him.

I lock him in the car, though I leave the windows and the sunroof open a crack. Whatever his history, he is mine now. No one can take him.

He is mine.

CHAPTER THIRTY-FOUR

IN THE DINER, I open my electronic pin-filled map realizing only as I renew its acquaintance that I'd never planned on having a reason to open it again. I am sorry beyond thought that I was wrong and that I am forced in there again now.

My educated guess and a bit of luck over dinner in San Pasado had paid out so well that first time. I tell myself that there is no reason I can't do so well again. And though I know that, strictly speaking, it is foolish to think so, I feel that right is on my side. Wonder Woman with a gun.

Here's the thing, though: experience has taught me that right doesn't really have a side. If it did? The world would look quite different. The world wouldn't look the same as it does now. At all.

Looking at my map, one of the things I think about is that a rational person would not go to any of these places, alone or otherwise. They would be hiding from police and others. They would be a fugitive and putting energy into not being found. But this is William Atwater who I have researched extensively. I know about him. And one of the things I know is that he is *not* a rational person. That opens the door, in a way. It seems to me it makes the unthinkable and the impossible possible.

So then, a new challenge. What would an *ir*rational person do? Is there anything that can be counted on? I lack the experience to know. Which makes me think of something. Somewhere there has to be someone—or even a whole group of people—who might know, based on behaviors and archetypes. People who might be able to make an educated guess, better than my possible shot in the dark. It is a big county and, hell, Atwater might not even be here. Though it would be out of character, he might have left the area in order to go to ground somewhere. But maybe I don't have to guess. Maybe there *are* people out there who can offer some sort of insight.

For lack of any better ideas, I turn to Google. Someone has the answer I need. I apply myself to finding it.

On the Internet, I locate a doctor who specializes in serial killers. He does lectures, has written a book. There is a phone number on his website. I dial the number from my phone, right there at the table. To my surprise, the phone is answered. It is him, the author doctor himself. It catches me off guard. I'd planned on leaving some imprecise message. Something, perhaps, about my own book. But now I've got him in person and I had nothing prepared. I hesitate. And then I begin.

"It seems to me that the past history of a serial killer might help determine a present location," I say without much preamble. I have introduced myself. Not much more.

I hear nothing and then a deep chuckle. The sound is warm and present. It gives me hope.

"You're looking for William Atwater." It's not a question.

"I am." I cover my surprise, though I don't know why I bother. Clearly, the guy knows his stuff.

"Don't think I'm magic. It isn't rocket science."

"An educated guess?"

"Right. Because you're not the only one. There is a whole platoon of others. What gives you special insight? What makes you think you can succeed where so many others have failed?"

"I've done it before."

"I don't think I understand," he says. "You've done what before?"

"Found William Atwater."

Silence. And then, "And what was the outcome?"

I think about how to answer before I say anything. What can I tell him without giving too much away? "It's complicated," I say at length.

"Is it?"

"It is."

"I'm sorry, miss." I hear an impatience in his voice I hadn't detected before. "Whatever delusions you have, I can't aid you. You are right to seek professional help, but there's no help I can think to offer. Perhaps talk to your physician for the recommendation of a doctor who can help you." There isn't even a click, just a sudden deepening of the silence that tells me he's gone.

I had hoped for help, but I am alone.

I choke back the sudden flood of tears that threaten to overtake me. I find them in my chest, my throat, but I push them back. There will be time for that at some point, but it isn't now.

What had I imagined, in any case? Of course what I'd asked him sounds insane. I can't even believe it myself. And briefly even *I* wonder at my own sanity. It's not the first time. Delusional, he said. I hold my hand in front of my face, turn it around. It looks real enough. I catch the waitress looking at me. I scowl at her and she scurries away.

I put her out of my mind and study the lines of my hand. I study my palm, my knuckles. I pluck at the skin near my wrist, watch the color drain and then return. Yes. It all seems real enough to me.

Pick yourself up and go on.

It's all I really know how to do.

Unbreakable.

I consider everything I know and the steps I've taken. I try to think if there's something I've overlooked. I mentally retrace my steps, not stopping until I come to my meeting with the reporter. I struggle for less time than one would have thought, then come up with his name: Curtis Diamond. He had told me something ridiculous; something I'd discounted at the time. I struggle briefly, then it comes to me: a psychic is what he'd said. Someone with sight who had gone to the police in San Pasado with information but had been turned away.

I try to remember if Curtis told me her name, but if he did, I can't think of it. And even while I'm running through all of these thoughts, I wonder if I'm seriously thinking about looking for a psychic. Then I cut myself some slack: What other leads do I have?

My smartphone is set to anonymize my number, so I don't have to worry about Curtis tracking me when I contact him.

I identify myself, then clear my throat before getting to the meat of the call.

"You mentioned a psychic," I say.

"I did?" On the phone he sounds even more newscastery than he did in person. His voice is all deep rumble and clear annunciation. If I didn't know what he did for a living, I'd guess correctly.

"Yeah. Someone who had tried to go to the police."

"Oh right. Yes. Sara Jane Samaritano."

"Whoa. Okay. I was trying to remember if you'd told me the name. Now that you've said it, I know you did not."

"Right? It's a distinctive handle. Why do you ask?"

"I'd tell you," I say, laughter in my voice. "But then I'd have to kill you."

"Well, we wouldn't want that. Good luck with whatever you're doing. And don't forget: call me if you want me to interview you. I know you've got a story."

"You don't know the half of it." It sounds like something you say, even if this time it's true.

You don't need to be psychic to find Sara Jane Samaritano. She has an Instagram feed, a Twitter account, a Facebook page, and a website. On the web site there is a form: you fill it out, plug in your credit card info, then you pay fifty bucks for what she calls a "preliminary interview." Once your card clears, it says, she'll call you and get down to business.

I realize it isn't even a long shot. It's a crapshoot. A shot in the dark. A desperate attempt. But it's fifty bucks and I don't have any better ideas, so I pull out a credit card, make the payment, then wait for the call. Truly, what do I have to lose?

The callback comes more quickly than I would have expected.

"Just call me SJ," she tells me when I greet her. "And tell me who you're looking for."

The voice on the other end of the phone is surprisingly youthful and energetic. Not what I'd anticipated. I'd expected a professional psychic to have a wizened face and craggy old hands. But this young woman sounds like she could be on a skateboard.

She has the voice of a kid. At first contact, I'm already regretting spending the fifty bucks.

"I'm looking for William Atwater," I say. "A reporter told me you contacted the police and they sent you packing."

"That's right." She says it flatly. I feel relieved. I don't know why. Atwater feels like a secret I've been carrying and here is someone to share it with.

"I'm trying to find him, too."

"Why?" she asks.

"I am going to kill him." There seems no reason to be coy with this anonymous voice on the phone. Sara Jane Samaritano. But, truly, she could be anyone.

"Oh," she says. "Oh! You mean to do it, too. I can hear that even over the phone. My. My." There is a wisdom in the voice, along with the youth. I don't know how to explain it, but that is my impression.

"Will you tell me what you were going to tell them?" I say.

She hesitates, but not for long. "What I was going to tell them is no longer relevant. Time has passed. The thing that would have mattered doesn't anymore."

I feel my heart sink. "So you can't help me?"

"I didn't say that. Understand the nature of my art, please. It's not conclusive. In some ways, I seldom get anything more than impressions. But they're strong. And I feel certain I am right."

Her voice tells me that she feels she is telling the truth or what she thinks of as the truth. In for a penny, in for a pound. Or, in this case, a psychic.

"Okay," I say. And why the hell not? It's not like I have any other big ideas. "Go ahead."

"Well, first I will tell you, as I tell everyone, that my particular insight is somewhat imprecise. That is, I see certain visuals, have certain impressions, etcetera, and when all is working well, those visuals will have more meaning for you than they possibly can for me. Do you understand? I will rely on you to interpret what I see. Make sense?"

"I think so. Do you think you'll see visuals in my case?"

"I already am," she says. I can hear the smile in her voice. She sounds kind. I'm glad.

"Okay. Lay them on me."

"All right. I'll begin by saying these visuals mean even less to me than many of those I am given."

"Ah," I say, sensing the preamble of a faker.

"No, it's not that," she says, startling me. It is as though she has read my thoughts. I chide myself, but settle in to listen.

"It's just that these visuals are . . . well, they're remote. And imprecise. There are no markers for me. Nothing I recognize. I will describe them to you and hope you see the meaning."

"All right," I say, my expectations low.

"First, a gas station. And it's dark. There will be a choice. You'll fork to the left."

"Fork to the left?" It may be imprecise, but it also seems quite detailed. Specific. I hadn't expected that. I sit up a little straighter, paying close attention. I begin taking notes. This seems like something I might be able to use.

"Two roads. You understand? Go left."

"All right."

"Then much, much darkness. Of spirit, but also in the world." Her voice sounds more distant. Dreamy. If she's faking, she's good. "It's a country road. No streetlights. Nothing, really, to distinguish this place from any other."

"That makes it difficult."

"Yes. Sorry. I realize. I warned you."

"Go on."

"Right. Okay. So darkness. That seems to be key." A hesitation. Then, "This is a bit of a jumble, but stay with me."

"Yes."

"I'm getting *verde*, which, of course, is Spanish for green, yet somehow I am certain we are not in Mexico. Or Spain, for that matter."

"Okay." Again, specificity. More notes.

"Maybe Camp Verde or Verde Road or something like that."

"Finding something called *verde* in California. Well, *that* should be hard."

"Right. Well, okay. Still. That's what I'm getting. Then there is a long road, whether this is Verde anything or not is unclear. But it is *not* a highway. Like a back road? Unpaved. It ends at a white cliff."

"I must be careful not to fall over it?" I feel as though I am humoring her now.

"No, no! The cliff is *above* you. Sorry. I shared that imperfectly."

"Above me. All right. Got it. A cliff."

"And I see three boulders blocking a path. I'm sorry. This seems especially meaningless to me, but it's just the visual I'm getting. Just stay aware and alert for them."

"Three boulders. Right."

"Yeah. Big rocks. Blocking a path. It's as though they have been intentionally used to stop cars, you understand what I'm getting at? Like not boulders that have fallen here by nature's hand. They are large rocks. Intentionally placed. Across a path or narrow road."

I take more notes. "Okay. Got it."

"That is not the end of your quest, but I sense it is part of it. A distinct part. And then another. This feels like a whole different reading. I should charge you another fifty bucks."

"Really?"

"No. Sorry. Weird psychic humor."

"Don't give up your day job," I say dryly. We both laugh, though I think mine has a nervous sound.

"So the different reading part. The visual I am getting now is another location. Not near the first. And nothing to do with the boulders. I see an empty house on top of a mountain. The sea is nearby. And he is dead there." I'm imagining Snow White, some wicked dwarves. I'm imagining a whole bunch of pictures that make no sense. "Or badly injured," she continues. "Sorry. I can't tell. But he is flat out."

"Who?"

"I don't know. But it's a male form."

"He's dead there now? Or whatever? At this abandoned house?"

"Empty," she corrects. "I didn't say abandoned. And no, I can't see that. This is a future vision. I'm fairly certain. It hasn't happened yet."

"Fairly certain," I repeat.

"Yes. That means that there's no surety to any of it. Or even less surety. That's because our actions in the present can impact whatever is coming towards us."

I've seen enough sci-fi-type movies to know what she is talking about. Time-space continuum, that sort of thing. But I feel pretty skeptical. "Is that everything?"

"Yes, that's all I've got."

"Well. . . thanks."

"You're welcome." Her voice is warm. Almost effusive. "And good luck on your quest!"

"My quest?"

"Yes. William Atwater. I think you will be successful. Whatever that means for you."

CHAPTER THIRTY-FIVE

AFTER THE CALL, I think about what I've learned. More to the point, I think about if I've learned anything at all. Verde something. A cliff above me. Three boulders. An empty, but not abandoned, house at the end of a road. This does not seem a lot to go on, and I feel as though the fifty bucks might have better been spent on gas or hamburgers or maybe toys for the dog. But it's all I've got, and the competent and friendly sound of her voice encourages me forward. It was more, in any case, than I'd gotten from the doctor.

And so, with my notebook and my laptop beside me, I order a cup of coffee and I begin.

The first thing I do is look for occurrences of the word *Verde* in San Pasado County. Like I figured, there are many: it's an area that has a lot of green and aspirations to green. There is a subdivision called Verde Springs, but it is on the other side of the county. I discount it because that was never Atwater's territory and I have no reason to think he would suddenly go so far afield. There are several roads called "Verde." There is a Verde Court Motor Inn and a Verde Chili Restaurant and a couple of Verde Beaches: North and South. For a second, one of these last two seems like a possibility until I realize they are also far out of my pinned area.

Of the "Verdes" in the area I had mapped for him, I find three that seem like real possibilities. Verde Park is at the eastern edge of the mapped area. One of the Verde Roads occurs close to where the day care Ashley was taken from is located and where I had found Atwater the last time. There is also a Verde Field, a small military airbase that, when I Google, proves to have been closed for the last twenty years.

The old airbase seems a good bet. It would be the kind of place I would hole up in if it were me doing the hiding. That seems as good a reason to try it first as any. I pack up, go back to the car and the dog, and we set out.

The drive to Verde Field is pleasant. Picturesque. If I were not currently so concerned with finding my prey, it is a ride I would enjoy. Gnarled oaks line a lonely, crack-sided highway where white-faced cattle graze in fields that look as though nothing new has grown there for months. Years. I find myself feeling sorry for those cattle, shuffling hopelessly across arid fields. Do they carry the memory of springy green under their feet, I wonder? Or is today the only memory that matters, and no other reality came before?

After a while, I make a turn and the road becomes even more desolate. I drive on an old and unkempt highway for half an hour and don't see another car. I remind myself that California has a population of around forty million souls. As I drive, I wonder idly where everyone has gone. Forty million take up a lot of room. But they're not here.

Then, suddenly, the road ends, and I find myself startled. I had been expecting an old airfield, no one around. What I find is different. I see a chain-link fence seven or more feet high with three strands of barbed wire on top. A weathered sign at the gate announces that this is "Camp Verde." Even though it is supposedly a decommissioned military base, the fence appears to be perfectly serviceable: there are no holes that I can see, though even without the sign, I would have had no trouble determining that I was in the right place. The old hangars and the airfields themselves are distinctive. Purpose built. And I see what I imagine would have been barracks as well as other buildings whose purposes I can't discern from a distance.

I follow the fence as far as I can in the car. This turns out to be not terribly far. Much of Camp Verde is off the road. After I've driven as far as I can, I drive a little further and park at the nearest pullout.

The day isn't hot, but I pull the car into shade. Though there appears to be no absolute need to do so, I put the dog on a leash and walk him for a bit. I don't have a clear idea of how long I'll be gone and I'd like him empty. More to the point, if there *is* anyone around, a lone woman walking a dog will invite little interest and it gives me a chance to look around unobserved, though on our brief walk we don't see anyone at all. I hear the buzz of high-tension wires from somewhere nearby, though I don't see them and the air is redolent with the scent of things growing and dying. Pleasant forest smells, nothing to cause concern. I stay alert for any change in the air anyway.

After our short walk, we return to the shady spot where I parked the car. When I open the door, the dog jumps onto the back seat happily enough. I crack the windows, lock the door, grab the Bersa from the trunk. I load the gun, then once again pop it into my purse, even while I think that, considering the way things have been going, I should maybe get a little backpack or something I could sling over my shoulder. It seems possible I will have to scramble or possibly even climb. Doing that with a designer handbag over one shoulder seems somehow wrong, and never mind impractical. A fashion crime that also doesn't help move things forward.

Back at the fence, I begin a circumnavigation. I don't bother keeping to cover because I haven't seen anything that makes me think I need to be cautious. I see long gray runways. Cracked. Weeds poke through the concrete here and there: in the end, nature always wins. The whole scene is like a poster for a place that is asleep. And then a sign of life: I think I see a feral cat near one of the buildings, but when I look again, it has disappeared.

At the fence, I am able to see something I couldn't from the road. Parked beyond one of the buildings, and I can only see a sliver of it, but there is no doubt: it is a white van. My heart lurches when I realize what it is and what it might mean.

At the sight of it, I fade back into the shadows. If it *is* him, I need the support of surprise on my side even though, at a glance, the situation is hopeless. The fence looms high above me, topped with razor wire even if it wasn't impossibly tall. I can see no way in. But *he* is in there. And if *he* is there, I can get in there, too.

The gatehouse is boarded shut. It doesn't look like anyone has used it in a really long time. There is graffiti etched on it in yellow paint. "Go hard or go home," and other shouts of defiance, meaningless without context.

I follow the fence line for half an hour. The ground is uneven in places and the going is hard. I am thankful that the day is neither hot nor cold. Either of those would have made the exploration less pleasant. But it is a perfect Central Coast early afternoon, the weather so lovely you don't notice it at all.

When I am as far from the road and the gatehouse as possible, I find a break in the fence. It is small. I have to get down low and wiggle through, pulling the Coach with its deadly load through behind me. At one point, I feel my shirt catch and tear. I don't think the rip is very big, but it hasn't done much for the health of my shirt.

Despite the drama and the dirt and the rip, after a while, I do get through. It's taken a few minutes, but now I am standing on the business side of the fence, brushing dust and plant debris off me, ready to move forward.

Though I have that in mind, I am somewhat frightened of the moving. I hadn't really thought I'd be able to find a way in. Now that I have, I'm not quite sure what to do with myself. Once again, I am asking: What do I hope to accomplish? Why am I here?—And it's not a philosophical question.

I move forward anyway.

Up close, the buildings are as dried out and unused as they had appeared from the road. They are mostly boarded up, with broken windows and other signs of abandonment. I am quiet, and I keep to the shadows. Beyond the element of surprise, I don't have much going for me. It would be good to understand the situation fully before I make any kind of move. But it's a big place. I have to find him first. Atwater. And by now, I am certain he is here.

Still sticking to the shadows, I move towards the van. Moving as slowly as I am, it takes a while for me to cover ground. The base is big and the white van is not as close as I'd thought at first. Perspective is everything in life, that's what I've learned.

Even while I move, I keep alert, listening for any motion or other sign of life. But there's nothing. After a while, I feel myself begin to relax. The world is full of white vans. There seems only a very slim chance that this particular path will lead me to Atwater.

Just as I begin to breathe again, I hear a motor start. My heart starts up with it, accelerating so quickly, I fear it will flutter out of my chest. I'm still not certain it is Atwater, and now I might lose him before I find out. I crouch low while I pull the Bersa from my bag, attaching the suppressor in a single, practiced motion, and when the van moves in my direction, I don't waste time or energy on identifying the driver. Instead, I take careful aim and, as the moving vehicle picks up speed, I am pleased with my accuracy as I shoot out the front tire on the driver's side.

The van is moving fast enough that it jolts to one side as the shot hits home. The van stops and the driver emerges, scratching his head at the unexpected blowout. At the sight of him, I feel a disappointment so sharp it feels unrelated to me: it is not William Atwater. Worse: the van I've immobilized belongs to the U.S. military. There are logos on the side and the man scratching his head at having a mysterious blowout is in uniform, though not fully. The pants and shoes look Army issued, but he's wearing a bright green T-shirt and I can't be certain at this distance, but I think I see something that looks like "Gabba Gabba Hey" printed on the front of the shirt. It makes me think of the Ramones for a second. How they are everywhere. Forever.

The man from the van appears to be alone here, and I wonder if he is some sort of forgotten security detail, left alone to mind the store. And I have damaged his vehicle.

"Shit," I mutter, pulling more deeply into the shadows.

Now he is done examining his tire and he's looking around for the cause. Just my luck: a military man. He will certainly know the difference between a common blowout and the damage caused by a bullet. He's shielding his eyes from the sun and peering in my direction and I realize I am in luck: I am backlit by the late-day sun and it is shining in his eyes. More luck: he appears to be unarmed.

I stuff the Bersa into my bag and scurry back towards the hole in the fence, feeling like a fox going to ground. Once I get in motion, I don't look back. I don't know if he's following me and I don't want to know; I just want to get back to the car, the dog, the hunt.

I can see the gap where I got in and feel the beginning of relief flood my body along with adrenalin moving me forward at speed. I am preparing to duck in the direction of my escape when I feel the hand on my shoulder. He has caught me. He recovered quickly and was faster than he looked.

I swing around and face him, and see he is astonished. He is surprised by what he sees. I am not surprised by his surprise. If someone sneaks into a military base and shoots out the tire on a van, she is not expected to look like me.

"What are you doing here?" he says. "Why did you attack me?"

"I didn't," I say, fumbling from the beginning. Wanting to explain and knowing there are no good words for this. "Maybe you had a blowout?"

He raises his eyebrows at this. We are no longer in shadows. We are standing right at the gap in the fence, and I realize I was moments from making good my getaway. He is much larger than I am. He would not have fit through the hole.

"You shot out my tire," he says again, ignoring my denial. I may as well not have spoken at all. There is wonder in his voice, though and it is doubly clear that, whatever he was expecting, it wasn't me.

I don't say anything. For the moment, it seems the wisest course. After all, what can I say? He doesn't wait for words, though, and he's caught me unawares. I'm not quite sure why. There is him, this military man in his fatigues. And then there is me, clearly in the wrong. So, when he snakes out one meat-like fist and squeezes my left arm behind my back in a half nelson, I am unprepared, though I should not have been. Even as I think that, I realize the fruitlessness of the regret. He had the jump on me, plain and simple. I could have played it differently, but I'd probably still be right here.

"Your weapon, please," he says politely. Calmly. He may look ineffective, but he is duty trained. I should not have expected less.

"I told you," I say through my discomfort. "You had a blowout. I don't have a weapon. The blowout had nothing to do with me."

He puts some pressure on my arm, bending it upwards, beyond the place where it is meant to go.

"Please don't make me break this," he says. There is no malice in his voice, I note. But I can also tell he doesn't believe in the coincidence of his blowout and my showing up.

I don't respond, and he pushes a little further on the arm I'd already thought was close to breaking.

"Okay, okay," I say, through my pain. "Uncle." The squeezing stops right away, but doesn't disappear. I can feel him waiting.

"Gun is in my purse," I choke out. It is heartbreaking to me, this giving up of the Bersa. But better my heart break in this way than my arm.

He lets me go and scoops up my bag in the same motion. With the Bersa in his hand, I imagine I see a smirk, but in the next instant it is gone so quickly I wonder if I didn't imagine it in the first place.

"Handy little gun," he says grudgingly.

I keep my mouth shut. It doesn't seem like anything I could say at this point will move this situation ahead. I am silent and watching. There are a number of ways all of this can go. Mostly none of them are good.

"Who are you here with?" Now that the gun has been secured and tucked into his waistband, I am no kind of threat. He looks around in comfort, trying to see whatever accomplices I might have. Clearly, I can't have done this thing by myself.

"I am alone," I say. It's not quite the truth, but I don't think the dog counts.

CHAPTER THIRTY-SIX

I AM SCRAMBLING through my brain for ideas, but nothing is coming. I want to say something that will make it all better. Will make all the bad stuff go away while also making him give me my Bersa back. I am scrabbling and scrambling but I know I don't have much time and no big ideas are coming to me.

"Are you a terrorist?" His face has no expression when he asks. Whatever else he is, he is a trained soldier. And me? I have never felt more alone.

"Do I look like a terrorist?"

"I don't know," he says. Clearly, all of this is outside of his experience. As well it should be to a nearly forgotten soldier playing security guard at a shut-down military base and airfield in rural California. "I don't think so. No."

"I'm not a terrorist."

"I don't think a terrorist would say they were one," he says as though considering. I search his face for a trace of humor at the words, but I don't see any. Instead, he looks like he's trying to work something through, but nothing is lining up.

"I'm not a terrorist," I repeat, but I see the growing doubt in his face. He is younger than he should be to be posted out here by himself. And there is the faint hint of a gin blossom growing on both cheeks, probably, I think, the result of too much time spent on his own with nothing for company besides a bottle. If I weren't in such a weird predicament, I'd feel sorry for him.

I see him trying to process who I am and how I fit into his reality while he also figures out what to do. This is outside of the routine. Beyond the every day.

"Well, I'll have to report you," he says, as though talking himself through what should be done next. "Even if it was a blowout." He eyes me suspiciously, but I can see him adding things up in a way that doesn't compute. One-plus-one-equals-six or something like that. All of the pieces together don't come to the right equation.

"There's nothing to report," I say. I can't afford the connection to my real identity or for weight to be put on the identity I carry. I can afford no connection. "I . . . I just got lost."

If I have any hope of this being easy and him just letting me go and forgetting he ever saw me, it goes out like a blown-upon flame with his next words.

"Let's get to the office, and we'll figure out what to do."

With his van offline, we are forced to walk, and I trudge next to him towards an office in one of the hangar buildings. I have to trot to keep up with his long-legged stride. I shake my arm out a bit while we go. It seems likely to me I will bruise where he was holding me. Or worse.

When he pulls open the big barn doors, I am met by the smell of dust and disuse, abandonment and forty-year-old motor oil. It's not a scent I'm moved to dab onto my wrists.

In the office, he indicates I should take a chair while he goes to the desk and fires up his computer. The computer is not as old as the rest of the stuff here, but it is clearly not this year's model. I am trying to think fast, but I am running out of steam. As lame as it is, I am in a military installation and there is only so much I can do.

"They'll probably have me put you in lockup."

"I can't be in lockup," I say. "Please."

"Look around," he says, waving a hand airily. "You've broken into a United States military base. Do you think I can just let you go?"

I see his point. See the precariousness of my situation. But still.

"I understand, truly. But it would be just so much better if you did not phone this in. Please." His face is implacable, and I decide I have nothing more to lose. I will try the truth, or as close to it as I can get. "I am hunting William Atwater."

"The murderer?"

"Yes. Last seen driving a white van."

"Ah," he says. I see a light dawn. Whatever he makes of my statement, I know he believes it.

"Right. I thought you were him. And listen, it's really important I find him. I think he has a little girl with him. I'm . . . I'm trying to save her."

I've hesitated because, out loud, the words sound ridiculous, even to me. Who am to I think I can stop a murderer? I see I have his attention though. Even if he doesn't believe me, it's an interesting story, and he's got nothing but time on his hands.

"It's a U.S. military base," he repeats needlessly. "You know I can't just let you go."

I nod. And I get it. Really. I do. Here's this low-man-on-the-totem-pole soldier stuck here most of the time on his own. And then I plop into the middle of everything. Clearly, that's going to be nothing but trouble. If I were him, I'd do the very same thing. Keep things simple and moving forward. I'm beginning to plot desperate measures doomed to fail when he speaks again.

"Atwater, huh?"

I nod.

"He's the one killed the little kids an' then got loose?"

I nod again, daring to feel the faintest hope flutter in my chest.

"What makes you think you can get him?"

I consider before answering but, when I do, I can see I chose the right words.

"I've got nothing to lose."

He grunts while he nods agreement. "I get that," he says and I can see he means it. "Guy like that," he says. "Would be better if he was dead."

"I aim to kill him." My voice is calm and determined.

He smiles at my words, but he isn't laughing at me.

"Yuh. Better or worse, I think. That's your aim. Can smell it on you." Then a little more seriously, "I know that smell," and then I understand that there is more to his story than just being shunted off to a backwater. Something led him here. Something happened first.

"I can't let you go," he says, and I feel the slender hope I'd held die at the back of my throat. It tastes like sawdust.

"Oh," I say. I just don't have any more words.

"Yuh. Can't just let you go," and I can hear him thinking now. I can almost hear the clicks of the wheels speeding up. "But maybe you got the jump on me."

It takes a second for me to understand what he's getting at and, when I do, I feel something grow in my chest. And the taste of sawdust is gone.

"Jump," I prompt. Because I am not sure.

"Yeah." His voice is brighter now. He can feel a purpose. "Because you had a gun. I couldn't safely disarm you and you held it on me and . . ." He has an idea. I can tell because of the smile that floods his face. He is having fun with this. And maybe fun doesn't come to him every day. And my mission? It's a good one. He knows that, too.

"And I ran away? Scrabbled back through the fence?"

"Naw," he says. The smile has dimmed to a grin, but it is still beautiful. "Or maybe. You got away from me. And then you hid or whatever. I didn't see you get away. Don't know where you went."

He turns his back. Pulls the Bersa from his waistband and plops it on the desk. Raises his arms over his head like I'd told him to stick 'em up and says, "Good luck."

I hesitate. And then I don't. I move forward cautiously, in case it's a trick. It's not though, because he stays there like that even after the Bersa is back in my bag.

"Thanks," I mumble.

"Don't," he says. "Just get 'er done."

I put my hand softly on the back of his head—a silent thanks—and then I scurry away.

CHAPTER THIRTY-SEVEN

I HEAD FOR the exit. Getting out of the compound is easier than getting in had been. Though I had feared some drama, in the end, it is easy. I just walk out the front gate.

Back at the car, the dog is ridiculously happy to see me. Ludicrously, rapturously happy. I open the door, and he practically pours out of the car in his joy. Maybe he'd thought he was a goner, trapped inside a car in the wilderness. I let him run around and do dog things for a few minutes, but I keep one eye on the empty road. From my perspective, the sooner we leave the area, the safer we will be. We get on the road, and I track us back to where I made my phone calls and it all starts again.

It does not take long before I come to the gas station at the fork in the road. It seems right. Correct. My excitement grows. Viewed from the north looking south, the gas station is located in the deepest part of a vee. Take the left road, she'd said. And so I stop. First, I take the dog around. It just seems the right thing to do. Then I park the dog and go inside.

I use the restroom. Buy a muffin and two large bottles of water. Garbage in, garbage out.

Among the chips and cookies and beef jerky and cheap electronic crap they are selling in the store, there is a rack of poorly made T-shirts. "San Pasado," one declares, a map of the county front and center. "It's where my story begins" is printed on the back. I take one off the rack, and if the clerk notices the rip in the shirt I am wearing while I pay for the new one, he doesn't say anything. Some things are best unremarked. Most people know that.

In the car, I pull the shirt on over the one I'm wearing, then go back over my notes. She had been very clear. "*Two roads. You understand? Go left.*"

And am I actually following the advice of a psychic? I chide myself for maintaining even the faintest glimmer of hope that young Sara Jane Samaritano's predictions will pan out. At the same time, I'm excited, though trying to hold that excitement down. The doctor I'd spoken to before I connected with the psychic is probably the one who is right: therapy is likely what I need, but I have a hunt on my hands. For better or worse, I put my head down and lean in.

After the dog and I do another round of the parking lot, we get back on the road. It is now fully dark, but my energy doesn't falter. I am in the home stretch. I can feel it in my bones.

First, a gas station. And it's dark. There will be a choice. You'll fork to the left.

When I move through the parking lot and back to the car, I don't see anyone moving in the shadows. Even when I pull back onto the highway, I don't notice the car following me, and the dog is still riding comfortably.

I continue on my way to Verde Road, having taken the left fork. The road is convoluted. One of those coast-to-canyon minor highways you find nowhere quite as they are in California.

When I come upon three boulders blocking a roadway just as Sara Jane Samaritano predicted, I am so excited I nearly drive off the road. Clearly, I should have listened to her in the first place.

I park in front of one of the boulders and get out of the car and use my smartphone flashlight to illuminate not much of the darkness. When you are trying to find your keyhole in the dark, it seems like a bright light. But here in pitch darkness, it is almost nothing at all. It is only by luck that the light catches a bit of a road sign reflecting out from the dried grass dying at the edges of the boulders. And when I pull the sign out to inspect it, I'm not even surprised when I see that it reads "Verde Lane." Even in the dark, I can see the white cliffs looming above me and I have no doubt that this is the correct Verde. Too many of the signs are right. And my heart expands slightly to send quick thoughts of thanks to Sara Jane Samaritano and to allow for the idea of magic in the world, at least for a while.

From my position, I have a sense that, if I were to turn my head to the right, in daylight, I would see forever. Mile upon mile of waving wheatgrass and stubby hills in the direction of the sea. But it is dark. The sort of velvety night that envelopes the soul. And I suddenly feel that, from here, it all winds down with the inevitability of a candle burning out. It's as though there's only one way it can go.

By bumping through a shallow ditch, I bypass the boulders blocking the road. The dog looks at me quizzically at this suddenly bumpy ride, but he doesn't comment.

From there, I inch the car ahead slowly, foot upon careful foot. It is so dark that a light up ahead on the slender track I follow seems to glow in the darkness. I stop the car when the road becomes too uneven to continue and get out into fragrant gloom, once again leaving the dog behind. This time, I feel only faintly ridiculous carrying my purse into the velvety night. Into the wilderness. The heft of the Bersa inside the bag restores my confidence. There isn't much anyone would ever need to face that the Bersa could not help with, that is my thinking.

I pull a hoodie on against the cold and creep into the night. The scent of green oak drifts up to me as leaves crush under my feet. The sound of night birds and brash insects. The harsh hiss of a biting bug in my ear. And always ahead, the light, calling me forward. I push back the excitement I feel. After all, it truly *is* wilderness. If it is not what I am searching for, what else could it possibly be, here where we are miles from any houses or other signs of civilization?

After a while, I hear a thin cry. Light and feminine. I indulge myself in the sound. Not a woman, I think. A girl. I move more quickly, but keep my wits sharp and on edge. I stay aware of every current of air, every sound. I am close now, I'm sure of it. And a mistake at this stage could be fatal. For her. For me. I'm not sure, but fatality seems a distinct possibility. Its potential is all around me.

Closer still and the object of my search takes a shape. There is a tent tucked into the side of the looming cliff, the forest thick around it. Had it not been for the light, I would have missed it altogether. And it is like a replay of that time, weeks before, when Arden and I crept through the forest not far from here. I can't help having a sense of déjà vu that I also know is real.

I approach the tent cautiously, the Bersa ready. I don't know what I'll find. And I jump, startled, when a branch breaks behind me, then stand still until no other sound follows. Some nocturnal animal, I think, as startled by me as I am by it.

Close to the tent, I can see how it's made. The structure is a classic shape, maybe Army surplus. Pale, rough canvas. Crude and utilitarian. A center pole. Illuminated from within.

I am so close now, and then the cry again. Soft. Not desperate. Almost an aside. As though maybe hours of more strident sound have led to this pale mewling. An animal sound. And there is nothing of hope in it. It is the sound of a creature beyond hope.

The plaintive sound makes me bold. And it isn't something I can walk away from, even if I wanted to. And I've come so far. And I don't want to.

The Bersa is in my hand. As I push the tent flap aside with the muzzle of the gun, I don't think about the unlikelihood of having hunches pay out twice in a row. I don't think about psychics or odds or lottery tickets or any of the things that would have indicated I would never find this needle in a haystack. All I can think about is the child in front of me inside the tent.

In a heartbeat, I take in the scene. She is exposed to the night air, something horrid in that: her childish body, naked, spread-eagled, and tied on the tent floor. I can see now that her whimpering had been abject and without point or any real hope. If there had been fervor in the cries that came earlier, the ones I did not hear, she is spent now, almost hopeless against the torrent of what she has experienced. And she is alone.

"Emma," I whisper, putting the gun aside, entering the tent more fully. "Don't worry. I'm a friend."

Her head swivels towards me, and I feel as much as see the relief in her, though the relief is not complete. There is still fear, and still the sound of a slight whimper under a ragged breath. But there is hope on her face, in her eyes.

I pull off the hoodie I am wearing over my San Pasado T-shirt. I settle it over her as I untie her. The hoodie covers her small form completely.

It's where my story begins.

She sits up and instinctively begins to rub her ankles and wrists where circulation has been cut off. The whimpering stops as she sets herself to this new task.

"Do you know where he is?" I ask.

She looks at me, still sputtering. Shakes her head. I feel maybe she is in shock. And no words come. If she has information for me, it is lost in a column of horror and terror. I don't even want to know what she has seen. Right now, there is one thing only of greatest concern.

"We're going to get you out of here, okay? We're going to take you home."

She looks up at me, then looks beyond me and screams, a sound so piercing I wonder if I'll even still have hearing after the ringing stops.

If I hesitate, it is only half a beat of a heart. I am pure reaction. I raise the Bersa two-handed as I rise from where I've been crouching next to the child and I spin.

He is in the tent's entrance and there is a chain in his hand. As I raise the gun, I see him see me and drop down to the embankment beneath the tent. Still, I feel certain I catch a piece of him. I hear something that sounds like "oof" as the slug hits home, and then I catch the white of his T-shirt retreating more deeply into the forest. I begin to follow him, but a shrill wail brings me back.

Ridiculously, I fire several rounds after him, feeling quite certain I won't hit him, but wanting him to understand the depth of my capability and the completeness of my desire. I drop back next to Emma and gather her in my arms, collecting myself as I go. I am so conflicted. Relief at finding the child alive. Self-recrimination for letting Atwater get away. Fear, because we still have a bit of a hike to get back to the car, and he could be out there in the darkness somewhere, hopefully bleeding, but maybe not. I take some small comfort in the fact that he ran in the direction opposite of where I left the car. But still.

Emma's whimpering slows, then stops, as I half lead, half carry her back to the car. The shadows are filled with bogeymen. Anything seems possible. I don't take awareness away from my gun and my surroundings. My training and experience leave me ready to put the child down and pull the Bersa out of my purse and shoot with a moment's notice. But, in the end, there is no need.

The car is only a few hundred yards into the forest, but with the weight of the little girl on my heart and the fear of Atwater on both of us, it feels like miles. And it is too easy to imagine him jumping out from behind every tree and bush. I have no illusions: he is larger than me and stronger, too. If I lose the slight advantage of my gun, all is lost.

At the car, I unlock it and we get moving quickly. I am still imagining Atwater jumping out at us from behind each bush and bend in the track. Emma is likewise silent, the only sound a ragged breath upon breath. She is not very old, but it is my sense that she knows what's at stake.

At the car, the puppy greets us stoically, like he's been waiting for us, which I suppose, in a way, he has. I see Emma relax visibly when I pop her onto the back seat next to the young dog and he snuggles against her instinctively. It's like a new level of safety has been revealed to her. Safe when she was with me, safer still in a slightly larger pack that includes a canine.

Once they're settled in, I get us moving, still ever watchful, even though the doors are locked with us inside. Despite my fears, the bumpy forest path remains clear. I don't breathe until I get to the highway and then, when I do, I hit the accelerator as soon as I drive back around the boulders and feel the smoothness of pavement under my tires. With my foot heavy on the pedal, the car jumps ahead.

"Hang on, honey," I say, reaching back to steady the little girl's shoulder with my hand, trying not to read too much into the motion when she flinches away from my touch. She looks at me with shadowed eyes. I want to weep with joy, anger, relief.

I want to weep.

Before we get to San Pasado, I consult my phone for directions to the hospital. It seems the only choice I have. I know I take a risk going there, but I don't feel there are any other options. The child needs professional care. That's apparent to me right away, even though I don't see any injuries. I know they are there. The ones you can't see.

I park at a distance. She protests at leaving the puppy behind, but then gives it up without much effort when I make it clear the dog can't come. There's not much fight left in the child. I note this with sadness. I suspect she'd given what fight she had up in the forest. She holds my hand passively as we walk to the reception desk at the emergency entrance.

"Hello," I say when it is our turn. "This child is Emma Schwartz. Does that name mean anything to you?"

The woman at the desk looks back at me openmouthed. She nods but doesn't say anything. I don't mind because, really, there's nothing I need her to say.

"Good. Then you know she needs an examination on every level. I . . . I have to go."

"But you can't—" In her world, my entire speech has been outlandish. So outlandish, she doesn't know how to process it.

She is sputtering. I feel a little sorry for her. What's happening here is unprecedented, and stopping to explain will endanger me. I know it's only a matter of time before she thinks to call the authorities. And then where will I be? "There's the paperwork," she says, indicating a clipboard. "The necessary forms..."

I ignore her. Drop down to Emma's level.

"I'm sorry to leave you, but I have to go..."

"But the paperwork." This from the desk above us. I ignore it further. Emma just looks at me with her large, pale eyes. She doesn't say anything, but I see she has calmed considerably since I found her. It seems to me there is a chance she'll be all right. But what do I know?

"They are going to take super good care of you, Emma. And your parents will be here soon." I think I can see a gleam of life ignite in her when I say this. I hope so. There are a lot of things to hope for this little girl. The child is breathing. She appears unscathed. I have reason to think that hope is not misplaced.

CHAPTER THIRTY-EIGHT

AFTER I LEAVE Emma at the hospital, I drive pointlessly for a while. It's like I have a decision to make but, in truth, I've already decided.

I *want* to head my car east; head my car home. I'm really tired. I want to go back to my forest. I am longing for it now. I want my peace and maybe some lamb stew.

But it isn't what I *must* do. That is just as clear.

I'm passing a strip mall and I pull in, park the car. Slump in my seat. Rub my head with my hands.

I'm tired. Just so tired. It's all beginning to take on the shades of a nightmare that won't end. The kind where you wake up thankfully, glad it's over; then fall back to sleep and it's all still there.

As I sit there, I think the last few hours over. Did I hit him? I felt sure I had. And then, seconds later, I feel equally sure I did not. Whatever the case, I have to calculate my next move carefully. I need to find him. I need to hunt him down. And I need him to know he is hunted. I reason that if he knows he is hunted, he won't feel comfortable enough to hurt anyone else. That is my hope.

What else to hope? Is he lying there in the forest? Has he bled to death? Has he gotten away? Do I go back there and scour the forest in the vicinity? And, if I do that, might he be speeding on his way? All of these things roiling around and I suddenly feel incapable of making a coherent decision; organizing my next strong move. I am overwrought. Jangly. And I can't remember the last time I ate. There is a Starbucks across the parking lot, open, even though it's late.

Inside I choose a cheese Danish and a latte, figuring that the milk will counteract the caffeine. I'm not worried about it keeping me up, anyway. When am I planning to sleep?

"We've got to stop meeting like this." The voice jolts me. I squint at the speaker. He's wearing thick-rimmed glasses and his hair is tousled, like a wind is blowing it even though we're inside and so there is no wind.

"Curtis, right?"

"Yeah. And you're the writer lady with the weird party habits."

I feel myself color slightly at the memory of running into him at Walmart, but I don't actually feel offended. His tone is genuine and warm and, certainly, the combination of things I was buying *was* weird. I don't tell him that though.

"Weird is a bit of a judgment, wouldn't you say?"

He laughs and you can tell that comes easily for him: laughter. Warmth. For a second. I envy him that. What must that feel like? The ability to put back your head and just laugh.

"Okay. Fair enough. *Weird* is a bit strong. Someday you'll have to tell me, though."

And I nod, because that's polite. But I can't imagine the future that has me telling him that.

"What are you doing here?" I ask.

"Getting coffee," he says, deadpan.

"Shaddup. You know what I mean. I would have thought you'd be back in L.A. by now."

"I am," he says. "I mean, I was. I've just flown in. Meeting my crew here. We got a tip. He's at Morning Bay."

A beat. And then, "He's not," I say with confidence.

"He's not?"

"No."

"How do you know?"

"If I tell you, is there some kind of ethical rule that keeps you from telling people how you found out?"

He regards me evenly before he answers. I can see him wondering what the author lady might be sitting on. But then the weird stuff at Walmart. He's not quite sure what he's dealing with.

"Sure. If you tell me stuff no one knows that can lead to a story, you're a source. You can tell me anything and I won't tell."

"Like with a doctor?"

He grins his deeply charming crooked grin.

"Yeah," he says. "Something like that."

I look him over. Up and down. Is there any chance in hell he's going to believe me? And, really, what part of the story am I going to tell? The least amount possible, I decide. Just enough to get his help for what has to happen next.

I look into his eyes. They are a clear cerulean and I find it is difficult to look at them fully without flinching. I do it anyway. I want to be watching him closely when my news lands.

I lead him away from the center of the room and pitch my voice low. "A little over an hour ago, I shot—or I'm pretty sure I shot—William Atwater. Not dead," I add when I see his look.

"What?"

"Yuh. He had a little girl with him. I dropped her off at the hospital a little while ago. Now I'm deciding what to do."

He kind of rocks back a bit on his heels and looks at me, clearly perplexed. I understand this. My little speech would be outlandish to almost anyone. And he looks at me, not as though he doesn't believe me, but like he can't quite believe his ears. After a while, he speaks.

"How did you find him?" Coming from him, this is understandable. He and his team have been hunting. It's what he's doing back in town.

"It's a long story. Let's just say your psychic tip panned out."

A raised eyebrow. A speculative look.

"Oh-kay."

"So, yeah. I don't have anything to show you that will help explain or demonstrate this is true. That said, I think it would be helpful—and what the hell do you have to lose?—for you and your team to follow me to where I last saw him and, I dunno, help me or whatever."

"Why should we do that?" He doesn't look like he's not believing me or challenging me. He looks like he just really wants to know.

"Because I'm tired, Curtis. I'm tired of doing this alone."

He keeps looking at me for what seems like a long time. I start thinking he's going to turn me down flat.

"Okay," he says, after a while. "I mean, what the hell, right? Morning Bay isn't going anywhere." And besides, he doesn't need to add, if what I've said is true, he gets a better story than any of his colleagues. He wins. And you can tell just by looking at him that winning is something he likes to do.

He asks how far we are from the spot where I last saw Atwater. I tell him maybe half an hour. He nods. Reflective. I know it's a half hour to Morning Bay from here, too, but it's the other direction.

By now, his crew has arrived. They are solid-looking. This is the biggest story in the country at the moment, so we've got the first string.

Curtis pulls them aside—two battle-scarred old cats—one bearded and one with what looks like it's probably a perpetual five-o'clock shadow—and a petite young woman with a fierce stance. I stay where I am, letting him talk his team through it. They either will or they won't, I figure, and nothing I say is likely to influence it either way.

After a while, Curtis saunters back to me. A crooked grin. "Yuh, we're in," he says with a smile. "Like I said, we got nothing else to do."

And I know what he's really saying: worst-case scenario, he loses a couple hours. Best case? They have an exclusive story. Odds are probably against the latter, but it's worth a shot. And so off we go.

I lead the way in my Volvo, dog in the back. The news van follows, but Curtis rides with me.

"You seriously got this tip from the psychic?" Curtis prompts.

"Yeah," I say, eyes on the road. Not giving anything extra.

"And you said you shot him. Tell me again why you were carrying a gun."

"I didn't tell you. Nice try though."

He lifts his hands in a helpless gesture. And I like him for not reminding me he's a reporter and it's his job to ask questions.

And then we're upon it. The boulders. The reflective signs. The track into the forest. I park where I parked before and the van stops behind me.

"Now what?" Curtis asks.

"Now we hoof it."

We follow the track in a little mob. We have one of the seasoned old dogs with us and the girl and they're both lugging gear; just in case. Both of them turn out to be camera people. The guy left behind is some kind of tech, left to operate the space-age gear in the van. They might not think this is going to pan out, but they're manning their battle stations. It looks like it's just how they roll.

When we reach the spot where the tent was, we find nothing at all.

"He's gone," I say needlessly. And I have to admit, I'm surprised. I had been so sure I'd injured him. Breaking down the tent and getting the gear away so quickly would have taken strength and agility, something an injured man would surely lack.

I feel like an idiot and I avoid Curtis's eye so if he thinks I've made something up, I don't see it on his face: I'm not looking.

The more bearlike of the team is ahead of us with a bright light. Rocky. I'm glad to see the young woman sticking to his heels. No matter that it seems like Atwater has cleared out, it doesn't seem to me to be a good idea to be alone out here right now.

Rocky stops suddenly and calls us towards him.

"Look at this," he says as we approach.

The light clearly reflects the area that held the tent. The earth is bruised in some spots; the sparse brush growing there is pressed down. Branches are broken. All in a pretty obvious ten-by-ten-foot square. It is on a slight embankment and the forest falls away quickly behind it.

"This is where the tent was," I breathe, nearly sagging in relief.

The young woman is holding a flashlight; casting the light all around on the ground; searching. She spies something, walks over, and picks it up. Brings it to us. It is a black nylon strap, a few inches wide, a few feet long. An innocuous enough object, but it looks new—not as though it's been out in the weather for months—and its presence and location seem to confirm the possible recent presence of a tent.

"That way," I say, pointing into the forest. "That's the way I saw him go." And then more quietly, "I shot after him, but he was moving and it was dark. At first, I thought I hit him, but now it doesn't seem like it."

At this admission, three heads swivel towards me, and Curtis articulates the question, but I saw it coming anyway.

"Who the hell *are* you?"

And I can't help but laugh a little, not unkindly. Because the way he says it—his tone and demeanor—he may as well be talking to Batman, even though I'm anything but that.

"It's a long story. It's complicated."

"Are you even an author?"

"Yuh," I say. "Something like that."

I head in the direction I'd seen Atwater run, and the team troops behind me, as I'd hoped they would, their questions on hold for now. Rocky and the girl keep their lights going broad, and we can make out trails here and there, but we see no further signs of either humans or vehicles until we come to a crude road in the forest that heads in the direction of the highway. It hasn't rained recently and in the dark we can't be sure if a vehicle has been this way, even when we search with the aid of lights.

"Well, if he was here, he's gone," Curtis says needlessly.

"Yeah," I say. "And I don't know where this road ends up. Pretty sure it's not connected to the one I took off the highway."

So it's another dead end, but oddly I don't feel like the team disbelieves me. As we troop back through the forest, the girl suddenly calls out. "Wait," she says. "Look at this." She has a .380

caliber slug in her hand, and on inspection, it looks to have something that might be blood on it. It's flattened on one side and looking—to my admittedly not knowledgeable eyes—as though it was prised out of something. Or someone. I don't dare hope that.

"You said you shot after him," Curtis says. "This slug from your gun?"

"Yuh," I say. "It's a thirty-eight."

"Backs up your story," Curtis said.

"You believed me anyway," I say.

He nods. "I did."

"How did you even find it?" I ask the girl. The thing is miniscule: maybe the size of a peanut. The odds against seeing it would have been huge.

"I know, right? Got lucky. My light just hit it the right way."

One of those things about chance and fate. And odds. I am encouraged. Maybe things are going our way.

We traipse on.

"So now what?" he says when we're back at the vehicles.

I let the dog out of the Volvo and he races around us happily, clearly glad to have extra people around to pet him. Instinctively, he goes to the young woman who coos over him happily as he rolls onto his back, offering up his unprotected belly. It would be a charming scene if I weren't focusing so sharply on what Curtis is saying.

"I have a feeling you're not going to consent to an on-screen interview."

"You're one smart cookie," I tell him, grinning. "But I have a story for you anyway. It's only been a few hours. I have a feeling it will still be an exclusive."

I tell him about Emma. The hospital.

“How will I say she came to be there?”

“If you could find it in yourself to say you don’t know, it would help me a lot.”

He nods to let me know he heard me and is considering.

“Yeah, so I’ll talk with the team, but I think we’ll do it. Thank you. But I’ve got something for you, too.” I regard him silently. Waiting. “I told you, we got a tip: we were heading to Morning Bay when we ran into you.” I still wait. “That’s it, really. Someone called our tip line: spotted him at a gas station on the way into town. We thought we’d deploy and just come check it out, see if we turned anything up, do some location spots while we were here.”

“And look what you turned up,” I say.

He laughs. “Yeah. So, anyway: Morning Bay. We’ll head down after we see what this Emma business is about. We can connect down there, if you like. Swap notes. Let me give you my number.”

He reaches for his card, but I wave him off. “I’ve got it,” I tell him. He shoots me a look, but I’m already calling out to the dog and heading for the car.

CHAPTER THIRTY-NINE

Morning Bay.

I'm working at remembering why the name resonates, and then I do: Atwater's mom. Morning Bay was a name she had mentioned and I'm having a hard time recollecting why. Maybe he'd just liked it? So before I head to Morning Bay, I feel myself turn the car back towards San Pasado, thinking to try the mom one more time.

I dig the address out of my notes, then find it without much trouble: San Pasado's wrong side of the tracks is mercifully small and uncomplicated.

The place looks just the same as it did on my first visit, even though it's night. This time when I rap on the door, there is no feeling of being watched, and I realize, in the same breath, that the gray car is also nowhere to be seen. The scary-looking dog that had been chained up outside last time is gone, too. And the house is dark.

I knock harder. When no one answers, I try the door. It's locked but I'm sure no one is inside. I creep around to the back of the house. I am prepared to take out the Bersa, use the butt of the gun to break a window, but there is no need. A low window is open at the back of the house, to let in air, I presume. I open it wider and hop right inside.

"Mrs. Atwater?" I call into the gloom.

It is so quiet; I feel I almost hear an echo.

Instinct leads me. Sometimes it is the only thing we've got.

When I reach out and snap on a light, I hardly even realize I've thrown stealth out the window until light floods the room, illuminating a squalor so complete, I want to step back. Everything is mean. Nothing here is fine. And there is a smell that I don't recognize right away. It's not bad, exactly, but for me it does not have a good association. I snuffle it a bit before I realize what it is: it smells like a low-rent thrift store. The kind of vast establishment that makes you regret your consumerism, because it is the kind of place plastic clothes go to die.

There aren't a lot of clothes, though. A visit to the bedroom shows drawers open, their contents mostly gone. I'm beginning to get the feeling that Mrs. Atwater has cleared out.

It's all catching up with me and I'm suddenly very sleepy. I find myself fighting off the urge to lie down on the unappealing bed, Goldilocks-style, and get some much-needed shut-eye. I don't though. For one thing, it's gross. For another, I just feel it would be a really, really bad idea.

I press on. There are other rooms. I come to a back bedroom even dingier than the ones I have passed through. I'm guessing it is or once was Atwater's, though I have no way of knowing for sure. It's a small room that houses a saggy bed, a chipped dresser, and a damaged bookcase. I run my eyes over the spines of the books there, stopping at *A Catcher in the Rye*, whose inclusion would amuse me if I were in a mood to be amused. I keep going, and pass over—and then come back to—*A History of Califor-*

nia's Central Coast. The book is old, and when I open it up, I see that it is "Property of San Pasado Junior High." I figure he's got a decade or so of late fees to cough up.

A page midway through the book has been folded sharply down. "The history of Morning Bay." There is a photo of one of the founders of the region and he is standing on the porch of the house he built in 1929, when his original 1880s house had burned down. The cutline says the house is situated above the town, with a view out to sea at the end of San Miguelito Ranch Road.

A big house at the end of the road. I have the feeling it is abandoned.

All at once, I know where I'm going.

CHAPTER FORTY

As I DRIVE, I think to call Curtis.

It is strange to me, that I should feel pulled to do so; I who have been operating alone so long. But I like the way the team has felt on this one. And somehow, I like Curtis, trust him. It feels good to have someone at my back.

The call goes straight to voicemail and I imagine that, even now, the team might still be at the hospital. Interviewing Emma. Interviewing her folks. Waiting for outcomes. Waiting.

I tell his voicemail what I've been up to. Let him know I'm heading to Morning Bay and that he should call me as soon as he's free so I can tell him what I've discovered and we can swap notes. When I disconnect, I wonder at the easiness I feel in this bit of sharing. It's because we both have an interest in the outcome, I tell myself. Our goals are not so very different, even if our methods are entirely.

As I drive, the dog's head suddenly pops up from the back seat, looking for attention. I realize he is balancing his back feet on the seat, with his paws on the console that divides the front buckets. He couldn't have managed this stunt even a week before. He is growing. Less of a baby already. More like a young dog. But maybe it's just because of all he's seen.

When I get to the Morning Bay turnoff, I have to stop at a gas station and ask for directions: Google Maps doesn't list any San Miguelito Ranch Road. But, as I'd hoped, the kid working in the store knows exactly where it is: a local secret, in a way, he tells me. The road is not official, and maybe it's on county or private property: he is unsure. But he tells me how to get there. He tells me which way to go.

The track is deep and windy. A forest road that every so often turns in such a way that you get a glimpse of lights. I have the feeling that, if it were daylight, there would be beautiful vistas out to the sea. At night, though, there are just different intensities of darkness.

I press on.

I have a strong feeling that, when I get to the house, I will find Atwater there. With that in mind, I cut the lights and coast along in darkness for a bit. I go slow so I can make out the twin ruts in the road.

The trees thin and I feel I am near my destination. I stuff the Bersa into my purse, tell the dog I'll be back in a while, and head out on foot.

Walking, it is dark. So dark. Once my eyes adjust, I can see the old road I am following, but only just. I stumble along carefully, hoping I won't be stumbling too far. It's hard going.

After a while, I turn a corner and feel rather than see the trees thin out completely. And there is a house in front of me. None of the windows are illuminated, and I feel hope sink to my stomach. No one is here.

I find the entrance easily enough. It is large: twice the height of a normal door. I am certain it will be locked, but I try it anyway, surprised when it opens. Inside, I understand though. This isn't someone's home. It is a grand old house, maybe long abandoned. It smells that way, anyway. Something of damp. And dry rot, though I'm not fully sure what that smells like. Somehow my instincts know, anyway.

I don't try the lights, but I suspect they won't work. I risk my flashlight app, though, because I want to be able to explore in the dark. In the flashlight's dim illumination, I can see that even though there are some furnishings, the place is not what anyone would call furnished. More like the party house you go to when you're a teenager. Or the squat house that is closed for demolition. Whatever the case, as I ramble through room upon room in the old mansion, I feel absolutely alone.

And then I don't.

I'm not sure what the shift is, but I feel it. I am alone . . . and then I am not. I strain into the darkness to try to isolate what I've felt. A motion, almost like a whisper of sound. It is the kind of place where one might expect ghosts, but I don't believe in them.

I creep forward, pushing away the unease I feel. Telling myself I'm being foolish. Encouraging myself.

I suddenly have a clear image of the ludicrous thing I have done here. It is a moment of pure unreality. Like it isn't happening at all. Like I'm sitting on a couch in some comfortable living room, watching TV. And I'm sitting on the edge of my seat, saying to the faceless partner next to me, "What is she doing? That foolish girl! Why did she go in there by herself? Argh! I can't look."

And yet it's me. I am the foolish girl. Moving slowly through the abandoned house. In the dark. Feeling the stirring of a creature. Yet, faced with it, I understand the foolish girl—all those foolish girls—better now. There are times in life where you simply have no choice.

And here I am.

As I move through the house, my eyes adjust to the full darkness and, with the help of my weak little flashlight app, I can make out edges of grandeur. This isn't just a big house. This is the sort of high-rent pile where robber barons of a certain era parked their wives to keep them from finding out about their mistresses.

From the spacious foyer, there is a large living area to my left, a dining room to my right, and a spiral staircase that sweeps up. Having circumnavigated the entire foyer, I stand in the center of it, deciding. I hear no sounds and nothing to inform my decision, so I head up the staircase if for no other reason than I can't think why I should not.

I creep up slowly, single step after step. I am being cautious in the dark. Watchful of my feet, but also listening for any type of noise. I don't hear anything.

At the top of the stairs, a long hallway goes off in either direction. When I look to my left, I see a dim light at the end of the gallery. I taste blood and realize I've bitten down on my tongue. Hard.

I stand there, at the top of the steps, briefly motionless, feeling like a deer and the headlights are bearing down.

A part of me—the grown-up, sensible part—thinks I should turn around, go back down the stairs. Maybe even back to the safety of the car; the dog. But forward seems safer than back. There is a reason for the light. I don't want it behind me and begin to inch in that direction. I am afraid, but I remind myself that's why I'm here. On the one hand, I am afraid to find him. On the other, it's the only thing I want. I draw the gun from my bag, prepare it for action, and start inching forward again.

It's a long way from the top of the stairs to the room at the end of the hall. At least, it seems that way to me, every muscle coiled and ready to spring. It's like some special kind of yoga, that's what I tell myself. One that tests every part of my resolve and stealth. It tests everything that I have trained.

And I tell myself that this is it. This is the thing I have worked for all of this time. I coach myself to silence. I remind myself of every single thing I have learned. Finally. I have him almost in my sights. I won't make the same mistake this time. I am shaking slightly, but I know it is with excitement as well as fear. William Atwater dies today. I make my heart into a stone.

When I finally reach the end of the hallway, I hold myself back from entering the room. I will myself to perfect stillness. Suspend, even, taking deep breaths. The ones I take are measured, practiced. It's a kind of meditation, this waiting for the perfect moment. Kundalini yoga: take a deep breath and hold it. Hold it until you can't. Then breathe deeper still.

In my breath-suspended state, I listen from the deep, shadowy darkness of the hallway; I listen for sounds of motion or activity. I don't hear anything. And then I do. Breathing: rapid in, rapid out. And a skittering. Like claws on wood. I imagine a giant rat.

I know I can't stay there, hidden in shadows, in the hallway, any longer. It comes to me suddenly that nothing moves forward until I do. And so I enter the room, gun held in front of me, two-handed and ready for anything. Or so I think. But I am not prepared for what I see.

The first thing I am aware of are the puppy's golden eyes. They brighten when he sees me, and his tail wags hopefully, but that's all that is in him: less than what is usual. He is afraid.

I have this moment of complete disorientation. I am certain I had left the dog safely in the car, as I always do. And yet here he is. I don't understand it. Then I move more deeply into the room and I do.

William Atwater is there. Leg irons very much like what I used on him in the RV are around my dog's neck. The puppy appears to be unharmed, but I can see that if Atwater falls, the leg irons will snap that sweet golden neck like soft butter. The pup looks so small to me right then. He is meant to grow to be a very large dog, and he has the big feet to prove it. But just now I can hold and carry his squirming self in my arms with only the smallest amount of difficulty. I long to reach for him and do that now, but I know that would seal both of our fates. I have to deal with the business at hand.

I refocus my attention on Atwater. His upper left arm is crudely bound. A dirty scrap of cloth partly dampened with dried blood.

"Yes. You did that," he says. He's followed my gaze. "It's giving me hell, but I'll be okay. I can't die, you know?"

I look at him flatly. "No," I say. "That is not something I know."

"But surely you must. Otherwise, I'd be dead already, you see?"

"How do you explain that?"

"I don't. I am one of the immortals."

I level the gun at his head. "We'll see."

He opens his arms wide, exposing, I'm imagining, his heart. "Go ahead," he says. And the dog wheezes at the motion when the irons tighten around his throat.

"Fuck," I say, though I'm not even sure it's out loud. "Fuck fuck."

Atwater smiles then. And I want to kill him as badly as I've wanted anything.

"You can't, can you?" And he seems satisfied. I've failed some kind of test. Or I've passed it. I'm not really sure. "You can't risk the dog."

"Let him go," I say, though I have zero expectation of compliance when I say it.

"You know what you have to do."

"Sacrifice myself for a dog? That's what you think I'll do?"

"No," he says instantly. "That would be idiotic. You're a hardened killer. You told me so yourself. There's no way you'd do that."

"What's the deal?"

"Put your gun down and I let your dog go. Then things are even between us, you see? And we'll see how it goes from there."

I play this out in my mind. See the flaws. So flawed.

"I can't do that, William. You know I can't. If I put the gun down, there's nothing to stop you from killing the dog anyway."

"Mexican standoff." He smirks.

"Something like that."

"You'd kill me in a heartbeat," he says with confidence. "Yet right now I sense you'd do almost anything to save that dog. Interesting."

"Not that interesting," I say. I'm thinking fast, but I don't see an easy answer. "Anyway, I thought you couldn't die."

He shrugs.

I want Atwater dead. I will kill him—and I have no doubt he *will* die. But the dog. Somehow, I can't make myself risk the dog, even though I know it's the right answer. It should be an easy trade: the dog for a serial killer. There's nothing difficult about that. And yet. I scramble, trying to think of a different way.

"Yes, I think so. You've been following me a long time. So long, I was certain you'd arrive. And yet, here you have every opportunity and you're not taking it."

He's taunting me in a way that makes me wonder: does he want to die? Is that what this is about? His life or the dog's.

I raise the gun higher, as though that will make a difference. Level the gun at his head. He squeezes the leg iron noose. The dog whimpers. Gags. I close my eyes and breathe. I just don't know what to do.

I level the gun at the dog's head. "I could take him out," I say. "Put him out of his misery."

"Well, that's the gamble I took, isn't it? That's the gamble I've known all along." And he sounds pleased about this, too. "You can kill him and me. Then you pass the test. Or you can just kill me and *I'll* kill him on the way out. Or you can put the gun down and trust I'll keep my word and *not* kill him. It's just such a super interesting dilemma, all 'round."

I know what I have to do. It will be humane if it comes from me, I know that. It will be more humane if I just kill the dog now. But in the moment I decide this, he looks at me with his golden eyes, and there is so much love and trust in them that I just can't. And I don't. And Atwater sees all of this and laughs.

"I sort of love you for this, you know?"

I close my eyes.

"I love you for being predictable in this way. And for your love. Not everyone has that. But I knew you would. You are so filled with love." He is so pleased with himself. So smug. And I try to think about a way out of this dilemma. And I can't. And I try to deny his words. *Filled with love.* How can that be? Yet that resonates, too, even if it's something I hadn't known.

I raise the gun. Take careful aim. I know what I risk, but I also know it can't be any other way. The trade that's demanded of me is necessary. It's not the answer I want, but it's the only answer that can be. Atwater simply must die.

It's like the killer sees the decision and knows, suddenly, that he's lost the round. He drops the chain and lunges toward me. The shot goes off, goes wide as Atwater's fist impacts with my jaw.

And then everything goes dark.

CHAPTER FORTY-ONE

WHEN I OPEN my eyes, I see nothing at all. I don't know how long I've been out, but I think it can't have been that long because no light comes in the window. Unless there's been a full circle of the sun since I lost consciousness, but I don't think so.

Even though it's you-can't-see-the-hand-in-front-of-your-face dark, I know I am on a bed. I feel the give of a musty mattress and warmth from a surface that absorbs heat rather than reflecting it back.

Despite everything, though, and against all reason, I know I am not alone. There is another presence in the room. I can't see anything and I don't hear any telltale signs. But I know.

I lie there silently for a slot of time that feels longer than it could possibly be. Five minutes? Less. I lie there, feeling the darkness. Reaching into it with my mind and my ears. Even while I wonder how it's possible, I know what I know and I keep my breathing deep and even, understanding instinctively that a change in my state will tip my hand.

I remember then and I wonder about the dog. My heart fills with concern for him. And then I remember to be concerned, also, for myself. It's then that I hear the slight and even breathing of another creature. Another human, I'm certain. But so quiet, it almost isn't there.

I think about my options, willing myself to remain calm. I am still breathing long and slow, conscious not to alter my outside state. Inside, though, I am seething with questions and the beginnings of plans. It is my nature to plan. To question. Without that, I know instinctively, I am lost.

I wonder if I am tethered. To test it, I pull ever so slightly on my hands and feet. Somehow that small movement alerts him.

"You're awake." The voice reaches into the darkness. It is so quiet; I must strain to hear. It is modulated for the middle of the night and I wonder if he knew I was awake before he heard something, or if he just got tired of watching and waiting.

"The dog. Is he okay?" I surprise myself by having this be the first thing I say. I didn't even know I really liked the dog very much, and here I am asking about him. Which sort of figures somehow, when I think about it.

"Sure. He's fine." I hear the sound of a foot connecting with fur-padded flesh. I hear a yelp. "See?" I tell myself not to ask about the dog again.

"I could tell you were awake by your breathing. Isn't it funny how we always can?"

"We have to stop meeting like this," I croak, fighting for composure. Fighting to sound strong and unafraid.

He laughs, like we're at a cocktail party and I've told a funny joke. I am not unbiased, but the mirth seems to have an unhealthy sound.

"It's fate, I think. You and I, we have things to talk about, don't we?"

"I . . . I wasn't aware."

"I'm not sure that's true."

"Sorry?"

"You know." He sounds confident. "You know we have things to talk about."

I take a deep breath. Send calming energy to my limbs. When I think about it, I *do* know what he means. The stuff we'd talked about in the RV. But then he had been bound, in my power, under my influence. Things are different now.

As though to illustrate this thought, he turns on the light. Backlit above me, haloed by the room's overhead light, his face seems larger than life. Something out of a nightmare or a horror movie. My fear had been passive and general before. It gallops away like a wild thing now.

"You look so frightened."

His voice is soft. A caress. And my blood slows. I can feel it creeping through my veins. I have researched him. Have seen his handiwork. The only thing I feel for certain: this situation that we are currently in, he and I? It does not end well. For me. I've seen photographic evidence of the outcomes of similar situations. There is no upside to hope for.

"It would be dumb for me not to be frightened; don't you think?" The words themselves are confident. But the delivery is not. I can hear the shake in my own voice. Leaf in wind. It has no strength, and the resilience? It is sapped away. I am as afraid as I have ever been in my life. Though I am not afraid to die. I am afraid of what he will do to me between now and the time that he kills me. I am afraid I won't die soon enough.

He smiles then. And again, that smile is warm, almost loving. A part of me wants to cry, to scream. But I don't. I know that, if I am to survive, I have to get to a different place. What makes this more difficult is knowing that, even if I achieve that higher ground, it might not gain anything for me. In the end.

"Are you afraid?" I ask, pleased when my voice sounds stronger than it felt when it was inside me, before it emerged into the air.

He looks at me. Cocks his head to one side, as though he is listening. As though he is a big, bloodthirsty dog. I can almost see his fangs.

"Me? Why would I be afraid? I'm standing. You are in my power."

"Am I?"

"Yes," he affirms. "Quite."

I try to analyze his expression, because it's a new one to me. It is one part righteous indignation, one part puzzlement, one part frightened child. I've hit a nerve, but I don't allow hope. I have a long way to go.

I close my eyes, force stillness, force peace. It is one of the most difficult things I have ever done. I want to cry and scream. Hide. But there's no place for it.

There is silence between us for a while. I hear him shuffle restlessly above me. He is standing there, still. I don't have to look to be certain.

I hear a ruffle of wind on shutters. I hear night insects, making a certain type of chatter. I hear him—gently, gently—transfer his weight from one foot to the other. And then back. I listen, but I don't hear anything from the dog. I try not to be concerned, but I am.

"What are you doing?" he says after a while.

I take a full minute to formulate an answer. And then, unhurried, though that is difficult, too. "It's been difficult. Coming out here. Following you. Finding you. I'm tired. I am resting."

"Why aren't you afraid?" Another shuffle, shuffle. And, maybe—faintly?—panting from the dog. I hope so.

And, of course, I *am* afraid, but I am gratified that it does not show.

"Should I be?"

He looks at me. Just looks at me, straight on. I think he might say something, but then he seems to change his mind. He takes half a step back and squeezes his eyes shut. Opens them. "I am tired now," he says finally. "I have to sleep." He still hasn't answered me and his exhaustion seems to have come on quickly. I don't know what any of it means. Is it loss of blood, I wonder hopefully. Or some malaise of spirit that drains him suddenly. I don't ask. Instead, I nod, as though I am less concerned and less curious than I am. As though I understand fully where his words might lead, though I don't.

There is an inexplicable moment where I wonder if he will lie down next to me and I fight a frightened revulsion. But then he nods again, seems to struggle with himself, then shuffles out the door.

I have this amazing moment filled with the inexplicable feeling of freedom. He will sleep and I will slip away. I breathe to calm myself. In a very little while, all of this will be behind me. I can almost feel the bullet I will kill him with: the force of it leaving the Bersa. The finishing of the job I should have completed when I had the chance. I am one stop from ebullience.

My excitement is short-lived. Before I can collect myself, he is back. The leg irons in his hand. There seems to be no escaping them. They look like the same ones I put on him in the RV, but I know that can't be right. The same ones, more recently, he had around the neck of the dog. I feel a coldness creep over me.

He tosses them in my direction. Stands at the foot of the bed with his arms crossed.

"You know what to do," he says. And it is then that I realize this is going to be a dance. He has every move planned. This is just the first one.

He isn't holding a gun, as I had been, but he is much larger than I am and not unpracticed with his hands. We both know that's enough.

I attach the irons as instructed, trying while I do so to stay alert to see if I can do it some half-assed way so I can free myself after a while. But there will be no easy out, not with him standing there watching me carefully. There can be no shortcuts.

When I'm finished, he secures the irons to the bed, then leaves without another word, looking as exhausted as he claimed he was. He seems to sway on his feet. I know it isn't true, but he appears to be barely able to stand; exhaustion pours off him in waves. He stumbles out the door, and I know I'll be alone for a while.

CHAPTER FORTY-TWO

I LIE THERE, unmoving. Something is happening. I can feel it.

I lie there, feeling the beat of my heart, the blood in my veins. Praying for a stillness of hand, of spirit. Praying for strength to see this thing all the way through.

Whatever that means.

The dog creeps to the side of the bed, licks my hand. I am relieved to see he appears to be fine. It was what I had hoped. I'd heard him cry out, but I hadn't heard anything crack or break. And, yes: to my eyes the dog appears to be okay. For the moment, at least.

"Poor pup," I whisper while I scratch behind his ears. "Poor little guy." He seems almost to swoon with the pleasure of the attention. I think back to the day I got him, his fat little puppy body wiggling up to his young master, dead on his own stoop. Should I have left the pup there? It would have spared him all of this, whatever this might be. Dogs are such simple things, really. I wish for some of that simplicity for myself. I wish for something to be easy. I don't know what that looks like anymore. Easy. I've lost the ability even to wish for it.

The dog settles down next to the bed and then there is nothing but waiting. Waiting for what? At first, I am not sure.

I don't know how far away Atwater's resting place is, but I don't take any chances. Before I do anything that will make noise, I give him the chance to fall asleep.

Once I'm as certain as I can be that he is no longer awake, I explore as far as my shackles will allow. It isn't far. I can reach the nightstands. I look inside them to see if there is anything of use, but there is nothing. I find a notebook and a pen, and while I've been told that the pen is mightier than the sword, I'm certain that reasoning won't work here.

I can't quite reach the dresser, but I figure that, even if I could, there would be nothing very helpful in there. The room looks as though no one has lived here for years. There's a small crack at the edge of the mirror over the vanity. Cracks on the wall. A couple of the dresser drawers are open—gaping—and the closet door is open, showing a whole lot of nothing inside.

I turn my attention back to the nightstand closest to me. Nothing in it, but then I get the idea to think about the things that are on *top* of the nightstand, including the unremarkable lamp that is the room's only source of light.

The lamp has a flat metal base. The simple shade is held aloft by a thin pole made of the same stuff. I realize I am viewing it as a potential weapon. It is not ideal, but it is all I have. Necessity, mother of invention and so on.

I stretch my arm out as far as I can, but even in that position, I can just rest my fingertips against the cold metal base. This is somehow worse than not being able to touch it at all. Like a tease.

I stretch further, but that really doesn't do anything but strain my muscles and I have this moment of a frustration so pure, I just want to relax into myself and cry. But I don't cry, if for no reason beyond the fact that I don't want to make a sound that might wake or alert him. I don't even want to disturb the dog. So I take the largest silent breath I can and forge on.

When it occurs to me to use my pillow as a tool to bring the lamp closer to me, it seems so obvious I am at a complete loss to see how I didn't think of it sooner. The pillow is awkward and not particularly firm, but I finally manage to use it to push the lamp ahead just enough that I can get my fist all the way around that firm, cold base. The simple act fills me with a feeling of pure accomplishment.

Once I have the stalk of the lamp firmly in my grip, I exhale for what feels like the first time in a half hour. The deep breath fills my lungs intoxicatingly. I am perspiring from my exertions and, once again, I feel like crying, but this time in relief. The dog senses my energy and looks up at me. His tail thumps dully on the floor until he subsides back into sleep.

So I lie there for a while, the lamp still in my grasp, but out of sight on the far side of the bed. I don't know how long I'll have to wait like that, but I'm presuming it will be a while. Atwater had looked all in: he'll sleep for hours, and I know I can't maintain this position for that long. Finally, I think to stash the lamp under the pillow, where I can get to it easily, but where it can't be seen.

Now I am tired, too, but I don't dare sleep. I might only get one chance at this, so I know I have to stay ready. Everything is balancing on it. I know what I'm dealing with; I have an idea of the future Atwater has envisioned for me. There is no future at all if I fail. There will be no do-overs and there is no second chance.

Time drags, though I can't watch it go by. My phone was in my purse with the gun. I can't see the purse in the room and I don't know what he's done with my things. Without my phone,

I don't know what time it is. And without that solid input of information on the passage of time, my mind reels around, reaching fruitlessly for proper information.

Staying there so still, I fight desperately against the stress sleep that keeps trying to claim me while pondering the squirrel brain of mine that's developed over the last few years, so keyed on my smartphone that I suddenly realize it's become difficult to think without it. This is the first time I've had that thought in a serious way. But after only an hour—or maybe it is two. I can't tell!—I feel a sort of easing from it. A freeing. The feeling is like a spell breaking. And I laugh to myself. I'd broken the smartphone habit, cold turkey. All it had taken was to have a serial killer chain me to a bed.

After a while, the darkness outside recedes and the hint of light drips through the window. Dawn. But after that, I slip back into a slurry of minutes and hours of enforced peace and it all ceases to make sense again. My new normal.

I journey like this for a long time. Hours. Minutes. Maybe it is even days. Time has ceased to have meaning for me. I fight sleep with everything I have and then, suddenly, everything I have is not enough and it wins. It is not a deep sleep. My worry has kept me skating near the edge of consciousness, ever aware that I have only one move. I am dealing with someone who has actually flayed people. And so much more. If my one gambit fails, I won't get another try.

CHAPTER FORTY-THREE

In the end, his footsteps on the floorboards are what wake me.

"How did you sleep?" he asks. He sounds like a concerned Airbnb host and I get a ludicrous vision of him making me fresh-squeezed orange juice with maybe a scone and offering up directions and suggestions to the local sights.

"What time is it?"

"Does it matter?"

I realize he is right: it does not.

"It's funny how we key on things. Time. And the passage of it." I marvel again at the calm sound of my voice. To my ears, anyway, it sounds clear and strong. The exact opposite of how I feel. I can see he notes the sound, too. He doesn't arch an eyebrow at me, but the effect on his face is the same. He regards me in silence with an expression I can't quite make out. It might be admiration, but it might be something else, too. I know I don't want to overestimate my position, which really couldn't be much worse. That's what I hope, anyway. I hope it doesn't go downhill from here. I have to hope that.

"You look very comfortable," he says again, still with an expression I can't read.

"I have been more so," I say like I'm admitting something.

I am aware of everything. The beating of my heart and the pulse at my brow. The lump that the lamp might be making under the pillow. The telltale cord following the lamp out of the bed, potentially sticking out like the tail of a puppy, though I can't gauge that from where I am. Any one of those things, as well as others I have not considered, might give me away. So I pray for luck to be with me. I pray like I still have a god and hope for an answer. I pray. It's all I've got.

"I'm feeling unwell," I say.

"What's the matter with you?"

"Maybe . . . maybe a fever? I can't tell. But I feel like I might throw up."

He looks at me without saying anything for maybe half a minute. And then: "It doesn't matter."

I meet his eyes. "I know," I say.

He sighs then. It's a response I might find comical if this were a different sort of event. But he sighs as though he has resigned himself to something, then he approaches me, drops his hand on my forehead as though he is checking my brow for a fever.

My hand is firm on the shaft of the lamp. I am holding it so tightly I can feel my nails pierce the fleshy part of my hand. When I bring my arm up, it is with the confidence of someone who understands how much force will be required to hit her mark in order to make any damage at all.

I aim for his face. It is possible that, after I break the bulb on his face or head, I will also be able to electrocute him. I don't know the mechanics of that, but it seems to me that electrocution is a possibility, and it is certainly my fondest hope.

I don't think about what it means if my gambit works: chained to the bed in this abandoned house with my assailant dead at my feet. It's a problem I long to deal with as I bring the lamp down on his head with my full force. I'm gratified to see the bulb pop as it breaks; to see a spark of bright light that I hope is electricity entering his body. Then more satisfaction when I note a trickle of blood run down his forehead.

He reels back, more surprised than injured. I feel my disappointment all the way down to my feet. It has been something. It has hurt him. But I can see right away that it is not enough.

"You bitch," he says. He pulls his arm back to strike me and I brace myself for the fist he is making, preparing myself for an onslaught that might potentially kill me.

But a movement at the corner of my eyes pulls my attention, and I see it when Curtis launches himself at Atwater out of the shadows. Has he been waiting for his moment? I think so. And maybe he has decided to make *this* his moment because he feels if he doesn't act now, Atwater might kill me.

Curtis is smaller than Atwater—not shorter but lighter—but he has the element of surprise on his side and, briefly anyway, it works. Atwater is toppled over. They grapple. It's happening so quickly; I don't have time to assess or determine. It's all animal reaction. I want Curtis to prevail for so many reasons, not the least of which is the fact that, despite my best efforts, I'm still chained to a bed with my best card played.

There is a moment when Curtis rides Atwater like a pony. I even see his legs dig into Atwater's flanks, for grip, for control, I can't decide which. Maybe both. It's not a good play, and I see it before it happens: Atwater stands, with Curtis clinging to his back like a monkey.

"Gonna crush you like a flea," Atwater grunts, smashing his back against the wall, and I don't hear Curtis's bones breaking, but a part of me can feel it. I know that if I can't manage to stop it somehow, Atwater will kill the reporter. And it won't take long.

I cast around for something—anything—to do and my hand connects with the cord of the lamp. I know right away that it's a shot. The only one I have.

Curtis sees me, straining at the end of my tether, my weapon again in my hand. They are just out of my reach. Curtis manages to maneuver the two of them closer. I hold myself back, so as not to blow what is likely to be my only chance, then chop again towards his head when I feel he may be close enough and will, additionally, momentarily be farther away.

I swing and basically miss. The broken bulb grazes his back and I see a trail of blood rise up, but it does not slow him down. He registers the pain, though. His attention is briefly diverted from Curtis. It isn't much, but it's enough. Curtis gets free. He is able to grab one of the antique chairs, swing it up, and crash it over Atwater's head. Atwater goes down and stays down. From the force of the blow, and from this distance, I can't even tell if he's alive.

Curtis doesn't check. He rushes to my side, his fingers going to the leg irons as he futilely searches for how to unlock them.

"Fuck," he says. "It takes a key."

"Check his pockets."

"Ugh," he says, but he's moving towards him. Bending over him.

"Careful," I hiss from the bed. "He's a pro at this." I don't add that Curtis, of course, is not.

I'm watching Atwater carefully while Curtis bends over him, but so far so good.

"Where's the team?" I ask while he searches. This all would have gone so much more easily with the team in play.

"They're down at the waterfront. There's a house there. Near the pier. We got a tip." He's talking between clenched teeth, while he searches through Atwater's pockets, a disgusted look on his face. I recognize the look. I'd been in that position before.

"Got it!" I recognize the triumph in his voice, too.

"How come you're here?" I ask.

"We got another tip. Some kid at a gas station called it in. It felt right."

It seems to me Atwater is beginning to stir. Not dead, after all. I feel relief and despair, all in one gulp.

"He's moving! Hit him," I hiss. Curtis looks a bit squeamish at this and I mime a hit theatrically. "Seriously. Grab the chair again. Bop him one. *Now*."

"I might kill him."

"Good," I hiss.

Curtis looks at me with wide eyes, but Atwater is truly stirring now.

"Do it!"

And, finally—luckily before my head explodes—Curtis leans over and picks up the chair again, then hesitates.

"Right on the noggin. It's okay. You can do it! I know you can."

And this last bit of encouragement seems to do the trick, because Curtis grabs the chair even more firmly, hauls back a bit like he's playing softball, closes his eyes, and brings it down on Atwater's brow.

"Yes!"

For just a second, Curtis looks back at me like a kid who just got praised.

"Gosh, that was hard," he says.

"I know," I say.

I can see even from my position on the bed that the blow was not as hard as it looked. The chair was heavy enough to pulverize

Atwater's head. But I can see the rise and fall of his chest. Not pulverized.

Not dead yet.

Curtis has turned his attention to getting me out of the leg irons. Until they slide off, I have this awful feeling that it won't work. That I'll be stuck in them forever, even though that makes no sense.

"Ohmigawd," I breathe when I'm free. "Thank you. You saved me. You're my hero!"

Curtis laughs. I'm relieved to hear the sound.

"Are you kidding?" he says. "We saved each other."

I bring my legs in front of me, rubbing the circulation back into them, feeling an echo of when I'd freed Emma—could it be?—just a few hours earlier.

"Now what?" Curtis says.

I'm saved from answering by the arrival of the team. We hear the van; hear the three of them clattering into the front hall. The shift in energy excites the dog. He pulls himself out from where he's been hiding, gives a "woof" that sounds more like greeting than alarm, then skitters downstairs to meet the visitors.

I glance at Atwater, but it's clear he's still out cold, possibly worse. There have been a lot of hits on the noggin in the last while, I muse. I fully expect that, after what he's been through, he might not ever rise again.

Downstairs, I am surprised at how good it is to clap eyes on this team again. The girl—whose name I've discovered is Juliet—looks so relieved to see us unhurt it's almost comical.

I'm pleased by their arrival, but curious. "Why were you worried?" Of course she'd had reason to be, but she also had no way of knowing that.

"Just a feeling," she says. "I can't explain it. As we were driving up here, I just suddenly got the sense that he was here. And then here you both are. Somewhere in there, I just started fearing the worst."

Curtis and I exchange a glance.

"Come upstairs," Curtis instructs the team. "There's something we have to show you."

The two guys look mystified; Juliet just appears a little more apprehensive. As we go up the stairs, I even see her nibbling on her nails.

We troop up there together. Curtis and I in the lead. Juliet behind us with the two guys right behind her, shielding her back as I suspect they often do; tacitly. The dog brings up the rear, following us, his nails making soft clicking sounds on the wooden stairs.

In the bedroom at the end of the hall, Curtis and I stop so short the others nearly careen into us.

"What?" This is Rocky. But neither Curtis nor I say anything at first. There is nothing to say. Less than nothing.

William Atwater is gone.

CHAPTER FORTY-FOUR

I AM REELING. Of all the things I had been expecting, it was not this. I am without speech. Curtis is not.

"I can't believe it." He's actually shaking his head. "Well, he can't have gotten far."

"What makes you think that?" Juliet asks.

"I thought he was dead."

I still don't say anything, even though I don't think what he's said is quite true. We never thought he was dead. *Dead* and *as good as dead* aren't the same thing. The empty spot on the floor drives that home.

Curtis gives the team an abbreviated version of what happened, then they fan out to look for Atwater in a manner that is so efficient, if you hadn't known they'd worked together on many occasions, you would now.

It's Juliet who discovers how he managed to disappear: a back staircase. I am astonished. I had not considered that a house might have two staircases to the second floor. The back staircase is smaller and narrower than the one that leads up from the foyer. Dimmer and darker, too.

"Service staircase," Curtis says, and I realize that makes sense: a path for the servants to take so the lords of the manor wouldn't have to see them or interact.

So that explained how he could have gotten past us, but not where he's gone, and I am aware of a sinking feeling. Like water through fingers. He's slipped away again.

"Ideas?" Curtis asks.

"Don't look at me. Look how often I've lost him." And I can't help it, but I know it sounds like I'm spitting up grapes that are sour.

"Maybe," Curtis says. "But you also keep finding him. So, there's that."

It's meant to be a comfort, but it does not comfort me. All of this energy. All of this focus. All this loss. Suddenly, all I feel is tired.

"I'm out of ideas," I say. "I'm going home." Curtis has no way of knowing that "home" is a more than six-hour drive, and he lets me go, totally immersed in his story and his team. What of all of this can be told? I hear them plotting their newscast as I call the dog to me and head outside.

My keys, my bag, and my phone have disappeared. I have to assume Atwater has taken them, but I'm not without resources. I'd long ago equipped my car with one of those little plastic magnetic key keepers that old men keep stuck to the underside of their bumpers. I'm pleased with myself now to reach under my car and pull it out, open it, and retrieve the key I'd stashed there. The whole series of actions restores some of my self-esteem. I have taken precautions; risen to the occasion. The puppy seems to be able to feel it somehow. He sits nearby watching me, occasionally thumping his tail in what seems like gentle encouragement.

I open the door and indicate that he should load himself into the car, and he does with his usual alacrity. Dogs and cars again. What's the deal?

I am about to take off when there is a shout.

"Hey, hey!" Curtis. "Rocky spotted him. Heading down the cliff. C'mon! Let's go!"

I actually hang my head for a second. It's an odd feeling. Malaise? Ennui? It's like everything has gone out of me. It's like I don't have anything more to put in.

If Curtis sees any of this, he gives no sign. He gets in the car, and it's like I am carried along by the spirit of his enthusiasm. I don't even feel like continuing the chase, yet I put the key in the ignition and head out after the van.

And then we're bumping back down the long road. I imagine a time when the road was smooth and new and carriages came this way. Maybe fancy ladies wearing gloves. They flutter their lashes at men in bowler hats. Everything is beautiful, but that was a long time ago. Not much traffic comes here now.

The clock in my car says it's noon, but that clock is always wrong so I know it is more like eleven. Still, the sun is reaching for the highest point in the sky, though without my phone, I'm not even sure what day it is.

The van negotiates the bumpy road faster than my car, and I soon lose sight of it. I'm not worried about it. I have absolutely no confidence that this chase will result in what I most desire. He has been *so* slippery, so elusive. He has been like a cat, with oh so many lives.

And then we round a corner and come out of the forest into a clearing and the van is in front of us, at the edge of an overlook that gives this incredible view of Morning Bay and the sea. It looks like a fairy-tale town and fluffy white clouds float above it, punctuating a perfect blue sky. Beyond the van, the team is heading along a ridge that follows the view, but takes them back into the forest.

"C'mon," Curtis urges, and I can see he is anxious to be away.

"You go," I say. "I'll be right along."

Curtis looks at me questioningly, but I urge him with a flutter of my hand. "Go. *Go.* Honest. I'll be there. I just have something to do." He hesitates another few seconds, torn. And then he's off.

I go to the hidden compartment in my trunk, where the darker twin of my Bersa is waiting. I load the gun, put the safety on, and tuck it into the waistband of my jeans. Carrying the gun that way feels ludicrous. I miss my purse, but it's what I've got. With the gun available, I feel a little bolder. I feel infinitely better equipped.

I am about to head out after Curtis and the team when a pale flash catches my eye. A man. At the edge of the forest and the ridge, in the opposite direction from where the team has run. I know who it is before I get close enough to determine. Who else could it be? And I know—I *know*—it can't be that he is waiting for me, and yet, I feel it all the same.

He is standing with his back to me, facing Morning Bay. Facing the sea. And it's like he is contemplating the view. Or maybe praying, though I can't imagine that could be the case. He is not at the edge of the cliff, but the edge isn't far. He couldn't hop there, but he could walk.

I move towards him carefully. Ready to shoot if he turns. And he doesn't. Even though I know he can hear me. I don't know why I'm holding back. I don't know why I don't just kill him. And then I figure it out.

"Renee Garcia," I say when I'm close enough that he can hear.

"What?" He makes the word a question, but I feel sure he has recognized the name.

"She is the only one not accounted for." My voice seems distant even to me. Detached. I can't decide if that's good. Or not. "The police are now thinking maybe you had nothing to do with her death. I guess you know that. They couldn't find her body in your garden. And her name didn't come up in the lists you shared. Was she . . . was she . . ." I don't finish the sentence, but I'm sure he knows.

He is silent long enough that I think maybe he isn't going to answer. Or maybe he actually doesn't know anything about Renee. Maybe her disappearance could be attributed to somebody or something else. When he finally speaks, he lays my hope to rest.

"Yes," he says after a while. "I remember her." Still without turning around, he pulls his shirtsleeve back and offers a scar in my direction. I have to get closer to see what he is trying to show me. And then I do. It is old and white, but the composition is clear: the perfect reflection of a small set of teeth.

"That was Renee," he says.

"She bit you?"

"Like a dog," he says.

"Wait. You're saying she got away?" I feel this odd little surge of hope. A bird in my breast. It dies at his next words.

"I killed her like the bad dog she was."

"You hit her—like you hit me." I suddenly have a clear picture. A fist connecting in retaliation. A tiny jaw, shattering, like so much precious glass.

He grunts ascent. I close my eyes. Just for a second. But I can't speak. And then I can.

"Why did no one ever find the body?"

"We were on the road. I popped her into a dumpster." He says it casually, and it takes a minute or two for his meaning to become clear. And when it does, I can't make the picture go away. He had thrown her away, like so much trash. And just like that, the trail had died.

I had seen Renee's parents on television at some point through all of this. Their grief was oldest and so their expectations were not high. The stoop in their shoulders had come from an old and grinding weight, not like the newly grieved who have been hit by a recent storm and for whom walking fully upright and erect is beyond possibility. Oddly, though, I'd noted that there was a little hope alive in each parent, even after all this time. Nothing more than a spark, really. A dull flame, ready to be ignited at the smallest hint of warm wind. And to hear him declare, so casually, what had become of Renee, with all of the caring one might have given a broken toaster, something in that chilled my blood. All over again.

"But that was a long time ago," he says.

"A long time," I repeat. My voice is so quiet, I can barely hear the words myself. "So why do you do it?" I hadn't known I was going to ask the question. And now here it is.

"Do you believe that no one has ever asked me that before?"

"Really?"

"No," he says, deadpan. "But it should be true, don't you think?"

I don't have an answer for that. And we both stand there, silently for the moment. Almost companionably. There is the sound of a light wind in the trees. Occasional hits of the music of children's laughter, wafting up from the beach. The sound is chilling in the circumstance.

The Bersa is trained at the base of his skull. I am ready to kill him at any moment. And yet. I don't. At first, I'm not sure why. I grapple with it. And then I don't grapple. We *are* different, him and I. I am not better. Because who can say they are better than anyone else? But also? We are not the same.

"It's like a pressure," he says out of the blue.

"What is?"

"You had asked why I do it. Before. You asked. And there is pressure. That's why. The pressure builds. I relieve it."

"Relieve it," I repeat without expression.

"For a while, after, it's okay again."

I wonder but don't ask what "okay" even looks like to him.

"And the garden?"

"Well, I didn't ever want it to be just for nothing, you know? It felt like it could give their lives real meaning. More than they ever could have without it. Giving back to the earth in that way." His voice has grown stronger with his explanation as he warms to the topic. He still doesn't look at me, and I can tell he is attempting to articulate something he has maybe never tried to put words to before. I don't point out the logic flaws. There seems to be no reason.

"And they were always kids," I say, my voice only loud enough to travel.

"Not always," he says, letting me know there is still another aspect here. "But mostly, yeah. And kids, well they're easy, aren't they? They're small and pliable. Easy to get your hands on. And just so sweet."

I feel my bile rising, but I hold it down. Steady the gun in my hands. Level it.

"You couldn't not do it, could you?" I ask, and I realize I am thinking about him like he's a vampire. One that must feed at intervals in order to ensure peak performance. I'm not asking because I am wondering about rehabilitation. That doesn't even seem like a possibility.

"We are the same, you and I," he says, surprising me with his words and by how closely they echo my own thoughts. "We are just the same."

I just look at the back of his head, at the view beyond and, for a moment, I fall into this. We *are* the same, aren't we? Then I mentally give myself a shake. We are *not* the same. To some people, the pieces might look similar, but the essentials? They're not the same at all. A pressure, he'd told me. Nothing in me has ever been that. And then his garden, the highest usage of those young lives, he'd said.

I think about the wholeness I have felt at times when I've killed, but that was never the purpose of the exercise. Or was it? Now I am becoming confused. Even so, I know there has always been mercy in my hands. And the killings I have done were never of my choosing. Except when they were.

The world swims a bit, in front of my eyes.

We are alike, he said. We are the same.

But we are *not* the same. I know that now. I take aim, take a deep breath just as the stillness of the clearing is disrupted by the arrival of the team. Cameras are rolling and I hold my fire.

Atwater senses my hesitation and powers forward, stretching for the edge of the cliff.

"No!" I shout, raising the gun, cameras be damned. I don't want him to escape, even in death. I vowed to kill him and, right or wrong, I want him to die. Even more than that, I realize, I want to know the job is done.

And yet, something holds me back. If I do this thing that I feel really should be done, am I still then better than him? How do I make that distinction? Who am I to decide? And I realize it is not a distinction I would have made a week ago. Two. I would have killed him without a second thought. The killing I have done has been business always. Cash—or bitcoin—on the barrelhead; someone killed by me when it could have just as easily been someone else. That doesn't make it okay, but it makes it different. At least, I've always thought so. Now I'm not so sure. Now I'm questioning everything I ever was and am.

This dithering within me happens over the space of the beat of my heart. Even so, when I hear the bark of an unsilenced gun, the first thing I do is look down at the weapon in my hand. Not me. Then I look behind me, astonished to see gentle Curtis with a revolver, held in front of him in a two-handed death grip.

"I couldn't kill him," I say softly, but he hears me anyway.

"I know," Curtis says. "I saw. But he had to die."

"Yes, you're right," I say, nodding. *He had to die.* But somehow, after all I had been and seen, I knew it couldn't be me.

* * *

There are times in all of our lives when everything is easy. When the road we are meant to take appears, and all of the pieces just seem to fall into place.

The dog and I leave California right away. We are back home at the forest's edge before the sun has a chance to set twice.

The dog seems happy to be back. Relieved maybe, though I can't imagine he knows how close a call we both had. Or maybe we had no close call at all. Maybe everything is written down somewhere and it all turns out just as it's supposed to. That's what I'm thinking now.

At the scene, the team had worked swiftly, ignoring me, surrounding their leader. Covering for one of their own. There hadn't even been a lot of discussion. No need. Atwater was dead. The world had killed him. I watched them agree that quickly.

Curtis had held the gun, sure. But Atwater had never quite belonged in the world.

Afterwards, all of the news stations reported Atwater's passing in stoic, heroic tones, like they'd had something to do with the outcome. Never knowing, of course, that one of their number had, indeed, put the outcome into place.

It's been confirmed: Atwater has been killed by person or persons unknown. Killed by gunshot, but no weapon found. A vigilante, one reporter floated. Maybe a bereaved parent or someone else who held a deep concern.

Curtis Diamond of WBCC Los Angeles had been the first reporter on the scene. A lucky break. He and his crew had been nearby, following a tip, and had actually been there minutes after the shooting occurred. Diamond will probably win an award for breaking such a significant story.

"It's important"—this from the same blond reporter with close-cropped hair and flat blue eyes I'd seen before—"to not take matters into your own hands. Always call law enforcement when you see something wrong. We have a detailed justice system perfectly designed to deal with these things in the right way," and so on. Warning us, all of us civilians, to leave well enough alone. She's right, of course. There is no place for vigilantism. The system breaks down if we don't all play by the rules.

We need rules.

On my fourth day home, I push the television back into the garage, cover it with an old blanket. While I'm still in the garage, I get a text. I pull my phone out of the pocket of my jeans.

"Hey, sunshine! How's life treating you?"

And I know it is a call to action. The beginning of an assignment. I stand there for a moment, in the musty gloom of the garage. I read the text carefully. Then I read it again. I don't think deeply about what I will say, though I don't send back the expected words: the words that are my code.

"*Fine*," I text back. "*I think I'm really doing fine.*"

Then I carefully turn the phone off and push it under the blanket with the TV.

Outside, the sun is shining. The dog joins me in the yard.

"It's so beautiful today," I say to him, turning my face to the sun. We head into the forest near the house. He gallops ahead a bit, expending a bunch of puppy energy. Then he settles in at my heel and we just trot along.

Everything smells warm and green. And then a wind comes up. I inhale it. Feel it on my tongue. It tastes like hope.

ACKNOWLEDGMENTS

THE FIRST THING I'd like to acknowledge is that I've never killed anyone. Not in real life anyway. Now that you have read *Endings*, that might not be apparent, so I thought I'd just say it, right out front.

I've never even thought about killing someone. I'm not one of those writers who goes around fictionally killing people who have done 'em wrong. IRL, I have a lot of love in my heart. Enough, really, to make a cynic kinda nauseous.

That said, as I set out to write the short story that would eventually grow up to become *Endings*, I spent a lot of time thinking about what it would take for a "nice" person—someone, say, like me—to kill someone for money. And once that thing occurred, who would I/they then be?

The story that emerged was deeply personal. And the readings from it I did at various literary events were passionate and prompted several of my colleagues to start prodding me: Sheena Kamal, Owen Laukkanen, Robin Spano, Sam Wiebe, and, in particular, Dietrich Kalteis all kept saying it had to be a book.

I didn't see it. Lady goes around killing people for money. Boring. That's not a book. "No, no," Dietrich said on a long drive back from a library event in a distant town. "It's about her redemption."

And suddenly the book-to-be came alive. Back in my studio, I could see how it all would go. That feeling that every novelist knows. The feeling of illumination when before the room was dark.

Of course, books don't get made by themselves. From darkness to full light requires so much support.

Many thanks to my wonderful agent, Kimberley Cameron, who saw even beyond the story I had.

I'm in love with Bob and Pat Gussin and the dangerously talented team they've put together at Oceanview. I am so happy and proud to be part of this lovely family.

Thank you to my husband, Anthony J. Parkinson; my son, the actor Michael Karl Richards, and his lovely wife, Kristen Houser; my brother, Dr. Peter Huber, and my brother-from-a-different mother, Roger Chow. As you guys know, I went the distance on this book. But I could not have without the support and belief that sometimes reached beyond my own.